THE DUKE AND THE LADY

JESSIE CLEVER

SOMEDAY LADY PUBLISHING, LLC.

THE DUKE AND THE LADY

Published by Someday Lady Publishing, LLC

Copyright © 2020 by Jessica McQuaid

ISBN-13: 978-1-7333262-9-2

Cover Design by The Killion Group

Edited by Judy Roth

Once upon a time, a teacher told me to live my dreams.

Well, Mr. Cusimano, I just wanted to let you know—
I am.

This one is for you.
Again.

CHAPTER 1

She knew what her sisters would say.

They would say how it was just like her to be brought down by a litter of puppies.

To be fair, she wouldn't have fallen for it if it weren't coming from Jonathan Devlin, the second son of the Earl of Westrick. Devlin was a watery chap who whimpered about flat champagne and wrinkled cravats. He hadn't committed any sin greater than wearing the wrong color waistcoat to a fox hunt, so why shouldn't she have believed him when he said the Marquess of Lumberton's prized Ridgeback had just birthed an extraordinary litter of puppies?

It seemed like such an innocuous thing, and something Devlin would have been interested in as it involved absolutely no effort on his part to enjoy it.

So she'd followed him.

The musicale was not overly stimulating. The Marquess of Lumberton had three daughters, all of whom possessed less talent than a tarnished teapot, and the evening drew on insufferably. It was probably this which had her accepting Devlin's story so quickly for in it she saw her way out.

The setting where the marquess's daughters performed was an assembly of drawing rooms with their doors opened to permit the gathering of all the guests for it was quite a turnout. While the marquess's daughters lacked talent, they did not lack in dowry, and all three were on the market that season.

Johanna, Louisa's younger sister, had jumped at the chance to attend for it fulfilled Viv's, their eldest sister's, quest to find them both husbands while also ensuring no such thing would occur that evening as all attention was on the Lumberton sisters. Johanna, ever reluctant to find a match, enjoyed the idea of being passed over very much.

Louisa did not.

While she was happy to do anything Jo wished, she was not so happy to endure the endless rendition of songs Louisa could not even decipher as the Lumberton sisters continuously mutilated the lyrics.

So if Jo were to gain something out of this, so would Louisa.

She was going to see some adorable puppies.

Devlin had easily slipped both of them from the crowd during a pause in the music as fortune hunters posing as eligible gentlemen surged forward to praise the sisters for their aptitude. Louisa and Devlin simply stepped from the room and into the empty corridor.

She should have known by how easy it was to escape that only bad things lay ahead.

The Marquess of Lumberton's townhome was much like the other homes of the peerage, and it was easy to navigate through the endless corridors toward the back of the house.

"Do you know where you're going?" She'd meant the question playfully as anyone who was familiar with dogs—and she was, thanks to her sister Eliza's love of collies—would know the pups were likely being weaned near the kitchens. They would simply need to find the servants' stairs at the back of the house.

That's why she startled when Devlin whipped about, his jaw firm, his eyes wide with indignation.

"Do you not think I know what I'm doing?"

The light was dim here as the guests weren't meant to be in this part of the house, and only a few sconces were lit along the corridor. The slanted light marked his face with valleys of shadows and spikes of light turning him suddenly ghostly before her. It was unsettling, but she shook it off. He was just being a spoiled child.

She picked up her skirts. "I didn't say that. Perhaps you misheard."

She didn't wait for a reply and moved forward. She could find the puppies on her own.

She'd only gone a few steps when Devlin came up behind her. His footsteps were so solid and swift the mere sound of them startled her. It was this that would be her first mistake. She pivoted to see just what his rush was about and in doing so, she was slightly off balance. She was certain this was why he was able to grab her arm so quickly and sweep her into a room off the main corridor.

They plunged into almost complete darkness, and her senses were left rattled and useless. Her first thought was the puppies couldn't possibly be in there. Who would leave a poor, defenseless pack of puppies alone in a dark room?

As soon as the question formed, however, she realized her mistake.

It was the same tragic tale of any number of debutantes in any number of seasons.

She straightened her shoulders, forced her ears to open, and willed her eyes to adjust.

She needed to get out of there.

"Devlin, whatever are you playing at?" She made her voice sound light and flirty.

The horrid look on his face moments earlier in the corridor danced all too clearly through her mind, and she knew she had to keep him calm. It appeared the dandy had a mean streak, and it was best not to rile him. Not until she could get safely away.

And then she would turn Viv on him.

She would turn all her sisters on him for that matter. Even Eliza's collie, Henry, would enjoy getting in on the fight, she was sure of it.

"This is no game." His tone was riddled with the moist sound of spit, and she wondered if he'd meant to sound menacing when, in fact, it only sounded as if he were too overcome to properly form words.

Carefully, she slipped a foot backward, testing the floor behind her. Judging by the softness beneath her feet, she stood on a carpet, but when Devlin had swept her into the room, she'd lost her sense of direction. It was likely the door was behind her, but she didn't know for certain if she was even near the door any longer. Was the carpet just inside the room? Should she try to find its edge and follow it to the door? She just couldn't be sure.

Achingly slowly, her eyes began to adjust. At the far side of the room was a bank of windows, their drapes not quite closed against the cold night. Moonlight spilled through the smallest crack, illuminating the outlines of the furniture that littered the room. There was a sitting arrangement, sofa and chairs, a dormant fireplace, and near-empty walls. It was likely an unused drawing room. The Marquess of Lumberton's townhome had so many, he probably didn't know what to do with this one.

For the first time, she felt a lick of fear.

If the room were unused, it would mean no one would find her because no one would have reason to come here.

She flexed her fingers, closing her hands into fists.

"Oh, Devlin, whatever do you mean?" She deepened her voice, hoping it would soothe him.

She heard him more than she saw him, shuffling somewhere in the corner across from her. There was the screech of wood against wood, and she realized he must have opened a drawer.

He was looking for something.

She slid her other foot back, thinking to widen the space between them. Quickly, she glanced behind her, but the darkness was too thick, the paneled walls too similar. She couldn't make out which was the door.

There was another screech of wood and a snap. He'd shut the drawer.

Suddenly there was a flash of light, and she closed her eyes against it. When she opened them again, her throat closed.

Devlin had found a candle and lit it, its wavering light striking those shadowy valleys across his face once more. The watery boy she knew from countless social obligations suddenly didn't appear so watery any longer.

The lick of fear grew stronger, and for the first time, she realized that noise she heard was her heart pounding in her head.

"Devlin, what is this?" The playfulness had gone from her voice, and her fingers fell from their fists to grip nervously at her skirts.

The candlelight caught the spittle that had gathered at the corner of his lips. "My father thinks I'm not a man. He called me weak. He called me a pansy. He called me—"

Whatever the last insult was, it was too great for Devlin

could not speak it. Instead his face twisted into an unknown pain.

She slid another foot back.

"Devlin, I'm sure whatever—"

"Shut up, you whore!"

The words more than their volume startled her into stillness. She'd never even heard someone utter such a base word, let alone hurtle it at her. It left her empty, shocked into nothingness. How could a single word have such power to completely undo her?

Several moments elapsed as she tried to regain her breath, to will the feeling back into her limbs, to realize that while Devlin held the candle aloft with one hand, his other hand was busy at the front of his jacket.

No, not his jacket. His trousers.

He was undoing the lacings of his trousers.

She didn't speak again, nor did she think. She threw herself backwards, her hands scrambling over the paneling to find the door. Her fingernails scratched at useless wood, slivers cutting through the fine silk of her gloves, but her hands found nothing.

He grabbed her before she thought he would, and the scream she had meant to scream got lost somewhere in her throat. He didn't hold onto her but instead threw her back into the room. She stumbled and fell against the back of the sofa. She gripped it, allowing it to hold her upright as she tried to slide around it, put it between her and Devlin.

He'd put down the candle. Vaguely, she was aware of it sitting somewhere to her right, the single point of light piercing the darkness. Shadows lurched at her, pantomiming until they became a sick chorus to Devlin's advance on her.

This was it.

This was her ruination.

She closed her eyes, her past swimming up to her in a single surge.

She deserved this.

The thought came from nowhere, like a swallow swooping down from the sky in a beautiful, pristine arc.

She deserved this because she had killed her mother.

When she opened her eyes again, she found Devlin had come closer but had stopped several feet in front of her. She became aware of pulsing along her arm where he'd grabbed her, and she knew there would be a bruise there.

Did it matter?

She waited for him to pounce on her, braced herself for what was to come, but it didn't happen. Instead, he stood in front of her, studying her with an icy glare that was far more violating than any touch. She blinked, but she refused to move her gaze away from his.

The moment went on, and she didn't know why he didn't move, why he didn't take his chance. She sucked in a breath, willed herself to calm, and tried to take in the rest of it. She was so certain of attack she hadn't bothered to look down.

His hand was inside his trousers, pumping furiously as he watched her, pinned against the sofa where he'd put her.

Bile rose in her throat as the last of her self-pity drained away.

The bastard.

She roared up, powered by a sudden rage, and flung herself at him. Her fist struck bone, but he was already moving to pin her, and the blow glanced off harmlessly. He snatched both of her wrists in his steely grip and tipped her backwards. Once more the hard ridge of the sofa pressed into her back, but now he was atop her.

"Be a good girl, and it won't hurt so much," he whispered against her ear.

She tried to turn her head to bite him, but he was careful

now, staying tucked under her chin so she couldn't move. He captured her hands between her back and the sofa and pressed harder against her, effectively making her powerless.

When his free hand began to lift her skirts, she remembered she should scream. It was the only thing left to her.

"No." The word came out as hardly more than a whisper, but behind it, a fire grew. Something wet and slimy pressed against her neck. His tongue. He was...licking her.

"No." This word came out firmer, louder, and she was ready to scream the next one as his cold fingers touched the sensitive skin of her inner thigh.

But the scream never came.

Because just at that moment, Devlin was bodily lifted away from her and thrown across the room as if he were no more than a dirty rug being tossed out for a beating.

She stared at Devlin's crumpled body on the floor for a second, but the man who'd saved her captured her attention for eternity.

"The lady told you no," said Sebastian Fielding, the Duke of Waverly.

* * *

HE FELT nothing as he stared down at the miscreant and tugged the cuffs of his shirt back into place.

Very little drew any emotion from him whatsoever now.

Very little except *her*.

He had no interest in complicating his life by taking a wife. That was why he found it so terribly inconvenient that he thought about her quite so much. He couldn't look at her now, even to see if she was all right. Every time he saw her he felt his control slip a little, and that would never do.

The sniveling fool he'd pulled off her crawled across the

floor, losing his balance more than once and crashing into the carpet only to scrape his chin against the wool of the rug.

"I shan't assault you further if you do not give me reason to. Perhaps you should take your time and gain your feet. You're sure to draw attention to your person when you leave here if you keep on like that."

He knew the young man was a son of the Earl of Westrick, but which one, Sebastian couldn't tell. They were all weak dandies as far as he could surmise. He'd been to Eton with the eldest, and Sebastian could tell the lot of them were no different. The sons of the Earl of Westrick couldn't help themselves out of a hand basket without a squadron of Her Majesty's finest men showing them the way.

He drew up his shoulders and turned only his head, steeling to look at her.

Louisa perched against the back of the sofa, her chest still heaving, her hair a mess about her face, her dress wrinkled and torn along the sash.

Rage surged unexpectedly through him, the feeling so rare it almost drowned him. He drew a careful breath to calm himself.

When he'd seen her slip away, he hadn't hesitated to follow. Last season Louisa's sister Eliza had married the Duke of Ashbourne, Sebastian's oldest and dearest friend, and now Sebastian's life had become inexplicably tangled with the young Darby sister. Since then, Lady Louisa Darby had been a pain in his arse.

She was all of those nonsensical things that inspired bards to write sonnets. She lit up the room by simply walking into it. She filled the space about her with laughter and warmth. She made him feel warm on a cold, rainy day.

All of that dribble, God damn her.

He couldn't be blamed for avoiding her.

He'd seen her at Christmas, of course. He wasn't capable

of refusing an invitation from Ashbourne, but he'd done his best to stay away from Louisa and most certainly was never left alone with her. He didn't like how easily she affected him. A simple smile from her had his insides melting, and it was objectivity that kept his world ordered. He couldn't have her...*changing* him like that.

He swallowed now as the rage that simmered just beneath the surface receded. He'd seen her slip out with the bastard Devlin, and for a foolish moment, he'd thought her smarter than to sneak off alone with a wanker like Devlin. But when they'd disappeared from the corridor, he'd methodically opened each door along the way until he'd found them. With each doorknob he'd grasped, he'd felt a surge of ghostly fear, the kind seated in one's belly from an old and faded trauma.

He didn't like closed doors. He knew only too well what could be hidden behind them.

"Are you all right?" He spoke the words clearly and calmly so as not to frighten her further.

It seemed to do little good as she only nodded her head quickly after several moments of silence, as if she had trouble interpreting his words. He didn't press her and turned back to the weasel still crawling across the floor in the direction of the door.

The chap had turned over now and at least faced Sebastian. The boy had little respect for others, but apparently, he had spades of arrogant pride.

"You bastard," he seethed. "How dare you lay a hand on me. Do you know who my father is?"

There was only the light from a single candle cutting a swath through the darkness. Sebastian knew the boy couldn't see him at the angle that separated them, so he stepped forward and picking up the candle, held it aloft. The moment the light struck his face the boy sucked in a breath, and Sebastian could have sworn he whimpered.

"Do you know who *I* am?"

"The Beastly Duke."

Had the room not been so still, Sebastian wouldn't have heard the words muttered like an oath.

"Then I believe you will not utter a word of what has happened here tonight as I'm sure you know what might happen to you if you do."

Even in the weak light, Sebastian saw the blood drain from the boy's face.

Devlin shook his head so hard spittle flew from his pudgy, wet lips. He said nothing else but suddenly scrambled to his feet, tripping his way to the door. He was out of the room, slamming the door behind him, before Sebastian drew his next breath.

He still didn't turn to face Louisa.

There was a tightness in his chest he feared, and he needed a minute to let it dissipate.

He held the candle aloft until he found the sconces on the wall. One by one he lit them until the room was no longer fraught with darkness. Only then would he allow himself to look at her.

She hadn't moved. She half leaned, half sat on the back of the sofa. In the light, he could see her dress hadn't torn. The sash had merely come undone from Devlin's assault on her person, but it could be fixed. He wasn't so sure he could help with her hair, but perhaps he could get her to a retiring room and fetch one of her sisters to help her set herself to rights.

He knew very well what might happen if any member of the *ton* suspected she was ruined this night, and he couldn't let that happen. The thing about living in a society like theirs was to control what was said about you. It wasn't an act of valor that had him thinking of how to prevent the fatal gossip. It was simply a matter of pragmatism. At least, that's what he told himself.

"Please tell me you didn't follow him out of some misplaced notion of love." He struggled to speak that last word, and even then, he swallowed hard against it.

She blinked, and her lips flattened.

In their shared history, he had learned she didn't balk from his succinct way of speaking. Others told him he was rude or more, crass, but not Louisa. Louisa had had the audacity to compare him to her sister Eliza. It was rather an awkward thing of which to accuse the Beastly Duke.

"Lady Louisa," he prompted when she didn't speak.

She closed her eyes and spoke a single word. "Puppies."

"I beg your pardon."

The rage that simmered just beneath the surface roiled again, and he wondered at its appearance. It wasn't usually a female over whom he would grow upset, but he wasn't surprised it was Louisa.

She opened her eyes. "He told me Lumberton's Ridgeback had had a litter of puppies."

"You went off alone with that tosser because he told you there was a litter of puppies?" He didn't raise his voice. Raising one's voice was only an admission of weakness, and it did nothing to further one's attempt to handle a situation, so what was the point in employing such a tactic?

"Yes." She didn't cower at the profession. She held his gaze, and he thought she almost dared him to question her.

"Puppies." He said the word again as though he hadn't ascertained its meaning.

"Yes." Louisa straightened so suddenly he took a step back, but she advanced. "Yes, I followed him because I wanted to see puppies." She pointed at herself. "I should be able to see puppies without thinking that some bastard might—"

Two things happened then.

Louisa dissolved into a fit of sobs, her words lost to tears.

Judging by the redness in her face, he thought it was rage more than fear that drove her to crying. It was something he could understand all too easily.

But then for some odd reason, upon seeing her distress, he pulled her unexpectedly into his arms. He cradled her head against his chest, wrapping his other arm around her shaking body, and just held her like that.

Her sobs stopped nearly immediately, but they stayed that way, entwined in the sudden quiet and stillness. The last thing he should be doing was holding her, and yet, he couldn't seem to let go. His steely self-control had suddenly evaporated.

He worried he might have crushed her, and lack of air was the reason for the sudden cessation of her crying, but he could feel the rise and fall of her chest matching his. It was a hypnotic thing, and he found himself trying to match her breath for breath.

He'd never been so close to a woman, not like this. He'd had his fair share of mistresses, but there had never been intimacy. Intimacy was far too dangerous.

However, just then, he wouldn't have stepped away for anything. That was, until Louisa spoke.

"You're not used to doing this, are you?" Her tone was nasally, and he realized just how firmly he pressed her head against his chest.

He relaxed his grip. "No, I am not. Is it obvious?"

"Terribly so."

"Then I must apologize." He didn't let go, though.

"Oh, please, no apology is necessary. Thank you for... well, everything."

He did step back now, but it was only so he could see her face.

"You needn't thank me. If I had my choice, I would have carried that weasel out of here by his balls and presented him to his father in the middle of the ballroom as the rat he is."

Her splotched face softened into a watery smile. "I should have liked to see that."

Neither of them spoke then, and he found himself in the precise situation he had avoided at Christmas. Now he could do nothing but stare at her beautiful face, her soft brown eyes and golden hair. She was an utter mess, more so now that he'd squashed her in his arms, but he didn't care. He'd never seen anything so beautiful.

Such beauty was dangerous.

He started to step back when he heard footsteps in the corridor.

Louisa turned to stone in his arms, and he could feel her heartbeat where she still pressed against him. It was an ethereal feeling, and one so intense it made him study the space between them, or rather, lack thereof.

"Someone's coming," she whispered.

Her eyes darted madly about the room, and he knew she was taking into account the same thing he had noticed upon entering.

There was absolutely nowhere to hide in this room. Even the windows were bereft of substantial drapery, and the only furniture to speak of were the sofa and two chairs, fit for nothing more than a Pomeranian.

They were going to be discovered, and Louisa's life would be ruined.

He couldn't let it happen.

In not more than a breath, his entire world shifted.

Sebastian and the things he expected of his life no longer mattered. The careful plans he had laid to ensure he'd never get entangled in anything as damning as love or marriage vanished. Studying Louisa's deep brown eyes and the utter terror that lurked there banished all thoughts of his own well-being.

He had to save her.

Again.

So he kissed her.

She gave a startled, indecipherable sound when he pressed his lips to hers, but then even more startling, she wrapped her arms around him and returned his kiss with far greater vigor than he'd anticipated.

He may have been inexperienced with comforting a woman, but he had ample practice when it came to kissing one, and he applied it now. Kissing Louisa was as blissful as he had imagined. Her lips were full and soft, and she tasted of lemonade and salt. He tilted his head, deepening the kiss, trying to get more from her, as simply kissing her was not enough.

It should have scared him, and it would prevent him from shutting his eyes once he reached his bed so many hours later, but right then, he wanted more. He wanted all of it. All of her.

He very nearly missed the door opening, and the sound of footsteps halting suddenly just inside the room. He didn't miss the exaggerated gasp nor the cry of a protective sister.

"Louisa!"

Sebastian thanked every god he knew that he had the power to pull away from Louisa's tantalizing mouth as he turned to face the intruders.

The Marchioness of Lumberton he had expected. The Duchess of Margate, Louisa's eldest sister, he had not. Not that it mattered. She would discover them soon enough.

"She's just agreed to marry me," he spoke the words clearly so as not to be misunderstood, but their faces only showed bewilderment. He followed their gazes to Louisa, still perched under his arm. He was surprised to find she no longer looked assaulted but now she looked rather…well, loved. He swallowed. "See," he said. "She's overwhelmed…with happiness."

It was a struggle for him to find that last word, but it needn't matter.

The duchess and the marchioness did not appear to believe him in the slightest.

CHAPTER 2

*A*ndrew Darby, the seventh Duke of Ravenwood and Louisa's older brother, shut the door in her face, which only meant Louisa had to open it before she charged into his study where Sebastian stood before the duke's desk as if awaiting the guillotine.

"I insist on being a part of this conversation. It's my future you're discussing."

Andrew pinched the bridge of his nose. "You should have thought of that before you allowed yourself to be compromised at a musicale."

"Your Grace, I accept full responsibility for the events of the evening. As I told your sister, we were overwhelmed by emotion on the occasion."

Sebastian gestured to her sister Viv as she sat on the sofa to the side of Andrew's desk, her color still rather piqued, probably because she hadn't expected to find her younger sister being thoroughly kissed by the Beastly Duke.

Poor Viv.

Louisa couldn't blame her. It wasn't as if Sebastian was

known for affectionate qualities. She eyed him now, wondering how far he planned to take this charade.

It was one thing for them to be discovered, and he had saved her honor by claiming an impending marriage. But it was another to pledge his life to her.

The Beastly Duke did not seem like the pledging type.

Sebastian continued. "I do hope you'll accept my apology for not speaking with you before I proposed to Louisa. I respected Louisa's input, and I did not wish to put her in an awkward position should she not wish to proceed with marriage."

Lud, even Louisa was beginning to believe him.

"Andrew, I must insist—"

"Louisa, there really is no part for you in this conversation. The terms of your dowry were set by Father before he passed. You know that. The only thing left to discuss is whether or not Waverly agrees to the terms of your dowry."

"No dowry is needed."

The words were spoken so coolly they were very nearly missed in the heat of the room. Viv pushed to her feet at the same time Andrew straightened from his desk, but Louisa could only stare.

Was he truly negotiating their...marriage?

And in that vein, was he refusing her dowry?

"You don't wish to wed her for her dowry?"

Louisa wished Viv's tone weren't so incredulous. Louisa liked to think she was a reasonable catch on the marriage mart this year. She wasn't particularly stunning, but she came from a respectable family with considerable wealth. Her demeanor was rather charming and her looks passable. Her sister need not be so disbelieving.

"No." Again, Sebastian spoke the word coolly and succinctly. "Her dowry is of no interest to me. I should only wish to have her hand in marriage."

She was sure her jaw would have fallen to the floor had it not been attached. She'd known Sebastian for nearly a year now, and romance was not a word used in his vicinity, and yet, had anyone come into the study just then, they would have declared him an utter romantic.

Andrew's brow furrowed. "You simply wish to marry Louisa?"

Sebastian gave a curt nod. "Yes, that is all."

Andrew's gaze turned to her and only just in time did she clear her own confused expression. She was, after all, supposed to be *overwhelmed* by Sebastian's desire to marry.

"Louisa, do you truly wish to marry Waverly?"

She couldn't help the frown that sprouted on her lips. "I thought I wasn't to be a part of this conversation."

She wasn't normally so sharp, but she was suddenly tired of the men about her dictating what happened to her. First the sniveling Devlin and now this. She was exhausted and quickly losing patience.

Andrew crossed his arms over his chest. "You don't need to be."

She straightened at his steely tone and leveled her glare at him. "I'm growing rather irritated with all of the male influence in my life at the moment."

"Well, then marriage should suit you perfectly." Andrew's tone was sardonic.

She took a step forward. It was time to tell the truth. Once they knew what had really happened and how Sebastian had saved her, they could discuss how to best resolve the supposed engagement to allow Sebastian to keep his dignity. This was all just nonsense, and if her siblings knew the truth, they would agree.

But her thoughts of rational discussion fled when Viv spoke.

"Louisa, I'm surprised at you. Do you have any idea what this could have done?"

"What *what* could have done?"

Viv stepped forward, her hands pressed together. "Any scandal now would have ruined not only your chances for a match but Johanna's as well."

The breath froze in Louisa's lungs, and her lips parted without sound emerging.

Viv was right.

Louisa should have seen that. It didn't matter what happened to her, but it did matter what happened to Johanna, her *little* sister.

She'd almost done it again.

She'd almost ruined her sister's life. *Again*. Wasn't it enough that Louisa was responsible for their mother's death? Johanna had grown up not knowing their mother at all. God, was there no end to Louisa's destruction?

Louisa licked her lips, but she couldn't draw forth any words, stricken mute in disbelief at her selfishness.

Viv continued. "We must keep this under control or Johanna's prospects will dry up." She turned to Andrew. "I suggest we move forward as quickly as possible."

Andrew eyed Sebastian. "Is that agreeable to you?"

It took Louisa a moment to realize Sebastian watched her and not her brother. She blinked and focused again to meet his gaze. Something troubled him. She could sense it, and with a sudden clarity, she realized.

This was going to happen.

She was going to marry the Beastly Duke.

All because of that sniveling weasel Devlin who thought he had the right to dominate her.

Her stomach clenched at the still-fresh memory, and she pushed her hands against her torso.

This couldn't be happening. It wasn't that she dreaded

marrying Sebastian. Quite the opposite truly. He was a fine man, if a little coarse around the edges and rather rude at times. Some might call him beastly, true, but...

All right, the word *beastly* was well applied in his case, but surely, that was hardly much to endure after what she'd done. Resignation fell over her like the sudden darkness that swallows a setting sun.

"I would like a moment alone to speak with Louisa."

While she had been watching him, she hadn't really seen Sebastian until he spoke those words.

She blinked, and it was like a fog was lifted. Sebastian stood before her much as he'd appeared earlier in the Lumbertons' drawing room. He wore all black, and his hair was cut too short and styled in an unrelenting sweep away from his forehead, accentuating his severe features.

But there was something about his eyes that didn't match the rest of him. His eyes were deep and dark, and for a moment, she thought they might hold all of his secrets. It was a ridiculous thought. The Beastly Duke didn't have any secrets. He was just...well, beastly.

"Haven't you already had enough time alone with her?" Viv's voice dripped acid.

Sebastian didn't seem bothered by it, but Louisa didn't suspect he would be.

"I should like to discuss the swiftness of this marriage as it affects her as well."

Andrew nodded. "I think that's reasonable. Viv, let us give them some privacy."

Viv didn't move. "I'm not leaving her alone with him again. Not until they're wed."

Andrew merely took his sister's arm and ushered her from the room.

Louisa said nothing until the door clicked behind them.

"It's my fault." She hadn't meant to whisper it, but she suddenly couldn't fathom the strength to speak properly.

Sebastian swallowed, and she could only imagine how he was feeling. He probably didn't want a wife. He likely saw her as a burden. She deserved nothing less. If she hadn't lived with the shadow of her mother's death, her stupidity in allowing herself to be deceived by Jonathan Devlin would have been enough.

This was her fate. This was what she deserved for being so foolish, for being so selfish.

She would marry the Beastly Duke and ruin his life as well, and that would be it. That would complete her swath of destruction in this life, for surely, it would be enough. Surely, her mistakes would leave her be.

But she couldn't help but wonder.

When would it be enough?

Never.

The word whispered its way across her mind as the only memory of her mother floated up, unbidden as it always did. Louisa sat on the floor, pressed up against her mother's knees as the rain pelted down around them. They were in the nursery in this very house, and her mother sang a song about butterflies and flowers that Louisa couldn't remember. She could only remember the tune of it. Her mother braided Louisa's hair as she sang, and Louisa closed her eyes against the memory.

When she opened them again, Sebastian had stepped closer, his hand reaching out as if in concern.

"It's all right," she said reflexively. "What's done is done. It's only...well, I must apologize. I shouldn't have brought you into this."

Her words likely didn't make sense to him as he'd saved her out of his own volition, but that wasn't what plagued her.

Her mind was overcome right now with the death of her mother and how it meant Johanna grew up motherless.

"Will a quick wedding be agreeable to you? I mustn't let my selfishness affect my sister."

If she hadn't been studying his eyes so closely, she would have missed the shadow that passed over them. She stilled, watching his eyes change, and she realized something she had said had affected him.

In the year she had known him, she had thought him impervious. From their first encounter in which he'd forced Louisa and her sister Johanna to exit their carriage in a rainstorm, Louisa had found Sebastian impermeable. He was like the coat of a dog which water simply ran off. Nothing could touch the Beastly Duke, but something she had just said had had an effect on him. She wondered what it was.

"A quick wedding shall be fine. I will speak with Ravenwood about settling the matter." He appeared to wish to say more, and she remained silent, fascinated by this sudden change in him. "Lady Louisa, I must tell you it's not your fault. What happened tonight. We are not guilty for the sins of others."

The words rang in her ears, and she wanted to believe them, but the past had a way of muting the present. It needn't matter what truths he lay at her feet. There were too many examples in her history to refute them.

But while she knew the words were for her, she couldn't help but gather a sense that he spoke them for himself as well. She wondered once again what secrets the Beastly Duke could possibly hide.

"But I *am* guilty in trapping you." As soon as the words were spoken, she couldn't help the small laugh that bubbled up. "Lady Louisa Darby traps the Beastly Duke. How absurd."

Sebastian's face remained unchanged at her statement, and she held out a hand to touch his sleeve in reassurance.

She stopped, her eyes riveted to her hand as it hung suspended between them. Besides their awkward embrace earlier, she'd never touched him, and suddenly, the entire situation seemed ridiculous.

"I'm sorry," she rushed to say. "It's just...well, you must admit this situation has gone rather awry, Your Grace."

"Yes." He spoke only the single word, and it left her feeling the burn of humiliation.

Could she do nothing to keep her whims at bay?

She cleared her throat. "It grows late. I'm sure you did not plan on such a lengthy evening."

"No." Again, only a single word.

She pressed her hands together. "Well then, I guess..."

How did one say good evening to one's forced betrothed?

"I will bid you good night then." Sebastian saved her with a neat bow as he turned to the door. He stopped before leaving, though, and turned back to her.

"Sebastian." She raised an eyebrow in question, and he went on. "You should call me Sebastian. Considering the circumstances, I mean."

He gave a small gesture to suggest their surroundings, and without another word, he left, leaving her to wonder why she wished he'd kissed her again.

* * *

HE SHOULD HAVE GONE HOME to bed. It would have been the prudent thing to do.

But he was too agitated for that. He was through the door of his club not twenty minutes later and seated in his preferred chair in front of a crackling fire, whiskey in hand in twenty-two minutes.

Only then would he allow his mind to make its way

through all the possible ramifications the events of the night could bring.

He was to be married.

Lady Louisa Darby was a good match by society's standards. The Ravenwood title was old, there wasn't so much as a whisper of scandal shadowing any of the sisters, or the duke for that matter, and by all accounts, Louisa would be well trained to manage a ducal household as she had been raised in one.

If only she weren't so damn ebullient.

He drained the first glass of whiskey and poured the second without taking a sip.

There was the matter of what was to happen after they were wed. The fingers of his right hand struck out a staccato against the arm of his chair, and he resolutely tucked his fingers against his palm to get them to stop.

He'd avoided marriage for this very reason. Marriage was complicated and messy. It led perfectly sound men to do irrational and stupid things.

Tap. Tap.

He switched the untouched whiskey glass to the other hand, hoping to preoccupy the traitorous fingers.

He was not being overly reactionary to the subject. He had only to remember his father to feel certain he was right. Marriage was no good, and he must formulate a plan to remain unentangled.

The word left a sour taste in his mouth, and he finally took a small sip of his whiskey.

He would remain loyal to Louisa, of course. He was a man of honor after all. But even thinking of what that would entail sent a shiver of trepidation down his spine. Surely he could separate a physical relationship from an emotional one. He was a gentleman, after all. He would do whatever was necessary to see that she bore children and was happy, and he would leave it at that. There was no reason to get his heart involved.

Tap. Tap.

He stared at the fingers of his left hand, a string of curse words silently directed at them as he admitted the truth to himself.

It would be impossible to separate the physical from the emotional when it came to Louisa. He knew that. Hadn't he spent an inordinate amount of effort on engineering circumstances not to be left alone with her whenever the situation should arise?

And now he was to marry her.

God, he was doomed.

The crackle of the flames pulled his attention, and for just a minute, he let his thoughts slip away from him. For an absurd moment, he wished to speak with his father about it. He'd always gone to his father for counsel, and this was a subject on which he required a great deal of insight. But even as he thought it, he realized what a poor idea that would have been. Even if his father were alive, Sebastian knew the depths of the man's weaknesses now. Speaking to him of any matter involving the relations between a husband and a wife was not wise.

Once welcomed, memories flooded his mind. He was usually so careful not to think of it, but with the hypnotic pull of the fire, the whiskey spreading through him with its delirious allure, he couldn't help it.

Unbidden came the image of his father when he had finally reached him that night. The blood soaking the carpet. The pistol lying spent on the floor like a forgotten toy, misplaced by a careless child. The sound of footsteps behind him as—

He snapped out of his reverie more effectively than if

someone had tossed a bucket of icy water on him from just a single thought.

He would need to tell his mother about his impending marriage.

As a rule, he eschewed speaking with the woman. They had never been close, and when his father had died, there was no reason for Sebastian to cobble together what was left of their tattered relationship. However, his father's demands that Sebastian respect the woman who gave birth to him were too hard to ignore when it came to a topic so life-altering as marriage.

He would need to speak to her, yes, but perhaps, just not right then.

His gaze drifted to his left, unoccupied hand, and he was relieved to see his fingers still and relaxed against the fine leather of the chair. He poked around in his head but the concern that the evening's events had roused seemed to have settled within him. It would be all right. He had control of the situation. He need only keep himself away from his future wife.

A piece of paper was snapped in front of his face seconds later, and he reared back, his eyes struggling to focus on the note that now lay positioned directly in his sight.

LOUISA TO WED WAVERLY.

THE SCRIPT WAS ENTIRELY FEMININE, and the briefness of the message suggested only one culprit.

"Johanna," he said before casting his gaze upward to find his best friend hovering over him.

Dax Kane, the Duke of Ashbourne, looked furious.

And rather undressed.

27

"Where is your cravat? You left home like this?"

"I did not leave home." Dax pressed the words between gritted teeth. "I was pushed from my home at an unholy hour in an attempt to stop my wife from running here in her nightdress herself."

"She should really have put on a cloak. It's rather chilly tonight."

Dax did not respond but instead took the empty seat beside him.

Sebastian nudged the second, unused glass sitting on the table between them.

"You look like you could use some spirits."

Dax waved the note. "Is it true?"

"Yes." Sebastian filled the glass when it became apparent Dax would not. He handed it to his friend who studied him with a wrinkled brow.

"Did you have another question?"

"You're marrying Louisa."

Sebastian sipped at his own whiskey. "That's not a question."

"Sebastian."

Dax Kane was Sebastian's only friend in the world and had been even after Sebastian had tried to constrict his obligations within society after his father's death. No matter how Sebastian had withdrawn, Dax had followed, and now Sebastian was grateful for that.

"I can't tell you what occurred. I owe a certain loyalty to Louisa."

Dax's expression cleared instantly, his eyes widening with curiosity and concern.

"What occurred? Is Louisa well?"

Sebastian thought of Devlin, sniveling at his feet, and rage poured through his veins involuntarily.

"I assure you her person is well. Circumstances required

what you see now." He indicated the note still clutched in Dax's hand.

Dax scratched the back of his neck, and Sebastian realized just how quickly his friend must have departed Ashbourne House. His collar was undone as noted by the lack of cravat, his waistcoat was buttoned unevenly, and his coat was a navy blue whereas his pants were more of a midnight, which made Dax appear as though he had had a misstep in a garment shop. At least he wore the correct boot on each of his feet.

"You offered to marry Louisa."

It was not a question, and Sebastian knew he could not lie to his friend. But his chest tightened as he remembered Louisa's face when the Duchess of Margate had accused her of nearly ruining Johanna's chance at making a match. For some reason, it was vitally important to Louisa that no one should find out about what had occurred that evening.

Not even her sisters.

Sebastian tugged at the cuff of his shirt.

"I did offer to marry Louisa, and she agreed to the proposal. Unfortunately, we were interrupted in our private conversation. I believe it was rather upsetting for her."

Dax didn't speak. He continued to study Sebastian, and while Sebastian was used to a certain number of quizzical stares, thanks to his reputation, it was another thing entirely to be scrutinized by one's friend.

But he could not betray Louisa, and so he sat, willing his fingers to remain still.

Dax finally cleared his throat and sank back into the chair, his fingers finding the glass of whiskey Sebastian had poured earlier. The man downed the drink in a single gulp, his gaze intent on the fire.

"You're going to be my brother-in-law."

Sebastian almost missed the words as Dax spoke them so

softly, but once their meaning set in, a warmth spread unexpectedly through him.

"I suppose I am."

The two men sat like that for some time. Sebastian quietly refilled his friend's glass, and they sipped in silence as the fire wove and snapped before them. After what seemed an eternity, Dax turned to him.

"What can I tell Eliza?"

Sebastian was not one to tread regularly in matters involving such delicate nuances as friendship, but he understood how important it was for Dax to return home and assure his wife all was well.

"You must tell her the truth," Sebastian began. "Louisa and I are to be married."

"The truth is hardly comforting in these circumstances."

Sebastian couldn't help the smirk he cast in his friend's direction. "The truth being her sister is marrying the Beastly Duke?"

"Eliza married the Jilted Duke, so I hardly see how that should be of concern," Dax said with a self-deprecating smile.

Sebastian cocked his head in mock concern. "I should think Beastly is a good deal more terrifying than Jilted."

Dax raised his glass. "Ah, yes, but Jilted would suggest there was something wrong with me. How horrible would it be to find one wed to a rejected specimen?"

"I'm not sure," Sebastian said as he took a sip of his whiskey. "I shall remember to ask Eliza the next I see her."

Dax's laugh was soft, and it tumbled off into the comfortable silence between them.

"Sebastian," Dax said softly after some time. "Are you sure you wish to be married?"

"No," Sebastian said automatically, for it was the truth. He had no desire to wed and he turned his attention directly to his friend and admitted as much. "I had no plan to wed at all until I met Louisa."

There it was. The plain truth of the matter, and a large part of the reason why he did his best to avoid her. If he were to ever step into the chaos of human interaction, it would only be with Lady Louisa Darby.

Dax continued to study him long after his words had faded.

Wanting to reassure his friend, Sebastian lifted his glass as if to emphasize his point. "I grow older every day, Dax. The title requires I wed and produce an heir. I can only stomach the idea if it were to involve Louisa. You can assure Eliza I have the best of intentions when it comes to her sister."

"The best of intentions. Isn't that what someone says before they do something catastrophically stupid?"

Sebastian stilled at his friend's choice of words, but his nerves settled when Dax laughed and setting down his glass, gained his feet.

Dax made a motion to fix his coat and soon realized he wore little more than a cutaway coat and no greatcoat or cloak. He patted his pockets and when he came up empty, Sebastian assumed he'd forgotten gloves as well.

"I believe I have enough to allow Eliza some sleep tonight, but you'd best plan on calling soon. She'll want to hear it from you."

Sebastian gave a nod of consent. "I shouldn't wish her to worry."

That at least was the most honest thing he had said. Eliza was the absolute best thing that could have happened to his friend, and he was rather sure Eliza felt the same way. He really did wish her not to worry over her sister's fate. While Sebastian was not inclined to emotional attachment, he was a gentleman and a man of honor. He would see Louisa cared for.

Dax gave a nod as if to bid him good night but stopped after taking only a couple of steps in the direction of the door.

He turned back, a single finger raised as if to clarify a point, a knowing smile on his lips. "Just understand, old friend, I know you don't give a damn about the title."

The parting words would haunt Sebastian long after his head hit the pillow that night.

CHAPTER 3

*L*ouisa thought one should be excited at one's betrothal ball, but she was nothing but an utter case of nerves.

At any moment, she expected someone to proclaim her the liar she was. Betrothal, really. Wasn't it more of a trial and this was her punishment?

As long as no one discovered the truth, and Jo was spared.

Unconsciously, she touched her arm where Devlin had grabbed her. As soon as she had scraped her gown off that night, she'd pulled her arm around to see if there was a bruise, but there wasn't one. Now, two days later, her skin was still unmarked.

She wondered if she'd imagined the whole thing. Perhaps, this was a terrible dream, and any moment now, she'd wake up.

She knew that wouldn't happen. There was no waking up from this. Perhaps she'd feel better once they were safely wed. Tongues couldn't wag at a properly married couple, could they?

She'd slept little that night and the night after that. She

wanted to say it was because of Devlin and what he'd done to her, but that wouldn't have been true. She hadn't slept because she couldn't stop thinking about Sebastian.

The way he had kissed her.

The way he had *held* her.

She hadn't known what it could be like between a man and a woman. Until then, her life had been dedicated to ensuring Jo's happiness, to making her sisters happy. She hadn't had time to wonder.

Now she wondered too much. She remembered how hard his body was, pressed against hers, how his hands dug into her back as he pulled her closer. Never before had she felt so...cherished.

For the first time, she thought about what her life would be like now. Absurdly, she had always thought she'd live with her sisters, continuing to ensure their happiness. She had always thought she'd be there for Jo, helping her to achieve whatever it was she dreamed.

But now suddenly she was to be wed, and it would be a lie if she said she had no desire to marry Sebastian Fielding. For while she still seethed with having her choice taken away from her by the actions of another being, the idea of marrying Sebastian was not an entirely poor one.

Not now that she knew what it was like to kiss him.

"Do you know I heard it's a love match?"

Louisa nearly spit out her lemonade as her ears tuned into the whispered voices behind her, her thoughts racing away as if someone had actually heard them.

"Love match? You must have that wrong. Who could possibly love a beast like the Duke of Waverly?"

"Oh no, it's true. I have it on good authority."

"And whose authority would that be?"

"Kitty's companion told my lady's maid she saw Waverly take Lady Louisa on a ride in the park last week."

It was all Louisa could do not to turn around and stare. Sebastian had never once called on her, not even to take her for a ride in the park.

"And her sister allowed such a thing?"

"As I said, it's a love match. What could be done?"

The voices were drowned out by the sudden arrival of a band of old women consumed in flounces of gray hair and strings of pearls.

Louisa swallowed convulsively, nearly choking on the last of her lemonade as her mind sped over the whispered rumors. They were utterly untrue, but their meaning...

People believed it was a love match. That would mean Jo would be all right. Jo could still make her own match, find the happiness she deserved for the rest of her life.

Louisa had only to marry Sebastian.

She became aware of the crowd around her. The ballroom at Ravenwood House was large, but as it was rumored the engagement of the Beastly Duke to Lady Louisa Darby was to be announced that night, the invitation to the ball had been coveted, and nearly the entire *ton* was there. Which meant finding Sebastian would be difficult.

She set down her empty lemonade glass on a passing footman's tray and picked up her skirts to go in search of her future husband. Soon they would be wed, and she could put yet another of her mistakes behind her. Until then, she would be acting the part of a doting betrothed.

She didn't make it very far as she ran directly into Jo attempting to free herself from a gaggle of matrons.

"It's quite a crowd in here, is it not?" Jo said, pushing back a lock of hair that had fallen loose in the crush.

"Quite," Louisa agreed.

"Do you think I could make it to the terrace alive? I should like a bit of fresh air."

Louisa shook her head, not bothering to look in that direction. "I think not."

"Louisa."

Louisa jumped this time, and Viv eyed her with a crooked brow of concern as she stepped from the circle of women behind Louisa.

"It's crowded," Jo supplied, gesturing around them. "It seems everyone already knows what is to happen tonight." Jo flexed her eyebrows with heavy insinuation.

Viv's frown was swift. "Surely not."

Jo nodded at a place behind her as if to indicate the crowd. "It's apparently common knowledge that Louisa has gotten herself a love match." Jo's smile was nothing if not mischievous.

Viv's gaze flew to Louisa. "Is that true? People are saying it's a love match?"

Louisa could only nod, but her gaze remained on Jo. How had her little sister heard such nonsense too?

Viv's smile was quick. "Well, that's simply splendid. Jo, this will do wonders for your own prospects. Love matches are so rare and all." Viv grabbed Louisa's arm before she knew what she was about. "They're about to start the dancing. Have you seen Waverly?"

Normally, this would not be a question one asked of one party of a betrothed couple at their betrothal ball, but there was nothing typical about their circumstances.

Louisa's chest tightened at the thought. It was her fault Sebastian had even been pulled into this. She should have learned by now never to let her whims take hold of her, no matter how innocent they seemed. She studied the faces of her sisters, and the guilt she had carried for so long came back as if it were new, cutting her once again.

She straightened her shoulders. "I haven't seen him, but I shall go find him." She patted Viv's hand that remained on her arm. "Nothing to worry over. We shall take care of everything."

Louisa craned her neck over the crowd and managed to see Andrew wilting over by the refreshment table as he played the dutiful host, receiving well wishes on his sister's excellent match, even if the official announcement had not yet been made. Sebastian, however, was nowhere to be found.

She pressed through the crowd, nodding at casual acquaintances, accepting fond wishes from old friends, until she found herself completely on the other side of the ballroom *sans* betrothed. She flexed her fingers in the skirt of her gown, her nerves suddenly firing as she pirouetted in place, neck craned, hoping to see Sebastian somewhere she had missed.

"You're going to hurt yourself."

Her heels snapped back to the ground as she whirled to face him.

"Where have you been?" It sounded rather accusatory, and she pressed a hand to her stomach to calm herself.

Sebastian looked as he always did, dressed in severe black, his hair swept unrelentingly away from his face, but this was the first time her stomach flipped at the sight of him.

Oh dear.

She clutched both hands against her stomach now.

What was happening to her?

She could admit to a certain fascination with the man as when she'd first met him, he'd reminded her a great deal of her sister Eliza, but this, her body, the things that were happening…she couldn't quite explain.

"Do you mean just now or before?"

A line appeared between Sebastian's brows, and for a

moment his question confused her. Why would she care where he had been before now?

She shook her head. "I've been looking for you. The dancing is about to start, and we're required to lead it off."

His expression blanked. "Then shall we?"

He offered his arm and she took it, but she stopped before moving toward the dance floor.

"Why would I care where you'd been before?"

She paused long enough to study him. She was certain he hadn't been in the ballroom mere moments before when she'd searched the room from one end to the other. So was she supposed to care where he'd been just previous? She again took in his costume of all black but noted now that he was clean-shaven as usual, the whites of his gloves radiant in the glow of the chandeliers and his breathing even.

That's when she noticed it. A single hair dropping onto his forehead. Sebastian wore his hair swept back and neat in an unfashionably tame manner. She'd never seen him with a hair out of place. She stared at it, unable to break her gaze away. Never before had a single lock of hair been so suspicious.

"Where have you been?"

He said nothing.

She turned more fully to face him and involuntarily, her hands went to her hips.

"You were late. To your betrothal ball. Do you know what that would have looked like had someone noticed?"

"Nobody noticed, so it doesn't matter."

"I noticed."

"You don't count."

His statement pierced her for the words were harsh, but in context, they really shouldn't have bothered her as the rumors were just that. Rumors. There was no love between them, and she should not care that he had been late to his own betrothal ball.

But that wasn't what mattered just then. Jo's happiness mattered. Viv's determination to see her wed mattered.

"If Viv knew, she would—"

The sweeping crescendo of violins interrupted her, and without further conversation, Sebastian tugged her bodily onto the dance floor. They spilled through the crowd, and indelicately, Sebastian pulled her into the required position.

Louisa didn't miss the whispers that swirled around her as she moved. It was rather an ungraceful entrance, and hopefully, Viv had not witnessed it. She could only imagine how the tongues would wag now at such an unseemly entrance.

Sebastian never met her eyes throughout the entire quadrille even when the movements brought them together at intervals. His features were arranged in absolute stillness, his touch polite but brief.

God, she wanted his arms around her again. It had been so long since she'd felt so safe, so precious, so...protected.

She clenched her jaw, forcing her thoughts to more practical matters.

What on earth would have made the man late to his own betrothal ball?

With a flash of realization, she realized he did not wish to be there. Of course he didn't. How could she have been so stupid? While Sebastian would perform as honor dictated, it did not mean he would enjoy the frivolity involved in a societal wedding. He would not care to navigate the intricate steps decorum required for them to be wed. She might know Sebastian better than most, but she knew above all else Sebastian only truly cared about himself.

Heat flared into her cheeks, and she hoped any onlookers would credit it to the vigorous exercise required by the dance. She hadn't seen Sebastian since that night, and she had no way of knowing how he truly felt about their predicament. She could only surmise that he was displeased. In fact, he probably hated her for what she'd done to him.

It seemed to take an eternity for their set to finish, and ever so coolly, Sebastian led her from the floor. As soon as a fold of guests enveloped them into a semblance of privacy, she turned with a harsh whisper.

"I'm very sorry to have trapped you. I promise I shall make up for it in future by being the absolute perfect duchess you require."

His eyes flashed, and his eyebrows went flat.

"What are you talking about?"

It felt as though someone had driven a knife directly through her breastbone. The guilt she carried over her mother's death was something she'd learned to carry, but now her guilt at trapping Sebastian threatened to suffocate her. Tears burned at the backs of her eyes, and she bit the inside of her cheek to distract herself.

"Just as I said. I promise to be the perfect duchess you require. I shan't be a burden."

"I don't require a perfect duchess. Where are you getting this nonsense from?" His brow folded as his jaw tightened.

She was only making this worse.

She found herself pulling at the silk of her gloves as her hands swelled in the heat of the room. She needed air. She needed to be anywhere but there where she could see the look of displeasure on his face at the same time her body yearned for his touch.

"Am I not clear?" She leaned in, lowering her voice. It would not do to be overheard and ruin what footing she'd gained in the society rumor mill. "I will uphold my role as duchess, and you needn't worry that I will embarrass you or entrap you in something that displeases you again."

He studied her for another moment before taking the smallest of steps back. It shouldn't have pained her, that small step, but it was as if someone had grabbed hold of the knife in her chest and twisted it.

"Very good." That was it. Just two simple words and an entire ocean was placed securely between them.

Her chest squeezed, and her stomach heaved. She shouldn't feel this way. She shouldn't care about what he thought. She knew the truth. Theirs wasn't a love match, and Sebastian truly was the Beastly Duke, caring only for himself.

So why was he marrying her?

That finger of doubt prodded at her, and the knife twisted yet again, her footing so uncertain now. She had to remember Jo. That was all that mattered now.

She wasn't sure how long they stood there like that, so much pulsing between them while neither spoke a single word. Only their gazes remained locked as if neither could look away.

Until someone spoke.

"Sebastian. I require an introduction."

Louisa turned at the sound of the slightly nasal, haughty voice at her side. A woman stood there, her back razor straight, her gray hair pinned fiercely to her head. Her features were sharp while her skin had taken on the crepe quality of an older woman, and her eyes were flat and dark.

Louisa stepped ever so slightly in front of Sebastian, not realizing why until Sebastian spoke.

"Louisa, this is my mother."

* * *

IT WAS impossible to stop the inevitable, but he wished more than anything that night he may have been able to at least delay it. Especially right then.

He had clearly upset Louisa, and he could not figure out why. Why was she prattling on about being the perfect duchess? She could withdraw from society completely once they were wed, hiding away at Waverly House until the rumors of whether or not she'd turned into a crone ran rampant through London, and he would not have cared at all.

It was precisely this kind of complication he wished to avoid, and so he'd agreed with her if only to make her stop arguing when he saw no argument to be had. That had only seemed to make it worse, and he suddenly wanted to be alone with her to force her to make sense.

And that right there was exactly why he was in danger.

He should not be alone with her. He couldn't trust himself if he was.

It wasn't as if he'd meant to be tardy either. It was only that the thought of seeing her again after being well and truly betrothed frightened him. He'd sat in his carriage in front of Ravenwood House for more than an hour contemplating his unease. God, he'd wanted to see her again. The pull of her was enough to have him sprinting from the carriage, and yet that was why he'd remained. He'd had to resist, because if he didn't, what would be next?

He would lose all control, just like his father.

Louisa dipped into a curtsy now, but he could tell it was more of a reflex as her eyes had gone wide.

"Your Grace," she said before Sebastian could warn her.

His mother straightened, snapping her fan against the opposite wrist. It was a deliberate move and one she'd perfected over the years to startle people when she disapproved of them. It only had him grinding his teeth.

"It's Lady, actually, but I can assume Sebastian has not seen to telling you that. How very characteristic of him. Lady Sonia Pryne, Viscountess Raynham."

Louisa never moved her gaze away from his mother. Lady Raynham had been known to force others to cower before her with a simple remark, but Louisa was hardly an ordinary woman.

"You really shouldn't make assumptions," Louisa said now, eyeing his mother. "It demonstrates a lack of perception."

Sebastian blinked, jarred by what he'd just heard. No one spoke to his mother that way, not even him, even if he should wish to. Not that he'd had a chance in his younger years when his mother was often absent, and now he found it wholly unnecessary to expend energy on managing his mother's narcissism.

"I beg your pardon." His mother's voice had turned to ice.

Louisa's smile was beguiling. "Were you unable to hear me? It is quite a crush in here." She stepped to the side just enough to put her arm through his. "No one wanted to miss our betrothal ball. You can understand."

His mother's eyes flashed between the two of them, and she seemed to come to some kind of decision because she snapped her fan against her wrist once more.

"I understand the ceremony is to be held next week. That's rather quick, isn't it?" His mother's eyes dropped surreptitiously to Louisa's stomach.

Something inside of him snapped. He stepped in front of Louisa and leaned down so his mother wouldn't mistake his words.

"I'm sorry you will not be able to make it. I understand your social obligations are pressing."

His mother did not react, and he had not expected her to. They faced each other for several breaths, and it was almost as if one were attempting to decipher the thoughts of the other, discover the weakest point, and determine the best way to strike.

Sebastian did not have the patience for that.

"I understand your new husband demands so much of your time."

His mother sucked in a breath at this.

It was a well-known fact Viscount Raynham spent more time at his club or between the thighs of his mistress than he did with his wife. Raynham the Rogue they called him, and that left Sebastian's mother the object of great societal pity, which he knew she hated.

Her upper lip curled over her teeth as she spoke. "It would seem he does. If you'll excuse me."

His mother's heels were crisp against the marble floors of the ballroom as she marched away from them.

Sebastian didn't hesitate. He took Louisa's arm and spun her in the direction of the terrace doors. Ravenwood House was much like any other of the social elite in town. The ballroom was outfitted with a series of doors that spilled directly out into what he presumed would be the gardens providing both fresh air and a respite from the congestion inside the ballroom. They had hardly made it onto the stone of the terrace before Louisa turned on him.

"That woman is despicable."

"Please do not show any politeness on my behalf."

She stopped even though he knew she had another barb ready and seemed to consider his words.

"I do apologize. I realize she's your mother."

"I had no say in the matter, so there's no need to apologize. I only ask that you do not allow my mother's words to offend you. She's a bitter woman, disappointed in nearly everything that's crossed her path."

She had stopped several paces behind him, and when he turned to look at her, he wished he hadn't. She stood suspended, vibrating with expectation much as she'd been the day he'd met her as she tumbled from her carriage in the rain at Ashbourne Manor.

"You wish to say something." He didn't know how he knew it, but he could feel it in the way her body pitched ever so slightly forward.

She closed the distance between them, and for one heart-stopping moment, he thought she would touch him. As if sensing her nearness, he felt the ghost of her hands against him, knew how her body would fit into his.

He took a step back, knowing he would need to find a widow or an unhappy wife soon. But even as he thought it, he knew he couldn't do it. Not anymore. He would be faithful in his marriage, loyal to Louisa.

He would always wait for Louisa.

His future loomed before him like a dark, endless night.

This was the very thing he had meant to avoid. But was physical pleasure as dangerous as love? Surely not. Desire was a need to be met. It was simple science that did not stray into messy emotions.

After what seemed an age, Louisa finally spoke. "I understand now why you are this way."

Her words stilled him.

"What way?"

"The Beastly Duke." She gestured at the ballroom behind him and presumably his mother. "If I had to grow up with her as a mother, I'd be beastly too." She spit the words as if they left filth in her mouth.

"Did someone say you weren't?"

He didn't mean to tease her, but he suddenly realized how alone they were. An entire ballroom of people was just behind them and God only knew who had trickled out into the garden, but right now, it was just he and Louisa on the terrace, and he realized with a start he was enjoying himself.

He loved to watch her fire, reveled in the way her ebullient nature turned into an inferno when sparked. Just as when her little sister's future was threatened. Just as when his mother had appeared before them.

She'd become a blaze because of him.

It frightened him at the same time it sparked a fire low in his belly. God, he wanted her. All of her. The line between physical and emotional disappeared, and he teetered on a dangerous precipice.

Her frown was swift. "A lady is not beastly. She is determined."

"Couldn't the same be said of my mother?"

"Your mother is a—" Her words stalled as if striking an impasse, but he leaned forward, anticipating her finish.

"Say what you wish, my lady. It's not as if stopping now will right anything."

"Was she like that when you were a child?"

It was not what he'd expected her to say, and he crossed his arms over his chest as he considered her.

"Fortunately, she was absent a great deal of my childhood. She preferred country parties to spending time with her family. I hardly saw her more than a handful of times a year."

His response did not seem to satisfy her as she worried her lower lip. He felt a tightening in his gut at the gesture, and he wanted to soothe her lip with his kiss. He tugged at the cuffs of his shirt and turned away.

He had to find a solution to this. He could not let himself give in. He knew he would lose all control if he did.

He turned back, and horribly, he found her just as enticing as before.

"Do you have any other prying questions about my family?" His tone was harsh, fueled by the war he fought inside himself.

He watched as her features folded, her eyes narrowing with hurt, and he hated it. Hated himself for causing it and even more, for being so selfish as to seek his own peace at the cost of her happiness.

Perhaps when they were safely wed, he could bundle her off to a country estate, never need lay eyes on her again.

It would kill him more surely than his unending lust for her.

She was in front of him before he realized she had even moved.

"I know I trapped you into this marriage, and I understand now why you are so hard. But would it be so difficult for you to treat me with a measure of decency?"

At her words, the fire that had kindled inside of him roared in defiance.

She smelled like almonds. The scent was pure and innocent and enveloped him in a quiet fog of his own desire. For as his brain connected with the scent, it conjured up an image of her tending to her toilette, almond oil in hand as she pressed it to her naked body.

He hardened just standing there in the cold air of the terrace in the middle of their betrothal ball arguing with an intended he never meant to have, and he wanted to hate her for it, but instead, he wanted nothing more than to kiss her.

"I find decency to be tedious."

He enjoyed the flash of annoyance in her eyes, and it only served to stoke the fires within him. He should not be encouraging this. If he had any shred of sense, he would end this conversation and return to the ballroom where all of London would be witness to their actions, holding him in check.

"You're insufferable." She was very close now, so close he could see the sparks of gold in her irises.

"You're beautiful."

He hadn't meant to say the words, and he wasn't sure whom they startled more. Her lips froze on another accusation as she stared up at him, and he flexed his hands into fists to keep from reaching for her.

"Did you just tell me that I'm beautiful?"

He nodded. "I did." Whether or not he liked this line of conversation, he was not a liar, and right then, she was stunning.

"You're still insufferable." She said the words like a shield, as if they held the power to deter him.

"You're still beautiful."

She chewed her lower lip, but he could only stare into her eyes. They'd gone dark with passion, and even in the dimness, he could see her warring with a decision.

"I can't love you," she whispered just before she pulled his head down, and her lips slammed into his.

CHAPTER 4

*S*he had expected an explosion, heat and fire, and passion.

But as Louisa was coming to learn with Sebastian, nothing was quite as she expected it.

Because instead of a fiery, passionate kiss like they'd shared in the Lumberton drawing room, this one was something else entirely.

He cupped her head in his hands, one at the back of her head, the other along the side her neck, so he cradled her, and the kiss was like something priceless. His lips were firm yet soft, his touch gentle yet exact. Her fingers curled into the front of his jacket as she yearned for more.

She wanted his arms around her but instead he traced a hand down her arm, trailing his fingers ever so briefly over the exposed skin between the sleeve of her gown and her glove so that her body sang in response, pulsing toward him. Soon that hand found the small of her back, pulling her just the smallest of degrees closer to him. Her heart raced when she realized how perfectly they fit together, and a sense of inevitability washed over her.

His lips left hers, and she whimpered, the sound plaintive and childish, but she didn't care. He soothed her with small kisses along the line of her jaw.

When his lips found the sensitive spot behind her ear, she bucked against him, her hands going to his shoulders as if to hold on, for surely she was falling. That was the incredible sensation that swarmed her then, cascading through her body as she let her head fall back to give him better access.

The press of stone against her back alerted her to the fact that he had moved them back into the shadows along the house. No one could see them now unless they searched carefully. The intimacy of the moment, knowing they could be caught at any instant, the sounds of conversation, music, and laughter from the ballroom behind her, all combined into a heady mix of anticipation and daring.

Louisa did not do things like this. She was always so careful. She was always so sure. She always put others' happiness first, so she didn't know what happiness could be waiting out there for her.

For surely this was it. This was what it felt like to have someone's attention wholly on you. And it was glorious.

One hand came around her back to shield her from the rough planes of the stone while the other explored freely, cupping her hips, her waist, his long fingers trailing over every dip and curve.

Unexpectedly, she realized she wanted more. Parts of her burned for his touch, wondered what it would feel like to have his lips where his hands were. She didn't know how to tell him. All she could do was show him.

She arched against him, pressing her body into his, and the moan that escaped her lips was unplanned and guttural, so base it almost frightened her.

But he seemed to understand.

His lips captured hers as his hand finally cupped her

breast. She jerked against the touch, her stomach tightening in response. Oh God, what was happening to her? She still wanted more. She pulled at him now, her hands desperate to keep him going.

"Sebastian," she whispered against his lips.

"Shhh." He pressed kisses at the corners of her mouth. "We wouldn't want to be discovered now, would we?" His tone was playful as they had already been discovered.

Only that time hadn't mattered. Not like now. Not when her body burned for him.

"Sebastian, I want...I don't know what I want." How was her voice so breathy? Was that even her who spoke?

"Let me show you what you want."

His tone had changed, deepened and turned gravelly, and low in her stomach a fire sparked in response. She became aware of a pulsing between her thighs, deep in her most sacred part, and she wondered again what was happening to her.

But his hands were already moving. The fingers that played at her breast traveled up, slipping her thin sleeve over her shoulder. Her bodice shifted, giving him room to plunge one hand inside.

Her eyes flew open, but the darkness was nearly complete where he had tucked them against the house. Only a sliver of moon broke through, and it illuminated the white of his hand where it touched her, stroked her, freed her from the confines of her gown.

He'd removed his glove.

When his callused skin touched her breast, she shivered, her knees weakening until only his arms held her up. The pulse in her belly grew until it tortured her.

"Please," she moaned.

She couldn't hold on to him any longer. Her fingers

clutched at his jacket, but the strength escaped her with every one of his touches.

That was when he dipped his head. She watched fascinated as he brought his lips to her bare shoulder, lower along her collar bone, down to—

She bucked as his lips closed over her exposed nipple, pleasurable pain shooting through her.

"Oh God, Sebastian." The words were hardly decipherable, her head thrown back against the stone.

He didn't stop. He sucked and licked, pleasuring her until she almost couldn't bear it.

"Sebastian, I need—" But still, she didn't know what she needed.

Vaguely, she became aware of her skirts moving against her legs and soon cold night air rushed up her legs, washing over her with much needed relief. But not for long. His hand was at her thigh, exploring the ribbons of her garter, teasing her bare flesh with the briefest of touches.

"Sebastian, what—"

But he stopped her with a kiss so ardent, she clutched at his shoulders to keep herself steady. His fingers, though, kept exploring, moving higher until they pressed into that part of her that ached the most.

"Ah, God, Louisa," he moaned against her mouth.

She let her body relax, the harsh plane of the stone at her back and Sebastian's hard body to her front wrapping her in a blissful cocoon that contained only the two of them. The rest of the world fell away. Her worries for her sister, her long-held guilt, her remorse at what she'd done—it just disappeared. Here there was only taste and touch and...pleasure.

His fingers moved, parting her folds so he could explore further. She'd only ever touched herself down there in her bath, and she couldn't imagine where it was he sought to go, but with each stroke of his fingers, her muscles convulsed involuntarily in anticipation.

Finally, a single finger stroked her, and her body sparked. She came up off the stone, her body arching into his.

"Sebastian." She spoke his name with troubled passion, and he captured her lips in a kiss.

"Shhh, my sweet. You don't want to be caught now. Not before I've pleasured you."

His words, so raspy and mysterious, burned their way through her like his touch never could. Just the sound of his voice had her aching, and she pressed into his hand, urging him to continue.

His laugh was soft against her ear.

"Do you like that, Louisa?"

She could only nod, her body wound so tightly, she knew she could endure only so much more.

"Tell me."

His fingers stopped in their exploration, and her body hung suspended on the brink of something no longer coming.

She opened her eyes, captured his gaze. In the moonlight, she could see only so much, but his eyes, his beautiful blue eyes, shone through the darkness. He didn't smile. He didn't smirk at the power he held over her. His jaw was tight, his expression earnest.

He really wanted her to tell him she enjoyed it. Somehow it mattered to him.

She laid a single hand against his cheek, the scrape of his beard rough against her palm.

"I love it when you touch me," she whispered.

And as if her words were an incantation, his fingers stroked against her, his head coming down to capture her in the passionate kiss she had expected earlier but which he'd withheld, knowing instead how he'd tease her into a greater frenzy of want.

His fingers were wicked against her, flicking over the small nub she had discovered once that she knew gave her great pleasure. Back and forth he rubbed it until the fire in her belly grew to be too much. He never relented, only shifted to slip a single finger inside of her. She bucked at the intrusion, at the sudden wave of ecstasy that crashed over her.

"Sebastian." This. This was what she had wanted. She hadn't known, but he had, and he gave it to her now.

Her hips moved of their own volition, her mound rubbing against his palm as he continued to stroke. Her pleasure grew focused, pointed, and she knew something had to happen.

And then it did.

The wave broke over her in a kaleidoscope of sounds and colors and sensations, her whole body seized with a pleasure so great she knew it could suffocate her. But she rode it, rode through wave after wave of beautiful color until there was only the sound of her ragged breathing, the pounding of her heart in her ears.

Sebastian still held her, his fingers stilled against her mound as if they contained the pleasure he had just given her. Her body vibrated, exhausted and yet charged. Sebastian's lips pressed against her temple, and his arm secured her to his body as he slipped his hand away from her, cold air replacing his warm touch.

Her eyes fluttered open as he stepped back, gently releasing her so her skirts fell back into place around her. With a sure hand, he slipped the sleeve of her gown back onto her shoulder, her bodice finding its way around her as if she hadn't just been ravished at all.

She didn't know how long they stood there, each

watching the other so carefully as if one of them might shatter into a thousand pieces at a single whispered word.

Something had changed. Something fundamental about who they were to each other. They were no longer acquaintances, but they were not yet lovers. There was a reluctance she could feel pulse between them as if each could not figure out the other. Confusion separated them as surely as a closed door would have.

"Sebastian—"

She stopped as he moved, but it was only to draw the single glove he had removed from his pocket. He slipped it on with the coolness of certainty, so very like him and yet not quite himself.

He had stepped back enough that the moon illuminated his face now, and she found it softer, the hard expression he usually wore somehow absent. There was a humanness to him, and she gasped almost imperceptibly as she realized she was likely the only person to ever see him like this.

Finally, her eyes met his, and in them, she saw that unfathomable darkness, and once again, she thought of all the secrets he must carry with him. But now, having met the woman who had given birth to him, his secrets didn't seem quite so mysterious. They just seemed human.

"Sebastian—" She stepped away from the wall, standing once more on her own two feet, a single hand raised as if to touch him.

But he stepped back and now the golden light of the ballroom struck him full in the face.

His eyes were flat, his jaw firm.

The Beastly Duke stood before her now, and a coldness replaced the pleasure that still simmered within her as if it never existed.

"We should return to the ball." His words were clipped, and he didn't wait for her response. He merely turned and strode back into the ballroom, swallowed up by the crowd that lingered within its walls.

She didn't know how long she stood in the darkness alone, but it was long enough for her to understand what she'd seen in his eyes.

Fear.

The Beastly Duke was afraid of something.

* * *

THE ONLY THING keeping him from getting outstandingly drunk was the memory of his father's dead body sprawled at his feet.

As imagined, it was an upsetting enough image to keep his behavior in check, if not his emotions.

He tugged at the cuffs of his shirt as he awaited the arrival of his bride in the small room at the front of the church. It wasn't exactly appealing, the idea of being married in a church, but as Louisa had already had very little say in her wedding, he gave her that one small thing. Although he had a suspicion it wasn't even what she wished as a church wedding had all the connotations of the Duchess of Margate. He was beginning to learn that Louisa made very few decisions based on her own pleasure.

She was marrying him after all, wasn't she?

He wanted to pummel that stupid Devlin boy. Did he have no idea how his actions had ruined a young woman's life? He needn't have finished what he'd begun. The whisper of it alone was enough to ruin everything for her. Why Sebastian felt the need to right that wrong was preposterous. He should have left as soon as he'd taken care of the matter and left Louisa to her fate.

Even as he thought it, he knew he couldn't do it. Not to Louisa. Anyone else maybe...

He scrubbed a hand over his face, turning to the wall of the small room so no one would see the gesture. His body still ached from their encounter at their betrothal ball. It was a stark example of the very thing he had tried so hard to avoid.

His emotions had overcome him, and he'd taken advantage of her. He knew she had been upset by meeting his mother, and he'd goaded her anger until she had erupted. It was entirely his fault. He was doomed to repeat the mistakes of his father no matter how he tried to stop it from happening.

There was no other thing for it. He must remain apart from his wife. He couldn't trust himself. Emotions made people do stupid things, and love was the most dangerous of all emotions. Hadn't he proven that night he couldn't separate the physical from the emotional? It was his heightened emotional state that had driven him to what he'd done.

But God, the way she fit in his arms was like coming home.

He drew a deep breath and turned swiftly, nearly knocking Dax into the wall as he did so. Sebastian had been so caught up in his own torment he hadn't heard the man approach. Now he stared guiltily, and a small knowing smile appeared on Dax's face.

"Nervous?" his friend asked.

"No." The word came too quickly, and they both knew he was lying.

Only Sebastian knew he wasn't nervous about the wedding. He was nervous about what would come later.

Dax crossed his arms over his chest. "Have you changed your mind?"

He had seen his friend give similar dour looks to any number of lesser men, and it irked Sebastian.

"Of course, I haven't. Are you mad?"

Dax's expression softened somewhat, but he did not uncross his arms. "You know you've put me in a ridiculous position. You're my best friend, and she's my wife's sister. I'm trying to protect both sides here, and it's impossible."

Sebastian was surprised to feel a smile prodding at his lips. "I do apologize for that. I really didn't think this through, I'm afraid."

Dax's eyes flashed, and Sebastian knew he'd let something valuable slip. Namely, that he hadn't planned on this hasty wedding to Louisa Darby. The two men eyed each other, but Sebastian would not relent. He'd lived through far more scrutiny than the stare of his friend, and he would survive this.

But he needn't have worried for at that moment his bride arrived. When one usually pictures a day as special and life-changing as a wedding, one pictures elegance and grace, he would have presumed. This was not the manner in which the Darby sisters arrived.

Their carriage pulled to a stop at the foot of the church steps and through the slightly parted doors he witnessed Ravenwood squeeze his way out of the carriage door and nearly topple to the pavement at his feet. A cacophony of gibberish followed the man like a noisy accompaniment, and both Sebastian and Dax leaned involuntarily away from it. Ravenwood righted his jacket and, without looking back or acknowledging the disruption behind him, took the church stairs evenly and sedately. When he reached the two men waiting there, he smiled politely and moved on, sinking into a pew at the back of the church where he remained, unspeaking and unmoving.

"You know Viv wants to marry off his sisters so the man can get on with his own life?" Dax spoke softly.

Sebastian couldn't help a sad shake of his head as he

considered the man's slumped shoulders. "I fear it may be too late."

Both men tensed as footsteps sounded on the stairs behind them, but Sebastian was grateful to see Eliza coming into the church, a soft smile gracing her features.

He'd expected a congratulatory remark but instead she bundled them both in the direction of the altar.

"Come now. Mustn't tarry." She ushered them with a singular focus, and for the first time, Sebastian understood why Louisa compared him to this sister.

He was already standing at the front of the church before he realized he, too, was smiling. Perhaps circumstances would not turn out as dire as he suspected they might be.

But then Louisa appeared, and there was some sort of organ music somewhere, and he forgot entirely any resolutions he may have had.

She was stunning.

He already knew she could take his breath away, and while he knew to expect it, he was not at all prepared for this. She wore a gown of such brilliant white silk it conveyed a sheen of almost ice blue. It was covered in droplets of small white flowers embroidered in lines along the skirt, hems, and cuffs, so she appeared like some ethereal creature stepped from the pages of a fairy tale. Her golden hair was swept up in a cascade of curls at the back of her head, tucked neatly beneath a small blue and white cap that perfectly accentuated her gown, tiers of veils falling to either side of her face.

The rest of the ceremony he could tell anyone very little about but what Louisa looked like, that—that he knew by reading the memory it had stamped on his heart.

By the time she reached his side, he was certain he was completely deprived of oxygen, and at any moment, his head would strike the floor as he fainted. But by God, that didn't happen, and he was just as surprised as anyone.

The clergyman—he could not have said if he were a vicar, a pastor, or a reverend as he both did not attend service nor did he have any wits left about him at the sight of his betrothed in her wedding ensemble—began to intone flowery words of either patterned nonsense or perhaps some kind of religious scripture. Sebastian paid very little attention.

The nerves that were so tightly strung at the beginning of the day were now wound tighter than he'd ever endured before then. But this was a different kind of torture.

The beautiful woman beside him—he knew the taste of her kiss, the feel of her soft skin beneath his fingertips, the way she fit against him, and the most precious part—the sound of her moaning his name.

He knew everything about her he never wished to know of a woman. He swore he would never make the same mistakes as his father, and now here he was, dancing the dangerous line of emotional torture, and he feared more than ever that he just might fall in love with Louisa Darby.

Nay, Louisa Fielding. Had they gotten to that part yet? He wasn't paying attention.

"And do you, Sebastian Fielding, Duke of Waverly, take thee, Lady Louisa, as thy loyal wife, to love more than all, to cherish without end, for better or for worse, in all manner of health until death should part you?"

It wasn't until Louisa nudged him in the ribs that he realized he was meant to say something.

"Yes." The word spilled from his lips with greater force than he had meant it to, but he was fairly sure he'd gotten his point across.

Louisa twitched beside him.

"Yes?" The vicar or whatever he was raised an eyebrow. "Are you consenting to wed Lady Louisa?"

"Yes, that's what I just indicated. Did you not hear it?"

Sebastian eyed the clergyman with growing suspicion. He had left the matters of the wedding to Louisa and her sisters for he had little care for it, but now he wondered if she had selected a qualified authority to marry them.

"You are to speak the words *I do*, Your Grace." The clergyman made a sweeping motion with his hand as if to indicate Sebastian should attempt the turn of phrase.

"Why?" A collective gasp of speculation rippled through the pews behind him, but he could only study the small man draped in cloth before him.

He'd already consented to the pledge. What more did the clergyman need from him?

Louisa twitched again, and he glanced to see if she were all right.

He could recall only too clearly the words she'd flung at him that night on the terrace. To treat her with a measure of decency. He treated her far better than he had anyone else, but perhaps that was not enough for her. He would do well to remember that when he felt himself drawing too close to her. However, he worried how it squeezed his chest to think he'd upset her.

But his eyes did not find a disappointed Louisa. Instead they found her attempting to hold back laughter.

"It's customary that the groom speak those words," the clergyman went on.

Sebastian wished to continue studying Louisa and the mirth he seemed to have caused her, but the clergyman was being so terribly insistent.

Sebastian turned back to the vicar. "Hang custom. I spoke my oath. Let us move on."

The gasps behind him turned to startled inhalations he was sure could be heard as far as Kensington Palace. Notably, the Duchess of Margate's exclamation he heard clearly as she muttered it just behind him, and now, he, too, felt the tickle of laughter at their situation.

Damn the woman anyway. He was tired of her high-handedness when it came to Louisa. Did his wife get no say at all in that which she wished for most?

He didn't know what that was, but he knew only too well now that she did what was best for her sisters, never thinking of herself. He wondered why he suddenly wanted to change that.

"Uh, very good then, sir. I—I—I mean, Your Grace." The vicar's hands shook on the Bible he held between them as he scrambled to find his place.

Louisa spoke, and Sebastian said some more things he'd never remember, and through the whole of it the tension in his chest grew until he thought he could no longer draw breath. This was ludicrous. He knew he was stronger than this. He knew a formality like marriage could never turn him into his father. It was only a subject of contracts. He agreed to some things while the Duke of Ravenwood had agreed to others.

There was no need to entangle matters of the heart. There was no place for them in marriage.

So why, when Louisa turned to him, her chin turned up, her lips ready for his kiss that would seal the oaths they had just spoken to each other, did his chest flood with a warmth he'd never felt, his arms loosen as though they might fly away, his mind fall into a peaceful silence filled only with the need to kiss his new wife?

So he did.

He pressed his lips to hers far more chastely than that night on the terrace, but even then, he couldn't stop the feeling that the world was closing in around him.

CHAPTER 5

*I*t felt more like she was trapped rather than celebrating.

The wedding breakfast Viv had insisted having at Ravenwood House was likely a more coveted invitation than the one for their betrothal ball had been. The drawing rooms overflowed, and every piece of china was put to service, every piece of linen employed. Viv was elated. Louisa wanted nothing more than to escape.

Finally, she had decided it was too much and slipped away for just a moment, hiding in one of the retiring rooms and soundly locking the door. Here she could rub at her throbbing temples where prying eyes wouldn't wonder if she were feeling ill because she was with child. Was that why she was marrying the Beastly Duke? Or perhaps they would attribute her condition to realizing the gross unfairness of her fate?

Either of those options were ridiculous, and they only served to add to the mix of emotions that swirled through her.

She wasn't sure how long she sat there, picking apart her

feelings one by one. There was the immediate overwhelming sense of the day. There were so many people, so many curious stares, so many people she had only known the names of who were suddenly interested in her well-being because she was marrying Sebastian. This only served to irritate her.

As she had never been fond of crowds before, today's turnout left her drained and wary. She was securely wed to Sebastian now, and for that she was grateful. Perhaps she could finally put her latest folly behind her. Jo was safe, her reputation untarnished. No one could ever find fault with the Ravenwood name now that Louisa and Sebastian were wed. Still, it left her feeling unsettled and cautious. She knew the power of the *ton*, had witnessed it in Eliza's own exile to the fringes of society based simply on her appearance. Her worry for Jo would never cease. Louisa knew that.

The thing that plagued her most, however, was her own dear husband. He hadn't called on her, and they hadn't spoken to each other since the night of their betrothal ball when he had thoroughly ravished her more than a week previous. That night stood out in the parade of nights in all of her twenty-odd years as a shining anomaly she would never forget. She hadn't known what her own body was capable of, true, but more, she could not have expected Sebastian would be such a skilled lover.

The thought still had her reeling whenever she mulled over it. The man was so hard and cold, so austere and silent. Who would have guessed he could kiss with such passion? Hold her with such care? Pleasure her with such preciseness?

The physical aspect of the night, while unexpected, was not what left her in such confusion. It was the look in Sebastian's eyes right before he ran away. The Beastly Duke was not one known for cowardice, but something that night had frightened him. For a week, she had fumed and paced, worried he would call off the match regardless of the comprising position in which they had been discovered. For a week, she ruminated over what could have possibly caused that look in his eyes, what could have made him run.

Through the whole of this, she had simply believed herself to be the one at fault. She was the one who had trapped him, and the guilt laid on her so thick and heavy she worried if she'd ever find relief. But after that night, she didn't believe her own guilt any longer. Sebastian had proven all was not how she believed it to be, and it only left her more befuddled.

How he treated her physically was so different from his words and his manner. He was still often short and rude, preferring to keep his words to a minimum. Being late to their own betrothal ball showed a lack of concern that should have been startling.

But he continued to contradict even that evidence of his feelings toward her.

And heavens, how he had looked at her when she entered the church that morning.

She hadn't wanted a church wedding, but Viv had insisted after Eliza was married in a chapel. Viv said it wouldn't do for all the Darby sisters to have small ceremonies, and none of them were brave enough to point out that Viv had had a great, flourishing church wedding. So Louisa was married in a church.

Jo had selected her gown, and while Louisa did not care for the icy nature of the white silk, she did enjoy the look on Sebastian's face when he'd first seen her. His eyes had gone round, and his lips parted ever so slightly. This equated to an outright emotional explosion for another person, and it left Louisa uncertain.

Sebastian wanted her. Even if he didn't say the words,

even if he was more often rude to her than not, he clearly showed his desire in those unexpected moments.

Was that what he was afraid of?

She sat up, her hands dropping loosely to her lap.

Was Sebastian…afraid of her?

Not her, exactly. He was afraid of what she made him feel?

A headiness overcame her. She'd never held that kind of power over someone, and the realization that she might over the Beastly Duke was…she didn't know. She didn't know how she felt about any of this, and that was why she was hiding in the retiring room to begin with.

She wanted to keep ruminating in her thoughts, but a sharp knock at the door told her her time was up.

"You can't keep hiding in there, Louisa."

She wasn't surprised to hear Eliza's voice. Louisa hadn't been lying when she said Sebastian reminded her of Eliza. They were both pragmatists of the highest quality.

Louisa pushed to her feet, and unlocking the door, pulled it open to smile brightly at her sister to convince her nothing extraordinary was the matter.

"Did your head ache on your wedding day?"

Eliza's laugh was soft. "My wedding was not the event of the season. Apparently, it's more of a spectacle to marry a beastly duke than a jilted one."

"How unfortunate." Louisa frowned dramatically even as her stomach flipped. "Perhaps a bit of tea will help."

She took her sister's arm and led her back toward the rooms where the guests had filtered in after the breakfast to enjoy the usual tea and cigars. Louisa felt her throat close at the thought of re-entering those rooms and stopped abruptly on the outskirts, tugging Eliza to an unexpected stop.

"I see Sebastian has been cornered by the aunts," Louisa

said, fabricating an excuse to leave her sister. "I shall go rescue him, I think."

She squeezed Eliza's arm, and throwing her one more convincing smile, she plowed into the crowd to reach her husband.

Sebastian was not cornered by her aunts or anyone else for that matter. He stood at the far side of the room with only Dax as company. Apparently, everyone wished to know of Louisa's decision to marry, but no one seemed brave enough to confront the Beastly Duke himself.

Dax turned just as she approached, and he gave her a nod as he disappeared in the direction she'd come, likely to find his wife.

Louisa took her place next to her husband, not knowing at all what to say and certain standing next to him was not any better than getting lost in the crowd.

"Your gown is…lovely."

Louisa peered around them to see if a stampede of rhinos had suddenly crashed through the doors, but everything seemed to be just as it was before. She turned a wary eye to her husband.

She had a glib remark on her tongue, but when she took in the tightness of his jaw and the way his eyes wandered anywhere but to her person, she took pity on him.

"Thank you," she whispered.

Sebastian's lips parted, and she hung on what he may say next, but she'd never find out. For just then, another voice pulled her attention away.

"Oh, if it isn't themselves!" shrilled a voice far too loud for polite company.

Louisa started and blinked, carefully drawing into focus the pair of older women who had stopped them.

"Dear Louisa, all grown up. Why, I remember when you were just a little thing. Don't you remember, Maude?" The woman speaking was short and stout, her gray curls poking out like broken springs around a tarnished tiara set far back on her head. Her face was doughy and round, but her eyes were sharp and bright, an incongruity Louisa found intriguing.

"Oh, I do remember, Martha. Has it really been so many years?" The second woman was just as short, but where the other was round, this one was far too slender. Her joints prodded at the elbows and through the fingers of her gloves. She, too, wore a tarnished tiara, but it nestled quite obviously on top of her lank, gray hair. Again, her eyes were disproportionately bright.

"I think it has," replied Martha, who Louisa understood to be the stout one.

As Louisa could only blink, Maude let out a trill laugh.

"Oh dear me, child, you don't remember who we are. It's quite all right. You were just a wee thing. I'm your Aunt Maude. Well, not truly an aunt." She chewed at her lower lip and looked to her companion for guidance. "I think we're cousins, aren't we, Martha?"

Martha took to studying the ground as if to piece the familiar connection together. Louisa could feel Sebastian stiffen beside her, and she could only imagine what he thought of this interruption.

He likely didn't have the time for such nonsense.

"Oh, Maude, you're quite right. Isn't it Wendy that is the connection? I do believe Wendy is a cousin, not an aunt."

"Are you sure she's a cousin? I thought she was Papa's sister?"

Martha shook her head. "No, I'm quite certain Wendy was a cousin."

Finally, the two women turned back to Louisa as if coming to a decision, small smiles playing across their identically small mouths.

"Well, child, whichever it is, we're so happy to see you. It's been so long you know," Martha said.

"We already said it's been a long time," Maude whispered. "We haven't seen her since, well, since—"

The poor little woman stopped abruptly, her eyes going wide as she took in Louisa, and Louisa suddenly knew what the woman had been about to say.

They hadn't seen her since her mother's funeral.

Louisa had never before seen these women, but funerals had a way of drawing together those who would otherwise remain absent from a person's life. The only other time in history Louisa could have seen these women would have been then, at her mother's funeral.

The realization rocked Louisa like a sudden storm sweeping across the moors. She swallowed and straightened her shoulders when she realized she'd inadvertently taken a step back and away from these women.

"How very kind of you to come today," Louisa found herself saying even as a flood of memories hit her.

Not now. She already carried too much. She couldn't think of her mother.

But the memories came anyway.

Those last few days of her mother's life. Everyone kept whispering. Doors kept shutting her out. The doctor kept coming at all hours. The housekeeper, or perhaps it was some kind of nurse, shooed the children away. Louisa had been too young to know who it was. Father, oh God, poor Father hiding in his study, too scared to see his wife dying.

Louisa had been scared, too, scared of her mother dying alone, so she'd done something terrible. The memories wouldn't stop now. The closed and dusty smell of the sick-room, something pungent and strong burning her nostrils as she got closer to her mother's bed. All of the bottles and rags that littered the bedside table. She still couldn't see her mother. She had to get closer.

After that, there was nothing but noise. First the doctor yelling for that other horrible woman, and then Father rushing in to scoop her up, his voice loud because he was trying to speak above the others, trying to tell her it was going to be all right.

But it wasn't going to be all right. It never would be. Because Louisa had killed her mother. Louisa had brought the influenza into the house.

This was her fault.

She didn't know how long she stood there, staring, concentrating on simply breathing, but these women must have said something because suddenly Sebastian touched her elbow.

She started at his touch, so soft and yet so sure and warm, and she swung her gaze up to his.

His eyebrows had gone flat, and he studied her carefully, and for one absurd moment, she thought he might care.

"Are you all right, dear one?"

Louisa turned her attention back to the women, but she didn't know who had spoken, her mind still in a place long ago and far away, and she didn't really care.

"I'm quite all right," she said, her face slipping into the practiced smile that came so easily now. "If you would excuse me, I must see to our other guests."

"Oh, of course, dears."

Louisa didn't hear the rest of it. She was already plunging back into the deafening cacophony created by her wedding guests.

* * *

Sebastian watched her carefully on the short ride back to his townhouse.

Their townhouse now, he supposed.

He would be the first to admit their wedding had not exactly been the stuff of a young girl's dreams. He could also admit his own role in that. Perhaps he should have not squabbled with the vicar at the altar, but really, the man was being unreasonable. What did it matter what words he spoke as long as they conveyed the same meaning?

What had occurred at the wedding breakfast, however, he knew was the final nail in whatever coffin Louisa viewed the wedding to have been. He didn't know who those women were, but he knew their effect on Louisa had not been pleasant.

In all the time he had known his wife, she was always effervescent, ebullient, charming, and warm. But when those women mentioned the last time they had seen Louisa, it was as if his wife had been replaced with another person entirely. Her dewy skin had gone cold and flat, her eyes swimmingly vacant as if she were seeing another time and place.

As the carriage bounced toward home, he studied her profile now, realizing for the first time just how much he didn't know about his bride.

He knew the father of the family had died in the last few years of simple and blessed old age, but he vaguely remembered mention of a mother who had died terribly young. He didn't know any more on the matter as it was none of his concern. But he was fairly certain those eccentric old women had meant they hadn't seen Louisa since her mother's funeral. Surely it was that which had made Louisa close in on herself.

And horribly, it now made him want to know about her mother's death.

He hadn't cared about another person besides Dax in a

very long time, and the tug of concern he now felt toward Louisa frightened him. This was the very thing he had meant to avoid. Emotional entanglements always led to these kinds of distractions, and before one knew it, he could be sucked into a turmoil he could have easily evaded had he not cared in the first place.

Sebastian released a breath.

It was too late for that. He knew it only too well. He already cared for Louisa, and he couldn't stand to sit there and watch her hold herself together so carefully.

He cleared his throat. "I trust the ceremony was to your liking."

She started as if he'd pulled her from the depth of her thoughts. "Yes," she said, but the word had an edge to it that suggested she spoke the answer she thought was warranted.

Her gaze remained focused out the window, but her irises did not move as though she weren't really paying attention. She just wished to look at nothing perhaps.

"I enjoyed the pudding. Ravenwood must employ an accomplished cook."

"Yes, of course."

The carriage rattled on for a few more beats.

"My favorite, though, was the parade of monkeys dressed in top hats."

"Em, yes."

He didn't know why he did it, but he could not stand the idea of carrying on such a one-sided conversation. So carefully, he reached out and slipped his hand under the one lying softly in her lap. She jerked, as he had anticipated, but he laced his fingers through hers and held on, capturing her in his grip.

Finally, her eyes moved, first flying to their entwined hands and then to his face. He smiled, hoping the unusual expression coming from him would hold her attention.

"I think it would be helpful if you were to tell me what you're thinking. I'm not sure I have the fortitude to withstand such an inane conversation. Should you carry on like that, your answers will grow so short as to be nothing at all."

"I'm sorry?" Her tone was confused, and he knew she didn't realize he had been talking the last few minutes or if she did, it only vaguely registered.

"Those women upset you. Not that you were particularly pleased before we encountered them, but you were at least pretending to be so."

She snatched her hand out of his grasp. "I was not pretending. It was lovely to see friends and family I do not always get to spend time with."

"Liar."

A line appeared between her brows as she frowned. "I am not lying. You just wouldn't know because you don't have family or friends."

Her words met their mark, and he felt the stab of them in his gut. But the shock that registered on her face quickly assuaged any lingering pain. He tried to assure her with a self-deprecating smile that it needn't matter how true her words were or that she'd spoken them, but there was no assuring Louisa Darby.

"I can't believe I just said that." She reached out now, laid a hand on his arm. "Sebastian, I'm so sorry. That was utterly cruel and inexcusable. I shouldn't have said it."

"Why? It's true, isn't it?"

Her hand slid from his arm as her eyes searched his face. "Just because they're true doesn't make them any less cruel."

"I'm glad you were happy to see your family and friends." He kept his tone even in hopes she would forget what she'd said, but there was no distracting Louisa either.

"You *do* have friends, you know. You have Dax and Eliza.

73

And even little George. You have your mother. Well, I can see where there would be more of a trial, but you do have her."

His heart slowed to an almost imperceptible beat as words he hadn't meant to say slipped from his lips.

"What about you, Louisa?"

The shock was better hidden this time, traced along the rounded curves as her eyes grew wide, but it was still there. Her gaze did that back-and-forth dance again, but he knew she was looking inside herself this time instead of at him.

Too late and too rushed, she said, "Yes, of course."

Her answer left a hollowness inside of him. He wanted to scratch at his chest as if to ease the pain, but instead he moved his gaze out the window.

It shouldn't matter. Louisa didn't marry him for love, after all, and he didn't want love in the first place. He had already learned to live with the loneliness. The loneliness was far simpler than anything else.

She didn't speak any more, and he didn't bother with any further questions. It was better this way. He had wanted a separation between them, and now he would have it. Everything could go back to what it was before.

The carriage dipped into a rather large hole in the pavement, sending him jostling against the side of the conveyance. His arm pressed into the box he had tucked inside his jacket earlier that day. In all that had occurred, he'd nearly forgotten about it.

He reached inside his jacket and slipped the slim box from the pocket where he'd placed it that morning and handed it to Louisa.

"I understand it's custom for the groom to give the bride a small token at the wedding."

She held her hands pressed to her stomach, her eyes riveted to the box.

"You got me...a present?"

"Yes." He gestured with the box for her to take it.

Gingerly, she held the box by the tips of her fingers.

When she continued to simply hold it, he said, "I believe at this point it's customary for you to open it."

Her eyes had been studying the box, so he was surprised to find them damp when she lifted her gaze to him. "But I didn't get you anything."

Once more he felt the stab of disappointment, and he pushed it aside. It didn't matter what she thought of him. He need only remind himself that theirs was a match of necessity, nothing more.

"I wouldn't expect you to."

He wanted it to be the truth but ever since that night in the moonlight when he'd held her in his arms, when he discovered just how powerful his attraction to her was, he had wanted something more. He knew it, he admitted it, and he toed the edge of the water where danger lurked.

He'd purchased the gift the very next day out of a compulsion that should have worried him. It was as though he needed to find something into which he could pour all of the feelings too dangerous to show Louisa. But the gift allowed him to express those emotions without uttering a single word to her that could one day haunt him.

She considered him for several moments before finally lifting the lid of the small jeweler's box in her hand.

His chest tightened as he waited for her response.

It seemed an eternity before she lifted her gaze to his.

"It's a hatpin." Her tone was neutral, if not slightly...disappointed? Confused?

"Yes. It's made of the finest gold, so you needn't worry that it not be strong enough."

She used two fingers to pick up the hatpin, the last of the light from outside the windows glinting off the yellow gold.

"Strong enough for what?"

"To defend yourself, of course. You don't want it to bend should you have need to stab an attacker with it."

Her lips parted as she absorbed his words.

"This is to defend myself?" She held up the hatpin.

"Yes. It's nearly twenty-three centimeters, so that should give you a strong grip on it. I thought the stone at the end would help with that. Give you something to wrap your fingers around."

She blinked, her brow knitting. "Why would you do this for me?"

He felt the words he wanted to say clog in his throat. There were so many reasons he wished for her to have the hatpin. Bastards like Devlin were all too common unfortunately.

"I won't always be there to protect you." He hadn't meant to whisper the words, but it was all he could do to get them out.

He studied her face, waiting for her response, but her eyes remained slightly unfocused, her lips parting as if she were blowing a kiss.

When she still didn't speak, he felt the silence begin to claw at him. "I'm sorry to say, not all men are honorable, as you unfortunately learned. It sickens me to think another man's actions can take away your choices. That's not fair, and it's largely beyond your control." He nodded to the hatpin. "That is the one thing I can do to give you a better chance at protecting yourself from less than honorable gentlemen."

She blinked once more and whispered, "Thank you."

"You're most welcome."

Something hung between them then, charged and pulsating. He could feel the tingly nature of it as if he were standing in the middle of a lightning storm. But then she blinked, and it vanished.

Carefully, she put the hatpin back in its case and snapped the lid shut.

"Those women were referring to my mother's funeral." Her eyes flew up, her gaze locking onto his, and for the first time that day, he found the fire there he was coming to crave. "That was the last time they saw me. My mother died from influenza when I was five."

She kneaded her lower lip, and he wondered if she wished to say more. She considered for some moments before turning away, holding the hatpin box clasped in both of her hands.

Once again he studied her profile, but now he knew more. He knew Louisa had a secret that was easier for her to keep than for her to speak. Something shifted inside of him, and he wondered if Louisa and he were not just the same— two creatures making their way through a world that had dealt them an unforgivable blow.

The carriage turned another corner, and although her head never turned away from the window, Louisa slipped her hand into his. It stayed there for the rest of the journey home.

CHAPTER 6

*T*he hatpin box lay open on her dressing table as she brushed her hair that night.

She couldn't take her eyes from the delicate gold that twined its way around the amethyst set into the head of the pin. The yellow of the gold and purples of the stone reflected in the candlelight with warmth and allure. It wasn't only functional: the piece was striking.

And Sebastian had gotten it for her.

The suggestions behind the gift were too great for her to comprehend even now that she'd had hours to digest it. Her husband not only cared enough to give her a gift but one so personal and meaningful. Only Sebastian knew what had happened that night in the Lumberton drawing room, and he'd chosen a gift of such heavy significance. She still couldn't wrap her brain around what it meant personally. That he was concerned for her safety, that he worried he wouldn't always be there to protect her.

Her heart squeezed at the memory of his words even as she brushed at her hair furiously.

Why did he do this?

Why was he so cold and rude one moment whilst the next he overset her with affection and care?

Why did he blunder his way through their marriage vows and then bestow upon her a gift of such…such…

Lud, were all men like this?

She wished Jo were here. At this point, she would even take Viv. Men were so vexing. How was a woman to navigate her way in marriage without the help of her sisters?

She stopped her hand, the brush caught in mid-stroke through her hair. The quiet of the house around her intensified as she realized how utterly alone she was. Her sisters weren't there. Jo was not in the room beside hers, and Viv was not down the hall. Louisa was completely alone now. Now. Now more than ever when she needed her sisters. She had never quite understood how challenging it would be to be married to the Beastly Duke, and she was without reinforcements.

A rustling behind her startled her, and she swung around only to see her maid, Nancy, putting the last of Louisa's gowns in the armoire. Waverly House had been rather dark when they'd finally arrived, and after greeting the staff, she'd gone directly to her rooms, wanting nothing more than quiet and a chance to lie down. She'd seen very little of the place, but her rooms were well appointed if the wallpaper was rather aged, the furniture worn. It was all fine trappings if perhaps a little old and well…unmatched.

Louisa wondered not for the first time about Sebastian's home life as a child. Waverly House reflected an existence of neglect, and she wondered if Sebastian were not evidence of the same.

"Nancy." Nancy was from Surrey and had grown up on a dairy farm. Louisa had never met a woman of such fortitude, and if anyone were to give her advice on how to manage the Beastly Duke, it would be the daughter of a farmer. "How are you finding things below stairs?"

Nancy tucked a stray ribbon into the armoire and closed the doors softly. "Waverly House is well run, Your Grace, if the other servants are rather quiet."

Louisa set down her hairbrush. "Quiet?"

Nancy folded her hands in front of her. The woman could not have been older than Louisa, but a hard life already showed on the dullness of her face and eyes. Moving households was hard for a servant. There was a new staff and a new housekeeper or butler to acclimate oneself to, not to mention the transportation and sorting of her mistress's things. The woman was likely as exhausted as Louisa.

Nancy gave a nod. "It's not that they're tight-lipped or unfamiliar, madam. It's only, well, they seem rather to simply not speak unless it's necessary. I get the feeling it's a rather taciturn household."

Louisa was not at all surprised to hear this.

"Nancy, may I ask you a personal question?"

The servant gave a quick nod, her expression unchanging.

"Do you have a beau in your life?"

"No, madam. It's unwise for those in service to form romantic attachments. It can make finding work difficult."

How very sad. "You have no one at all?"

"I have my family, madam. I do get to visit them twice a year."

Louisa pushed to her feet. "Nancy, you shall have tomorrow off. I know transitioning households can be difficult, and I plan to spend the morrow learning my way about this new place. I shan't have need of you. Would you like me to arrange a carriage to take you to your family?"

Only Nancy's eyes gave any indication that she'd heard

her mistress as they rounded slightly in shock. "Your Grace, I couldn't—"

"Unless you have any helpful information regarding one's relations with men, I think it would be all right for you to rest tomorrow." Louisa gave her maid a sardonic smile.

Nancy's mouth softened as her eyes took on a hint of understanding. "Madam, if I may, servants often hear the rumors of the *ton*, and…" The maid's voice trailed off.

"And I've married the Beastly Duke?"

Nancy looked about her as if searching for danger. "Well, yes, madam."

"It appears I have, but I assure you the rumors are far worse than his bite. If only he was better at communicating…" It was her turn to let her words trail off.

Nancy stepped forward, her expression earnest. "Your Grace, if I may. My mum is always saying how my da isn't quite how he seems. He's a burly man as you can expect from a farmer, but he's always been sweet on my mum. Perhaps His Grace has a harder exterior than his heart. You might just be surprised if you simply talk to him."

Here Louisa stood on her wedding night getting advice from her lady's maid. Not that the woman was wrong about what she suggested. Louisa was beginning to suspect the same thing.

She took the maid's hands into her own. "Thank you, Nancy. That should be all for tonight. I'm sure you'd like your bed."

Nancy's smile was grateful. "Thank you, Your Grace. Should you wish me to braid your hair before I leave?"

Louisa shook her head. "No, thank you. I'll see to it."

It would be nice to have something to keep her hands busy while she waited for her husband to arrive. With a flash, that night on the terrace came back to her, leaving her hot and unsettled. Would he do that to her again? Would he do...more?

Nancy gave a bow of her head as she moved toward the door, but Louisa stopped her.

"Oh, Nancy, it just occurred to me. You're lady's maid to the mistress of the house. I suppose I ought to call you by your family name now." Nancy had been with Louisa since her coming out, and it felt odd to call the woman anything but her given name. But Louisa supposed the rules of society dictated otherwise now that she was a duchess. And besides, Nancy had earned the recognition. "You must get used to me calling you Williams now."

Had the light been better, Louisa would have sworn Nancy blushed.

Her maid gave a small curtsy. "Thank you, madam."

Louisa watched the door shut on the only person who shared a connection to her childhood, and soon she was standing alone in her rooms as the Duchess of Waverly.

A fire had been laid as the spring was slightly chilly and the warm summer nights had not fallen on London as of yet. She concentrated on the snap of the flames if only to distract herself from her thoughts. Without knowing she did it, her hands explored her torso and stomach, anticipating the touch of her husband's hands on her body, discovering her every curve, feeling—

She coughed and twisted around to retrieve her brush. After a few furious strokes, she abandoned the brush and carefully plaited her hair into a loose braid over one shoulder. Her night-rail was a new one from her trousseau, and the lace edgings were still snowy white and crisp. With her hair in a loose braid and color high in her cheeks from the day's events, Louisa might have said she looked pretty.

But was this how one dressed when awaiting one's husband on their wedding night?

Nervousness swamped her, and she picked up her dressing gown, suddenly feeling exposed and raw standing in the middle of her room. Pulling the garment tightly around her, she made her way to the fire, welcoming its warmth. Tucking her feet beneath her, she slid into the chair closest to the fire and wrapped her arms about herself.

There was no need to be nervous. Sebastian had proven himself respectful and attentive, if he sometimes erred in his delivery of his intentions. Physically, he'd never hurt her. Quite the contrary, in fact. He had done nothing but made her feel utterly cherished every time he touched her.

When he'd slipped his hand into hers in the carriage after the wedding breakfast, she'd nearly lost what little she'd eaten, so startled was she by the simple, sweet gesture. She should have told him the truth then. She should have been honest with him about the guilt she carried, but something stopped her.

She wasn't sure where they stood and what their relationship was to be. It was so confusing and visceral. One moment he made her feel precious and the next he supplied one-word answers and made her feel as though she were the least important thing in his world. The man was trying, to say the least.

So she'd kept her secret. There was no reason to tell him anything about her past that he needn't know. She'd carried the guilt for so long. She would simply continue to carry it.

There was a small clock set on the mantelpiece, and she glanced at it now, wondering when her husband would make an appearance. It was just after midnight, and had this been any other night, she'd have still been in ballgown and slippers and dancing the night away with every eligible bachelor the *ton* had to offer.

But now it was different. That part of her life was over.

Now she was well and truly wed, and Jo was safe. Jo's future was safe. Perhaps Louisa could finally rest.

The fire tugged at her, but her eyes would not close, her body wound tight with anticipation. Should she wait for him in the bed? Was that what was expected?

She glanced again at the clock, a sudden thought striking her.

What if he didn't come?

Theirs was not a love match nor even one made of their own free will. There was nothing to dictate he should visit her tonight, only the obligation to consummate the marriage, but if he gave no credence to the marriage to begin with...

Louisa got to her feet, unable to sit any longer.

He had been late to his own betrothal ball. What was there to suggest he *would* visit her tonight?

He'd already made it abundantly clear that she had trapped him, that he felt the confines of his marital prison. She had never thought him one to marry, and now she had forced him into it, pinning him with the unyielding arms of honor.

Damn him.

She didn't know where such a strong thought came from, and it startled her. She pressed a fist to her stomach and sucked in a breath.

It was Sebastian's fault.

The whole of her life had been focused on making her sisters happy, and Sebastian had stepped into her world and shown her she had feelings of her own. Wants and desires. Passion. All of those things she had simply ignored because her sisters came first.

And now he wasn't coming.

He showed her the hunger that could exist between a man and a woman, and now he was going to leave her wanting.

That may have worked with another woman, but it wouldn't work with Louisa Darby.

She pushed up the sleeves of her gown and without stopping to rethink her actions, she marched to the connecting door and pounded on it.

* * *

HE WANTED nothing more than to drink the glass of whiskey he held precariously balanced between the tips of his fingers and the arm of his chair. But it was the second glass of whiskey he'd poured that night, and he never drank the second glass in its entirety. He might have sipped at it and savored it, but never would he toss it back like he'd done the first one.

His wife lay in the bed in the connecting room, and he was hard at just the thought of slipping in there and making love to her.

Whiskey was not enough to banish her from his thoughts.

He pictured her in a virginal gown of snowy white, tucked into bed with the covers pulled tight to her chin, her golden hair fanned out on the pillow behind her. He wanted to run his fingers through that hair, take fistfuls of it and bury his nose in her scent. He wanted her pressed against him, feeling the way she fit so perfectly, like nothing and no one before her.

But he knew if he gave just a little, he was doomed.

His father's dead body flashed through his mind, and reluctantly, he took a sip of whiskey, the only thing left to him to push away his torment.

The banging startled him so badly he choked on the small sip of liquid, coming up off his chair as though someone had poked him directly in the arse with a hot poker.

He knew it was sometime after midnight, and his heart

kicked up its pace as he went to the door and threw it open. The corridor was deserted, and he stared at the empty space for an interminable length of time as he willed his heart to stop pounding. Whatever was going on?

The pounding sounded again behind him, and he pivoted, casting his gaze back over his shoulder.

Someone was knocking on the connecting door.

If his heart was racing before, now it slowed to deadly levels.

Louisa.

Louisa could be the only one knocking on that door, and judging by the force with which she did it, she was not pleased.

He closed the door to the corridor, unconsciously throwing the lock as if to assure himself there would be no other intruders that night. He marched over to the connecting door and thankfully yanked it open before she could start pounding again. He found her standing there, fist raised as if she planned to continue her assault.

He stared at her without greeting as the pressure with which he was grinding his teeth prevented speech.

He didn't need this. He didn't need to see her like this. He didn't need to witness the stuff of his imagination come to life. Only the reality was far worse.

The snowy virginal gown was there, but so too was a satin robe that draped every curve of her body. Her hair wasn't spread across a pillow but instead hung over her shoulder in a braid that tempted him to unwind it.

It only helped when he took in her face, and her tight, angry lips, her hooded eyes, and narrowed nostrils.

"You're not coming."

He doubted she understood the double entendre, but it still forced him to surreptitiously adjust his tight trousers.

She had stated the problem precisely. He was not coming. She was staying safely in her rooms, and he was staying safely in his.

"I'm sorry?" He thought if he played innocent, they could reach the end of this conversation without him undoing eight years of careful control.

Instead, she stomped through the open door and turned on him.

"It is customary for the husband to visit the wife on their wedding night to consummate the marriage."

Even when she spoke with such clinical acuteness, it did nothing to lessen his desire for the act of which she spoke.

"It is customary." He folded his arms across his chest. "But what of our marriage *is* customary?"

He didn't know why he had asked the question. It would not at all encourage the end of this conversation and see her safely back in her rooms. But something compelled him to keep her here for just a little longer. Surely, he could control himself. He'd been doing it for so long now it was nearly second nature.

A shadow passed over her face at his words, and he felt a pang of regret, for what he didn't know. He'd only spoken the truth. There was nothing traditional about how they had come to be married, and he was only pointing out that fact. But his words had struck something within her, and a part of him wanted to comfort her. He took a step forward before he caught himself.

She retreated, however, her next accusation already on her lips. "How our marriage came about may not be customary, but we are still required to live with one another now that we are wed. Do you propose carrying on in a half state of existence for the rest of our marriage? You living your life while I live mine separately?"

"Yes." He hadn't meant to speak the word with such force, and it ricocheted through the room like a gunshot.

It was as if he had slapped her. Her mouth registered shock in a soundless *oh* as she took a quick step back as if the word itself had forced her to.

"Louisa." It was all he got out before she threw up a hand. It was his turn to react as though he'd been struck. The single gesture arrested him in his stance, his mouth snapping shut.

"I beg your pardon." Her tone was even, as if he had not just pulled the foundation from everything she clearly had expected of their marriage. "I hadn't realized you would wish this to be more of an arrangement. I understand." She did the oddest thing then. She smiled, but it was a smile tinged with what could only be pain, but somehow he thought the gesture automatic for her.

How often did she use that smile on her sisters? How often did she use it to placate one of them?

His mind blanked at the expression. He hadn't known he held the power to hurt her so deeply. He had never held such power over anyone. Having lived a separate existence himself these last eight years, he had forgotten what it was like to have one's words and actions affect another person. Now he'd hurt the one person he would never wish to. His chest tightened as he stepped closer yet again, but she was already turning back toward the door.

"I apologize for interrupting your evening. Good night." She slipped through the opening of the door with such cold grace, he hadn't realized she'd even moved.

Fear gripped his throat, strangled his words, but watching her disappear like that, knowing how he must have hurt her, he knew he had to fix it and fix it fast.

"I can't fall in love with you." The words were nearly shouted as he watched the door closing between them, but at his outburst, it stopped.

He hung there, suspended. Would she open the door or continue to close it? He wished he'd had more experience with this sort of thing, but he hadn't bothered as it was the very thing he wished never to encounter.

He may have blundered the entire thing, and could he really blame her for her escape? He'd just doomed her to a loveless marriage. Louisa Darby, the sunshine in every room, the belle of every ball. He'd just singlehandedly condemned her.

His chest hurt, and a throbbing had begun at his temples. He concentrated on breathing, but the door had still not moved. After what seemed an eternity, the door opened but only slightly. Louisa's head came around the corner.

"I'm very sorry, but did you just say you can't fall in love with me?"

He swallowed, unsure of his voice. "Yes, that's precisely what I said."

Her eyes narrowed in confusion even as she gave a brief nod that she'd heard him, and then worst of all, she withdrew her head and closed the door.

The click of the door shutting pierced him, and he turned away, unable to look at the place where she'd disappeared.

He should have told her. He should have been honest with her from the start that theirs would be a loveless marriage. But even then, he recalled her reaction to those women at the breakfast that morning. He couldn't be sure, but he thought it was more than just her mother's death that weighed on her. There was something else, something darker.

He couldn't allow himself to feel remorse. She had her secrets just as he had his.

Then why did he feel so absolutely wretched?

He strode over to the decanter of scotch he had left on the

table beside his chair. Forget the second glass. He wasn't stopping until he was well and truly drunk.

He'd just pulled the stopper from the bottle when the connecting door crashed open. He spun around so quickly, scotch sloshed in the decanter, and he quickly reset the stopper before any made its way out.

Louisa stormed in, dressing gown flying out behind her like an enraged goddess. But she wasn't enraged. A deep line was nestled between her eyes and her mouth was already working out what he knew would be an endless stream of questions.

"What do you mean, you can't love me?" She stopped several feet from him, her arms swinging madly as she gesticulated her question. "I know you're...well, different, but I happen to know I am quite fetching, and some would even call me pretty. You yourself called me beautiful. Why are you so certain you cannot love me?"

He set down the scotch. "You assume this has anything to do with you."

She crossed her arms, her satin dressing gown twisting about her. "I am your wife and the person in question. I should think it would have something to do with me."

"It has nothing to do with you. If anything, you make it extremely difficult for me to stay true to my course."

Her expression relaxed at this. "I apologize again for trapping you. I promise—"

"Why do you keep apologizing for that?" He cut her off. "I offered for you. You did not demand I wed you to alleviate the potential danger to your reputation. I chose to do that."

"You wouldn't have been forced to make that decision if it were not for my careless actions."

He took a small step toward her. "Careless they might have been, but no one dictates my decisions. You must not accept guilt for the position we now find ourselves in."

Her shoulders squared, and her chin went up at that. "It is not guilt. It is responsibility, and I take mine seriously. I promised to be a good duchess, and I shall. You won't be disappointed."

"I never suspected I would be."

They watched each other for several silent beats before she began to worry at her lower lip as he was coming to expect she did when she toyed with a problem.

"Out with it."

She dropped her arms, her hands going into tight fists. "I still do not see what any of this has to do with loving me." Her face went red at her declaration, and she closed her eyes, holding up both of her hands. "That came out entirely not how I meant it. I would agree I am an affable person, but I do not expect everyone to love me. I simply struggle with why you're so adamant about us maintaining separate lives so you can *not* fall in love with me."

"I find love does nothing but encourage people to engage in irrational and dangerous behavior. I swore off the notion long ago."

He'd stepped too close to her, and the scent of orchids toyed with him. He turned away, putting much-needed space between them, tugging at his cuffs as he did so.

She was quiet for longer than he expected, and he peered over his shoulder at her. She studied the carpet, her jaw working, and he knew she pondered what he'd said.

Finally, she faced him. "I can understand how you might draw such a conclusion. I, myself, often wonder why love leaves us open to so much heartache. But why would you commit your life to such emptiness?"

The fire snapped behind him, and the few candles that lit the room served only to create a bubble that contained only them. A feeling of security washed over him. He could say anything now, and she would listen to him. She may not understand, but she would listen. And for the first time in a very long time, he could lay down his burdens at someone else's feet.

So he told her the truth.

"Because my father killed himself over his lover."

CHAPTER 7

*S*he didn't know Sebastian that well, and yet she knew him better than anyone in the *ton*, including Dax. Knew his person more so than his past, and his revelation left her searching for words.

"I didn't know." The words came out hardly more than a whisper.

"No one does."

This took her back even further.

"What do you mean, no one knows?"

He turned away from her toward the fire, and she saw he'd been drinking before she entered. An empty glass and decanter of dark liquor sat on a low table by the chair next to the fire. The tableau it conjured in her mind was a sad one: Sebastian at the fireside drinking alone on his wedding night.

Every time she thought she had condemned him to the boar society thought he was, she uncovered another layer of him that left her gasping.

She watched him now as he paced away from her.

"My mother found him after the fact. It was shortly after

Christmas, so I was still in London at the time. I remember the red ribbons and bows festooned everywhere, the smell of holly and pine." He gave a harsh laugh then. "It was a shock to be confronted with such gruesome loss after walking through such cheer."

He studied the fire instead of facing her. She took a step closer to him, her feet soundless on the carpet.

"Sebastian." She could speak only his name. The picture he painted was too stark and heavy with sadness. She couldn't force him to continue if he shouldn't wish to, but she could let him know she was listening.

"I told my mother to keep the servants from the room while I fetched the doctor. He was a good friend of my father's, and I knew I could trust him to be discreet." Finally, he turned only his head to send her a wry smile. "You surely know how malicious society can be when one of their own steps out of bounds."

His words cut too close to the bone for her as she faced the husband who had been forced to wed her to avoid the same vindictive society. The same husband who had just told her he couldn't love her.

Had she thought he would love her?

It had never crossed her mind, not consciously anyway. Her intent had been setting on marriage to avoid hurting Jo. But now, in the stillness of the night around them, now that the danger to Jo had passed, Louisa could explore her deeper intentions, and if she were brave enough, she could admit she'd always been attracted to Sebastian.

Love?

Maybe not that exactly, but that ethereal pull that draws a person eventually to love? That was what she had felt for Sebastian. Possibilities. But there were no possibilities now.

It shouldn't matter. Jo was safe, and that was the most important thing.

"I do," she finally said, licking her dry lips.

"My father was buried before anyone could ask questions. I carefully placed the idea that he died of apoplexy and that the family wished for privacy. There's nothing society enjoys more than heartbreak, and a father and husband taken too young from something out of one's control was just what they wanted."

"Is that why you withdrew from society?" She wasn't sure if it was overstepping her bounds to ask such a question. After all, he had not seemed pleased with discussing this in the least, and she should have been satisfied that he had told her what he had.

But she couldn't stop herself, not when she saw someone hurting, and she itched to fix it.

The thought startled her. It had never occurred to her that Sebastian might need her. That she may be able to make his life...better than before he'd met her. Perhaps she could heal the wounds his mother had inflicted on the young boy, tamper the remorse and anger of his father's death. Maybe she could bring him back into the light.

As she studied the taut muscles under the shoulders of his jacket, the way his hands clenched into tight fists, it seemed an impossible feat. But didn't Louisa excel at resolving precisely such problems?

He seemed to consider his answer before he said, "It was the catalyst for the decision I had already made. I had been in society several years by that point, and I found I did not like it in the least. Why expend one's energy on such frivolity and nonsense?"

She wanted to ask him about that, but she wouldn't be distracted from the matter at hand. Namely, why her husband couldn't love her.

Again, not that she wanted him to. It was more about having the possibility of such a thing. There hadn't been a possibility at all, and now it was over before it had even begun.

And perhaps a few more kisses. One or two caresses wouldn't be a burden.

She gave herself a mental shake. Now was not the time for that.

"Do you know…" she let the question trail off as she took another tentative step forward.

"Who was my father's lover?" His voice was hard as he finished the question she couldn't. He shook his head. "I never bothered to search her out. What would have been the point?"

"It could explain why your father was desperate enough to take his own life. An act such as that is not taken lightly, I imagine. To take one's own life…there cannot be another choice in the person's mind, and they choose the most awful one because they think it's all they have left to them. Your father must have been terrified."

His jaw relaxed at her words. "I suppose he might have been."

She had reached the chair by the fire, and she placed her hands along the top of it. "How did he do it?"

"He used one of the dueling pistols his father had given him. Ironic that he should use it to take his own life rather than the life of another."

"I see nothing ironic about the affair."

He moved his eyes away from her and studied the fire for several beats.

"No, I suppose there isn't." His voice was gravelly when he finally spoke the words.

They fell silent then, and she let the crackle of the fire fill the space mostly because she didn't know what to say next. How was she to speak to him about love?

"I should have told you," he said after a while, and she looked up at his words.

He had turned away from the fire now, and his eyes were piercing as they focused on her. A shiver passed down her arms at the intensity of his gaze, but she shook it off. Hadn't he just told her they were to lead separate lives?

The horrid thought struck her then that she would need to seek a lover herself if she would wish for any of…the more delicate things that usually came between husband and wife. She didn't know precisely what those were, but Sebastian had shown her enough, so she knew there was more to be had.

It just wouldn't be with Sebastian.

The thought had her chest squeezing, and she stepped back, swallowing.

"It's no worry," she said, waving off his concern. "As you said, ours is not a customary marriage, and I am sure there will be much for us to figure out."

His fingers flexed against his leg, and her eyes caught on the movement. It was safer to look there than to return his dark gaze.

"Can I ask you one more question perhaps?" Her courage was quickly fleeting; if she didn't ask now she wouldn't. He gave only a nod, and she continued. "Do you not believe in love because of what happened to your father or do you not wish it for yourself?"

His laugh was harsh and critical. "I have seen the evidence of love and what it does to those who indulge in it." He stepped closer to her, lowering his head to capture her gaze as his voice grew earnest. "I assure you I want nothing to do with such carelessness. Love makes sound people do stupid things, and I will not fall victim to it."

The question she most wanted to ask was on the very tip of her tongue. She need only push it out. Her heart raced at the thought, but her tongue remained still, her mouth slightly parted as she stared at the shadows of her husband's face.

If he didn't believe in love, then why had he done what he did that night on the terrace? Why had he shown her passion and desire only to rob her of it for the rest of her life?

How could he be so cruel?

But that was just it. He wasn't being cruel. He was treating her the way she had treated him. She had ruined his life that night in the Lumberton drawing room. He might think he had a choice to not offer marriage, but she knew differently. Sebastian was a man of honor, and she left him no way out. Now she realized what a death sentence for him it was.

She shivered at the realization, rubbed her hands along her arms as if to warm them even as the heat of the fire scorched her face.

"Surely, you've seen what good can come from love. Eliza and Dax—"

"Are a rare exception." His tone was steely, and she shut her mouth on the rest of her words.

Well, that was it then. Her future loomed before her, empty and loveless. Had she really expected anything else? She wasn't sure. She'd never thought about it. She'd always believed once Jo was happy and wed, she'd worry about it then. But that wasn't what happened, and she'd never gotten the chance to worry over it.

The silence stretched awkwardly now, and she felt the tendrils of guilt ease into the tension.

She gestured to the connecting door, already backing away. "I do apologize…again…for my outburst earlier. I had thought—" She gave a shrug, embarrassment racing up her neck in a hot flash. "I had thought—" But again the words got stuck. She laughed to ease the moment, but he hadn't moved in the least from where he hovered across the room. He only watched her retreat, the space between them growing wider, impassable.

She abandoned what she'd been about to say. There was no point in it. Sebastian was determined not to fall in love, and she was rather convinced he couldn't be dissuaded. Sometimes people had to choose things for themselves if they were ever to change, and Sebastian was clearly a person who did not seem to appreciate change.

Her head suddenly pounded as though all the tension of the day struck her at once, and this was the final blow. She raised a weak hand as if to bid him good night, and she turned to open the door behind her. Escape seemed the only desirable thing then. Escape and darkness and sleep.

Except she paused with her hand on the doorknob, unable to move.

She shouldn't turn around. She should go through the door and give the man some peace. But that was just not in her nature. There was a missing piece to Sebastian's story, and she knew she wouldn't rest until she found out the whole truth.

She looked back at him. The room was dark except for the fire and a few stray candles, and she could see very little of his face from here. But she could feel how rigid he was, sense how tightly he was holding himself.

She asked the question anyway.

"How did you know your father killed himself over his lover?"

"My mother told me."

The words whispered their way across the room to her, and the tick of suspicion she'd held solidified itself in her belly. Maybe she was predisposed to distrusting the woman, but something about that didn't seem right. Louisa pictured her sister, raw and torn from discovering her husband's infidelity, and the tickle of suspicion grew stronger.

"Apparently my father had had a lover for years. They had agreed to be discreet about it. You know how those things are in society marriages. But when my father's lover broke it off, he was devastated, my mother said. She said she'd never seen him that way. It was like he was someone else entirely."

She nodded to let him know she'd heard, but she was too consumed by her own suspicions to respond. She merely raised a hand in farewell and slipped through the door, closing it softly behind her.

She stared at that door for several long minutes. The panel was thick enough that she didn't hear Sebastian moving on the other side. She wondered if he'd taken up his drink, resumed his seat in one of those chairs by the fire, ruminated on the grief of his past.

But even while she pictured it, her mind raced with all that he had just told her. In the end, she collapsed on the bed still in her dressing gown, and when sleep came, it was drugging and consumed her whole.

* * *

"You're distracted today."

Sebastian stopped rolling the tip of his pen between his fingers even as his eyes remained riveted to it.

"Marriage sitting well with you?" Dax gave a short laugh. "I can only imagine it must be."

It was only a few days later, and Sebastian found himself sequestered in Dax's study to go over the agriculture bill. They still needed more voting members on their side, and the vote was only weeks away. Dax had suggested the strategy session to determine who seemed like a good prospect to target in the following weeks to garner support.

Sebastian had welcomed the distraction from his own quagmire, enjoying the muffled sounds of the Ashbourne home with their quiet hints of domesticity. In Dax's study, his own problems were far away and easily ignored.

So why then was he twirling his pen like a child?

He set down the instrument entirely and scrubbed his face over his hands.

"I find marriage requires a certain bit of...adjustment." That seemed like the safest word to say just then.

Dax's laugh was stronger this time. "It does take a certain amount of getting used to. Is Louisa well?"

Louisa was damn well perfect.

Since their wedding night, he'd scarcely seen her. Only at meals and passing in the corridor, and then she'd been unusually silent. It wasn't that she was gloomy or taciturn. On the contrary, she readily answered his attempts at conversation and bestowed upon him her usual smile when-ever the occasion arose. It was more that he *felt* her misery. She no longer offered up a topic of conversation, never initi-ated a question.

It was as if she were doing her best to be the perfect duchess.

Just as she had said she would.

She was demure and polite, acquiescent and prepared. She'd seen to the menus and the shopping, instructing Cook on what to prepare and the housekeeper on what was to be stocked. He'd heard some nonsense about draperies and rugs and linens. Louisa had only offered up a topic once, and it was to ask him for the ledgers regarding the house accounts. He'd happily handed them over to her, and she'd thanked him. Politely.

The entire discourse had taken all of five minutes, and she'd turned away from him again.

He could hardly blame her. He'd given her no choice in

the matter. He hadn't told her it would be a loveless marriage when she'd had time to back out, but then, he knew she hadn't thought she could escape their marriage. She had to protect her sister no matter the consequence to herself.

He always pictured her as she had been that night, fiery and alive in her virginal white dressing gown, the outlines of her legs visible through the light fabric.

God, he'd wanted her.

He still wanted her.

So he was spending afternoons at Ashbourne House hoping to avoid her entirely.

"Louisa is well."

Dax set his pen down now. They'd commandeered a table in the study to use for their papers and correspondence, and afternoon light speckled the surface with sunshine. Dax leaned back in his chair, his expression lost to shadow as he moved away from the sun.

"Are you ever going to tell me what really happened? How it is that you find yourself married to my wife's sister?"

"Louisa agreed to it." He spoke the words dryly, even as his stomach clenched.

She hadn't told him her secret that night. That was what haunted him now. He had told her everything about this father, things he'd never spoken of before even to Dax. Yet she had remained close-lipped. He had thought perhaps she would open up to him after that night, tell him why it was she was so affected by those women at their wedding breakfast.

Only she'd closed herself off since then.

He could hardly find fault with that.

Sebastian stood and went to the teacart that had been brought in nearly a half hour earlier by a maid. He found the tea lukewarm, but he didn't care. He carelessly poured himself a cup and rather than drink, stared into it.

"What do you know of the Darby mother?"

He hadn't meant to ask the question, but once it was out, he felt some kind of relief as if he'd opened a valve.

Dax shrugged. "Eliza hardly speaks of her. She died when they were so young." His friend leaned back in his chair, resting his head against his knitted hands. "I have the impression the Darby children were largely left to their own devices. Their parents neither neglected them nor did they dote on them. They were just loving parents who wanted the best for their children. The best tutors, the best nannies, the best school for Andrew." Another shrug. "Why do you ask?"

Sebastian made his way over to the windows and stared out at the passing traffic.

"We encountered a pair of women at the wedding breakfast who seemed to upset Louisa."

Dax sat up. "It wasn't the aunts, was it? Maude and Martha." Dax gave a mock shiver. "They upset Eliza, too. Apparently they're her mother's cousins once removed or some such thing. They drove Eliza batty."

Sebastian turned back to his friend at this. "They did?"

Dax gave a sure nod. "According to Eliza, they only pop up at funerals and weddings, actually mostly at funerals. Rather unsettling if you think about it."

Sebastian mulled this over while he took a sip of the warm tea. Perhaps he was overthinking it. Maybe Louisa had nothing to hide, and those old women were simply a touch creepy in their eccentricity.

But why did he get the sense he was still missing something? He resumed his seat, setting aside his teacup to lean on the table toward his friend.

"Dax, I think I'm missing something," he said plainly.

His friend raised a single eyebrow. "I haven't seen you this engaged since Vaughn suggested a tax on shoe polish. What is it?"

"Have you noticed how Louisa caters to her sisters? For such a strong-willed woman, I find it odd that she bows to their every wish."

"If you speak of Viv, then I can assure you it's the nature of all the sisters to bow to her. The woman is formidable."

Sebastian waved off the suggestion. "It's not just her. It's Jo, too. She's particularly protective of her."

Dax gave a laugh. "I think the thing you're missing is common human relations. Johanna is the youngest sister. Of course, Louisa is protective."

He felt a sense of calmness at his friend's certainty that it was nothing more than normal familial connection. It still troubled him though.

"How do you know this? I don't see any siblings running over you." He gave his friend a wry smile, but the man only leaned back with a laugh.

"Why continue to produce children when you made a perfect one at the first off?" He asked, gesturing to himself.

Sebastian felt a smile tug at his lips, and the tension in his chest eased for the first time in days.

Dax was probably right. Louisa wasn't hiding anything from him, and he shouldn't worry so much over it. Only…he couldn't love her.

He toyed with his discarded pen, the ink dripping onto a scrap of paper to create a navy blue pool.

"Dax, would you consider your marriage a love match?"

Dax gave a bark of laughter. "I wonder what's brought this up."

Sebastian cast him a frowning glance.

Dax ignored his friend. "Yes, I am lucky enough to count myself among the men who have found a true match, but I think you already know that. What is it you're really asking?"

"Do you remember when you plotted to wed a wallflower to avoid falling in love?"

Dax's face grew somber. "We don't bring that up in this house. Eliza has shown me the foolishness of my ways."

"That's what I'm afraid of." Sebastian leaned back in his seat, steepling his fingers in front of him. "I told Louisa I cannot love her."

Dax gave no reaction that he'd even heard him. It was some time before Dax stood and bypassed the teacart on the way to the liquor cabinet in the corner. He poured each of them a measure of scotch and returned to their table, pushing aside the lists of names they had been studying. He handed his friend a tumbler and sat back in his chair, waiting, knowing Sebastian would speak when ready.

Sebastian held the tumbler between his hands, rolling the glass back and forth as the sunlight caught the liquor like the angles of a prism.

Like swimming in a cold creek, it was best to jump in all at once.

"I'm afraid that if I love her, I'll make the same mistakes my father did," Sebastian said.

"What mistakes?"

In all their years as friends, Sebastian had always trusted Dax with his secrets. All of them except this one. He peered across the table at his friend, and he realized that at some point they had grown up. They were not the young boys they had once been, hiding frogs in the beds of their enemies at school, racing their horses across the fields of their country estates to feel the wind whipping past them.

There were shadows under Dax's eyes, and Sebastian realized with a jolt George was likely keeping them up at night. His friend was a father now. No longer the carefree bachelor he had once been alongside Sebastian. Now he held responsibility for another human being, his son.

This realization struck a note deep within Sebastian, and he pressed a hand to his chest as if to still it.

"My father made some poor choices in response to his lover ending their relationship."

Sebastian couldn't bring himself to tell his best friend the truth. It wasn't because he wished to protect the title either. Deep within him, Sebastian still wanted to shield his father from anyone who might judge him for his deeds.

"You never told me about what happened with your father. You seemed to disappear during that time."

Withdrew from society was what Louisa had said. *Disappear* was a far more appropriate word. He could still remember the way he had felt during those first few days after his father's death. It was like he'd turned into a ghost, passing through the days as if he weren't really there. He could hardly remember what had even occurred during that time. He vaguely recalled his mother making the necessary arrangements, instructing the staff to rid the house of any trace of his father. He couldn't recall much after that. In fact, he had no memory of his mother being in residence after those first few days, but that seemed entirely possible. He hadn't done more than move from his bedchamber to his sitting room in those days. He couldn't very well know if his mother had been there.

Sebastian drew a deep breath. "My father killed himself because his lover ended their relationship."

It was easier to say this time, but he still felt the squeeze of his chest, the feeling that someone was watching.

Dax raked a hand through his hair and sat back in his chair, expelling a narrow breath. "I'm so sorry, Sebastian. I didn't know—"

"I didn't want anyone to know."

"You told Louisa." Dax spoke the three words like a proclamation.

Sebastian could only nod.

"How did she take it?"

Sebastian pulled up the image that had haunted him that night. Louisa so still, as if her spirit had left her body, her movements mechanical as she'd opened the connecting door.

"I don't know. She seemed to close in on herself."

Dax shook his head. "Have you not realized what Louisa's nature is? As her husband, I would expect you to know."

"If you didn't notice, we wed rather quickly, and I haven't gotten the chance to become acquainted with my wife."

Dax leaned forward on the table, bringing his face closer to Sebastian's. "Louisa fixes things, Sebastian. Now that you've told her this, she's going to try to fix you."

Sebastian straightened, the cloud that had been following him for days suddenly lifting. "She's going to do what?"

"She's going to fix you. It's what she does. Every time one of her sisters has a problem, Louisa comes to fix it. Do you remember how you first met her?"

He would never forget how he first met Louisa, sopping wet in the rain.

"She'd come to Eliza's aid."

Dax nodded and knocked on the table with one fist. "You've just given her a problem to solve. She's going to try to fix you."

"Why would she do that?"

Dax's grin was slow and knowing. "Because you told her your secrets."

"Secrets?" Sebastian stilled, not trusting the mischievous grin on his friend's face.

"You didn't marry Louisa for love or for money. I know you didn't take her dowry. Johanna is telling everyone of the fact. Which leaves only one thing. One thing which would compel Louisa to help you."

Sebastian's breathing slowed.

"You married her out of honor, friend. And now she'll want to make you happy."

CHAPTER 8

She hadn't meant to renovate Waverly House. It just sort of happened.

When she had awoken the morning after her wedding, she'd lain in bed for some time, letting the truth of her position settle over her. Her instinct was to jump immediately out of bed and go about righting the situation so as to ensure Sebastian's future happiness. But there were several things wrong with that notion.

First, Sebastian was not one of her sisters. She had no right to interfere in his life, especially in his past, and it wouldn't do for her to arrive unbidden and immediately stampede into a web of family secrets. The second issue was that Sebastian didn't wish to change. It wasn't something she could prove. It was more of something she could feel. He had created a world in which he thought he could survive after the unbelievable had happened. Who was she to upset that?

Only she already had by forcing him to marry her.

It didn't matter if he tried to deny it. He wouldn't have had to make a decision, honorable or not, had she not created the necessity for it.

If she couldn't make Sebastian happy, she needed to do, well, something.

She'd crawled out of bed that morning, her head pounding from the kind of sleep that tricks you into thinking it's welcome but really only makes one's head fuzzier and gone straight for the strong cup of tea Williams had brought her. She drank it down in nearly one gulp, willing the warmth to spread through her numb limbs and bring her back to some semblance of existence.

Only then did she think about what he'd said.

He couldn't love her.

She still didn't know how she felt about this declaration, but it wasn't immediate regret, which puzzled her. Perhaps because her attraction to Sebastian was still so physical. She hadn't been given time to explore her other feelings for him. Like the way she was inevitably drawn to him in a room, the way she often craved his practical attention to a problem, the way he rolled his drink glass among his fingertips.

The pain she felt in her chest was a loss of possibility, not a broken heart. It still hurt all the same. She touched her lips briefly, tracing the echo of his kiss.

Would he ever kiss her again? Would he ever make her feel so…wanted?

She blinked away the painful memories and became aware of the room around her. Williams had drawn back the curtains and bright morning sunlight flooded the room in a cheery yellow glow, which was a surprising contrast to the worn state of the place.

The already drab wallpaper was patched and peeling in the corners. The furniture was mismatched and scarred, the exposed wood nearly crying for attention. The carpets were musty and muted, and she wondered when they'd last been shaken out.

She set down her teacup with a resounding ring and

pushed to her feet. If she couldn't fix Sebastian, she was going to fix his house.

That was why three weeks later she found herself covered in fabric swatches as she waltzed about the first-floor drawing room, Jo following carefully behind as she held up samples to the wallpaper to determine the best fit.

"I still don't see how a duchess could allow the room in which she receives guests to be so…well, so…"

"Awful," Louisa finished for her sister.

Jo stopped in her perusal of fabric swatches laid out along Louisa's arms and placed her fisted hands to her hips.

"I mean really. She's a duchess. Clearly she didn't have Viv for an older sister telling her what she was doing wrong."

Louisa couldn't help the laugh. "Viv may be hard on us, but we're the better for it, don't you agree?"

Jo exchanged the swatch in her hand for another along Louisa's arm. "Indubitably."

She held up the mauve fabric to the pastel hues of the wallpaper and shook her head. "I simply can't imagine who would use a green such as that for the drapes in this room." Her little sister referred to the monstrosity that was the drapes, a study in green and brown that was most likely found in the pages of a mycology book. "I mean, this wallpaper is lovely. Why ruin it with something which too closely resembles mashed peas?"

Louisa gave a quick nod in agreement. She'd been lucky to find that at least some of the rooms had adequate wall coverings of an acceptable hue. But she could recall only too well what Sebastian had said about his mother being largely absent from his childhood. She would have been absent from this house as well, and it showed in the tattered and uncoordinated furnishings.

Jo held up another swatch. "I think this one is it."

The pattern she held was a pale blue with vines of green

and pink and white swirling through it. It complimented the pale wallpaper while highlighting the colors in what would be the new drapes.

Louisa dropped her arms. "Splendid."

The sisters exchanged mutual smiles of accomplishment before moving back to the sofa where they had spread out the various fabrics and wallpaper samples Louisa had acquired from the design firm she'd hired to assist with the renovations.

"We should probably move on to the dining rooms when you get here tomorrow. I should think it proper to host a small dinner party soon as duke and duchess. I'd like to send out the invitations before Viv reminds me I should."

"Louisa."

She stilled at the worried tone in her sister's voice. Turning only her head, she took in Jo's furrowed brow and pinched lips. Dropping the remaining swatches in a haphazard pile, she whirled swiftly and took hold of Jo's hands.

"Darling, whatever is the matter?"

Jo's mouth worked without sound coming out, and then finally, she said what she obviously needed to say in a blast of air. "This is all my fault." Her sister did not burst into tears as it was not in Jo's character. Instead she pulled her hands from Louisa's and speared her tightly pinned hair with her fingers. "I'm so sorry, Louisa. You really didn't need to do this."

Louisa could only stare. "Do what?"

Jo flung her hands wide, encompassing the room and more in their conversation. "This. Marrying..." she struggled with the words before flinging out an accusatory finger which pointed at nothing. "Him!" she finally said as if it were necessary to expel the word from her person.

"Do you mean Sebastian?"

Louisa always marveled at the way people seemed to fear him, but only she knew his secrets, only she knew he feared emotions others took for granted.

Jo collapsed in the chair behind her, sending up a cloud of dust. "Yes. You didn't need to marry him, Louisa. Not for me."

Louisa sat on the low table in the middle of the seating arrangement so she could put her hands on her sister's knees.

"Jo, darling, whatever on earth are you talking about?"

Jo leaned forward, her eyes ablaze. "I know what happened that night, Louisa. Don't act the innocent."

Fear shot through Louisa so quickly she choked on it. How did Jo know? Who else knew? She had to speak to Viv. What if this got out? What would happen to Jo's future?

"You didn't have to marry him, Louisa. I know it's tempting, and I know sometimes we want to dip our toe into the things we've been told is forbidden. I understand that, I really do."

The fear was abruptly muddled with confusion.

"What are you talking about?" she asked again, squeezing her sister's knees.

Jo placed her hands on top of Louisa's. "I know you were caught in a compromising position with Waverly. I know you married him because you were afraid of what might happen if people found out. I know you married him to protect me." Jo gritted her teeth through the last word, and real pain flashed in her eyes. "I'm so sorry, Louisa. I should have spoken up, but I just couldn't. You seemed...well, happy." She spoke the last words as if they were the most preposterous statement ever made.

Louisa sat back, pressing her hands to her stomach. "Jo. My dear Jo. I really need you to slow down and explain what you're saying."

She wasn't sure which surprised her more. That Jo knew

the truth of that night, albeit not all of it, or her observation that Louisa had appeared happy to wed Sebastian.

"I was eavesdropping that night outside of Andrew's study. I know what Viv said to you. How you could have endangered my future." It was her turn to squeeze Louisa's knees. "But you needn't have worried about me. You know I always come out all right."

Louisa shook her head. "You mustn't feel guilt over that, Jo. I crossed a line of propriety and I accepted the consequence of that."

"I know you did. And I know Waverly didn't accept your dowry. That was the only thing that kept me quiet at first. I thought he really was marrying you out of love." She sat back and held up both hands in a sign of surrender. "Now, don't get me wrong. The man is vexing. But perhaps I don't know or understand the whole of the relationship between the two of you. And as we got closer to the wedding, I tried to pay better attention." She leaned forward, her eyes imploring now. "I didn't notice, Louisa. I didn't notice until I was seeing how very much attached to Waverly you are. You were always by his side at the betrothal ball and then at the wedding breakfast. It was like you had found your match."

Louisa's heart beat faster, and her eyes threatened tears. That might have been, but then Louisa had thought perhaps one day they would find contentment in their marriage, if not true love. But she knew now none of that was possible.

She plastered on the smile she had grown so good at displaying and laughed a soft, trilling laugh. "Oh, Jo, I would never have pegged you for the romantic. You really mustn't fret so. I assure you it was no hardship marrying Sebastian." She gave her sister a wink she did not feel.

Jo laughed, the sound like a blast of relief, and finally her brow cleared of worry.

Louisa stood, pulling her sister up with her. "I do hope

you'll talk to me before you let yourself be carried away by such nonsense," she said as she led her sister to the door. "Now, where is Viv making you go tonight?"

Jo wrinkled her nose. "It's a dinner party Viscountess Mayfield is throwing. I'm afraid I'll be seated by that dreadful baron again. The one from the Lake District."

Louisa felt a twist of pain for her sister, followed by the immediate relief that she need no longer engage in such nonsense. Perhaps Sebastian wasn't entirely wrong about society, a thought which left her concerned for her own well-being if she were suddenly agreeing with her husband.

She gave Jo a short hug. "It will be wonderful. Perhaps you'll meet your own match tonight."

Jo's smile, which had only so recently returned, suddenly dipped, and her expression grew pensive.

"Whatever is it now?" Louisa asked, emotions roiling within her. She really couldn't take much more of this.

Jo met her gaze, her shoulders rolling back as if she were facing a difficult responsibility. "That's just it, Louisa. I felt so guilty about what you did for me, because, well, because it doesn't matter about my future prospects. I shan't find a match this season or any other season."

The air itself stilled in Louisa's lungs as she tried to absorb what her sister was saying.

"You can't be serious." Jo was rather bold and had no issue stating her mind, but she was kind and caring and she could make anyone laugh. Of course, she would find her match.

But Jo was already shaking her head. "You don't understand. You didn't need to marry Waverly because I'll never accept a proposal. My heart already belongs to someone I can never have."

A hundred questions flooded Louisa's mind all at once, but she could only blink at her sister as she tried to will her mouth to form even one of the things she wished to ask.

Johanna loved someone she couldn't have? For how long? And why? And most importantly, who?

But she could ask none of those questions for just at that moment, Sebastian came through the drawing room doors, his pace brisk and efficient as if he had an urgent matter to discuss with her.

Louisa never moved her eyes from her sister as Jo turned and nodded in greeting.

"Waverly," she said.

"Lady Johanna, I must insist you address me as Sebastian. All of these titles seem unnecessary in the present situation."

Jo gave another nod. "Then you must call me Jo." She reached out and squeezed Louisa's arm, but still Louisa could not move. "I'll see you tomorrow, dear sister," she said and left before Louisa could find her tongue.

She watched her sister go, and Sebastian must have mistaken her attention on the door for her readiness to receive whatever matter he wished to discuss for he stepped beside her and said, "You'll need to get ready for dinner. My mother has sent us an invitation."

* * *

HE HAD LESS than no desire to dine with his mother, but it would be unacceptable for him to decline an invitation as a newlywed, as it would be an advantageous opportunity to introduce his wife and new duchess to society through a dinner party at his mother's, the dowager duchess at one time and now the Viscountess Raynham. He would not refuse such an invitation, and he knew his mother likely understood that.

So it was that he found himself tugging at his cuffs as he made his way to the foyer that evening, anticipating finding his wife and instead discovering the vestibule completely empty. He went so far as to check his pocket watch, thinking he may have the time wrong, but a sound further down the corridor drew his attention. He replaced his pocket watch as he moved through the house.

He discovered his wife in the drawing room where he'd found her earlier, and he stopped in the doorway when he realized she hadn't heard him approach. She was dressed for the night in an emerald silk gown that was warm against her pale skin and set off the golden tones of her hair as if she herself were a jewel. He swallowed, the breath catching in his throat as he watched her. She'd removed one long glove and with her free hand, traced the design of a fabric swatch he could see had been discarded on the arm of a sofa. He moved his gaze between her wandering fingers and her intent gaze, wondering what it was that preoccupied her mind.

For she wasn't studying the fabric. Her vacant eyes suggested she was somewhere else, perhaps mulling over a problem she couldn't quite solve.

Maybe he was the problem.

He took an involuntary step back as he recalled what Dax had told him. Louisa fixes things, and she would fix him now. He was both thrilled and terrified at the notion that she would try to make him happy, to make him love her. He hadn't considered either emotion in so long, he wasn't even certain what either would look like for him.

Could he love Louisa without making the same mistakes his father had?

He shouldn't even be contemplating such a suggestion. He had already told Louisa how their marriage would be, and for the past several weeks, they had lived a peaceful existence.

Who the hell was he fooling?

The past several weeks had been torture for him. Everywhere he went through his house the smell of orchids taunted him. He was sure he'd find her around every corner, and when she failed to materialize, he was left wondering why he felt so bereft. He knew this couldn't go on forever, and he feared what the resolution might be.

What if he just let Louisa...fix him?

The very thought sent a rush of emotion through him that felt suspiciously like relief. It was an effort to avoid attachment, to keep oneself from forming relationships. What if he just let it all go and loved his wife?

He cleared his throat loudly and stepped briskly into the room to stop his wayward thoughts. She just looked pretty tonight. That was all. He shouldn't let it go to his head.

She looked up from where she'd been studying the fabric swatch, and it was some seconds before her eyes focused on him. She gave a soft smile as he approached.

"Is it time to leave already? I'm terribly sorry. I'm just a touch distracted, I guess."

He stopped several feet away from her, afraid to draw any closer.

He wanted to kiss her.

It wasn't that he was suddenly overcome with passion. It was quieter than that. Almost as if he would come down to find her every night, dressed so exquisitely, quietly awaiting his arrival before they left for their nightly social obligations. Almost as if he could get used to this, used to her, and every night she would tilt her cheek up for his kiss.

Except she didn't do that. Roughly, she tugged on her glove as she walked past him for the door. It took him a moment to realize she'd simply walked away, and she was already receiving her wrap from Milton, the butler.

She adjusted her gloves along the line of her wrap as she asked, "Did your mother invite many people this evening or is this more of a private affair?"

He stopped in front of her, considering her question.

When he didn't answer, she looked up and after a moment studying his face said, "Oh, you didn't think to ask. Quite all right. It needn't matter anyway, I guess. I don't like your mother with lots of people around. Why should I like her if there aren't any around?"

He laughed.

He wasn't sure who was more surprised. Louisa, himself, or Milton.

Louisa had been halfway out the door, and she turned back at the sound, her look curious if not a touch concerned. Milton, the good man, stepped to the side and busied himself with rearranging the gloves in the front hall.

"I insulted your mother. Did you just laugh at that?"

He gave a shrug. "I already told you. It's not as if I chose her as my mother. Who am I to care if you should malign her unpleasant demeanor?"

Her brow furrowed, but she said nothing more. She was distracted again once in the carriage, and the short ride to his mother's home was marked by the clatter of the carriage wheels rolling along the rutted cobblestones. Not able to take the silence from her, he leaned forward.

"Whatever has you preoccupied?"

She started at his question.

"I'm sorry. It's just…well…" Her voice trailed off as she finally turned her attention from the window to meet his gaze. "Do you sincerely care about this?"

The question stung, although it shouldn't have. He had made known his position on what he expected from their relationship. Namely, that there not be one.

"Yes." He spoke the word softly, carefully, as if he might startle her.

She considered his response before saying, "Johanna said something odd today is all, and it has me perplexed."

"Is she well?"

Louisa waved a hand at this. "Oh, she's perfectly well. It's just that—she told me a bit of a secret is all." She stopped and worried her lower lip briefly. "Well, I assume it's a secret. I don't believe the other sisters know, and she's certainly never told me."

"What kind of secret?"

He didn't want to be so bold as to suggest she tell him. He only worried that the younger Darby sister may be meddling in something she shouldn't. He was beginning to learn all the Darby sisters were dangerously head-strong, and he was concerned for the young woman's safety.

His wife considered him again, and he realized she was deciding whether or not to tell him *what* the secret was and not simply what kind it was. A note of concern rippled through him. He had no desire to be entangled with the other Darby women. He could hardly handle the one he was married to. But before he could stop her, Louisa blurted out her sister's secret.

"She's apparently in love with a man she can't have."

God, he didn't wish to be having this conversation.

"Then she should get over it."

She frowned at his words. "That's not really the point."

"Yes, it is. She's just proven once again that love makes people do stupid things. Nothing more. Tell her to have sense and not ruin her life."

"Are you saying I should ruin my life if I were to fall in love with you?"

He'd had a retort ready on his lips, but her question sucked the air from his lungs.

"That's not possible," he finally said, finding the practical answer to be the safe one.

She scoffed at his sensible response, however, and it left him nervous.

"How can you say that? You cannot control who falls in love with you."

He gave her a sardonic smirk. "But I can control how I behave around others, and I am certainly the most disagreeable and rude gentleman of my acquaintance."

"That doesn't preclude love."

"Why ever not? I am thoroughly unlikable."

"I find you remarkably likable."

It was as if the air itself had been sucked from the carriage. The very space between them vibrated with tension. His wife had the audacity to sit serenely on the bench opposite as he considered what she had just said.

He was not at all likable. He had done his best to ensure he wasn't, and yet, Louisa continued to move outside of all of the rules he had so carefully constructed around himself.

"Then you are the exception." It was his turn to stare out the window and avoid his wife's gaze.

"We thought Johanna wasn't interested in finding a match," Louisa went on, even when he did his best to ignore her. "But it wasn't that at all. It turns out she's already found him, and he's not available to her."

"Then she should find a better one."

"That's not how it works. You should know better than anyone you can't control who you love."

Now he did bring his gaze back to hers. "What is that supposed to mean?"

She raised a single brow. "It means exactly as I said. Aren't you the very person who told me love is irrational? Wouldn't it brook the argument that it is also uncontrollable?"

He felt a trap and progressed warily. "It would stand to reason that such an argument could be made."

"So couldn't it be said that you might fall in love without your permission?"

He opened his mouth, but no words came out. She'd

trapped him nicely, and oddly enough, he thrilled at her dexterity and ingenuity.

He tugged on his cuffs. "I would never allow myself to do such a thing. It suggests a dangerous lack of control. Something I eradicated from my person some time ago."

He wasn't sure if the carriage jostled them with a particularly strong bump at that moment, or if she had done it deliberately, but suddenly, her wrap slipped from one shoulder, baring an expanse of her décolletage to the moonlight that spilled through the carriage window.

His eyes fastened on that expanse of clear, pale skin as if it were water and he was dying of thirst. The moonlight played across the fine bones of her collar, dappled her neck, and teased his eyes to her face where he found her giving him a sultry smirk.

He adjusted his seat on the bench, hoping to relieve the sudden pressure in his trousers.

"And what if you were unfairly…tempted?"

Dear. God.

What had he done?

He'd not only stepped into danger, he'd invited it in, married it, vowed to cherish it for the rest of his life, and he was nothing if not a man of honor.

"I cannot be tempted." Perhaps if he said the words they would become the truth.

Except he knew how futile that course was.

He was more than prepared to take his wife right there in the carriage. If she but crooked a finger in his direction, he would fall to his knees in supplication. He was entirely hers to do with what she wished, and his only saving grace was that she didn't yet realize it.

But maybe she did.

She leaned forward, elbows to knees, and the bodice of her gown loosened just the smallest degree, but it was enough to afford him a view of her magnificent breasts. He knew how tender they were, had caressed them with his hands and mouth, had tasted her skin—

"Are you so certain?" Her voice had dropped, and the soft, coaxing tone had his eyes riveted to her mouth.

He leaned forward, matching her position, until their faces were so close he could have kissed her. But he didn't kiss her. He moved ever so slightly until his lips met her ear, and he whispered, "Yes."

He would thank God later that the carriage stopped in front of his mother's house just then because he knew that should she test his resolve, she would uncover him for the fraud that he was.

CHAPTER 9

She was flushed by the time she entered the drawing room where the other guests were shown to wait for the start of dinner. Louisa counted eight other couples upon their entrance, not including the viscountess and her husband. The viscountess, in fact, was noticeably absent.

She felt a modicum of relief at not facing the woman immediately. She was already feeling rather more vigorous than usual, and she feared her boldness would get her into further trouble that evening. She didn't know why she had behaved so on the carriage ride, but after Jo's startling revelation, Louisa was rather tired of the people in her life making decisions of which she knew little or nothing until their impact was felt on her.

For why on earth had she teased Sebastian?

Yes, she had felt a thrill of power when she saw her ministrations working, but it only served to drive her further into a frenzy. Her skin ached for his touch, her lips craved his kiss, and he had sat there with all the emotional response of an eel.

And now she was forced to dine with his mother.

Could this evening get any worse?

She rued the thought as soon as the couple beside her turned, and she was faced with Jonathan Devlin. She took an involuntary step back, only to have Sebastian's hand at the small of her back stop her. The touch sent a bolt of lightning through her as he had not touched her since their wedding day, and now was the absolutely worst time to remind her of how good it felt.

She blinked, forcing away all of her roiling emotions to focus on the man who stood in front of her. It wasn't Devlin at all. It was her own silly mind playing games on her. It was the earl himself, Westrick, and his countess, whom Louisa understood not to be Jonathan's mother but rather the earl's second wife. Louisa hated herself for being so jumpy and vowed to one day return the favor to that sniveling weasel.

For now she nodded in acknowledgment to the earl and countess and moved deeper into the room with Sebastian directly behind her. The other couples Louisa knew only by name and the brief occasions where they had passed during social functions such as these.

She felt the weight of the day and her responsibilities as the Duchess of Waverly suddenly press down on her shoulders. She didn't wish to be here tonight. She wanted to run back to Ravenwood House and demand that Jo explain what she had meant. She wanted to be at home, nestled into bed, waiting for her husband to come to her.

The last thought stabbed her directly in the chest for when had she come to think of Waverly House as home and why would she keep expecting Sebastian to come to her? He'd already made his position on their marriage perfectly clear.

She knew she would need to face that soon. Throwing herself into a household renovation was only an excuse to avoid the subject she knew she must confront. Otherwise, her marriage loomed before her like an endless swirl of social obligations and polite but distant interactions with her husband.

They had made it nearly to the other side of the room before Sebastian was accosted by the Earl of Bannerbridge. Louisa nodded politely to the earl's wife who stood meekly behind him. The poor girl, she was likely half the age of the earl, and it appeared as though she were expecting a child.

Louisa was not prepared for the way her chest squeezed at the sight, and she turned away abruptly, nearly colliding with the footman who had just arrived to offer the ladies some wine. She happily accepted a glass and quickly put it to her lips to avoid conversation with anyone else.

She'd only taken one sip, however, when Viv's voice sounded in her head, reminding her of her duty. Not for the first time did Louisa wish she'd had a sister who didn't care about her quite so much.

Louisa turned back, her practiced smile already on her face, to find Sebastian still deep in conversation with the earl and the poor countess still standing mutely to the side.

"Do you know Viscountess Raynham?" Louisa offered in an attempt to coax the girl out.

She smiled sweetly, and color immediately infused her cheeks. Louisa racked her mind to remember when the Earl of Bannerbridge had wed, but she couldn't recall. This girl was likely younger than Louisa, and she was already starting a family of her own.

Louisa took an overlarge gulp of wine and swallowed hard, steeling herself against the way her emotions rocked back and forth within her.

"The viscount and viscountess are acquaintances of my husband." Even her voice was soft and mild, and Louisa pitched forward just to hear her.

Except the woman said nothing else, and Louisa was left to conjure another polite question to draw her out.

"Well, that's lovely. How are you and the earl finding the season? I hear there's to be a new production of *The Magic Flute* at the Royal this year."

Louisa did not care for opera, but Viv had reminded her time and again it was an honored tradition of the *ton*, and it would do well for Louisa to at least be knowledgeable.

The countess gave no reaction to this question, and Louisa sipped her wine, letting the silence wash over them. She quieted Viv's voice in her head. After all, she had tried.

She glanced at Sebastian out of the corner of her eye, but it appeared he would not be surfacing soon from whatever deep discussion he and Bannerbridge were having, so she surveyed the room to see if there was someone else with whom to converse. Only to lock gazes with the viscountess herself.

"I do apologize for needing to step out. Poor Hamill had misplaced his snuffbox. You know how men are, dears." This last bit was directed at the Countess Bannerbridge while Louisa got the end of the sentence, which was mostly a cold press of lips in a disdainful smile. "If it isn't my daughter-in-law, the new duchess."

Louisa curtsied as was appropriate while her lips moved automatically into a smile.

"Viscountess. Thank you for your kind invitation this evening."

The viscountess showed her teeth now as she said, "I should have thought I wouldn't be required to send an invitation to my son in hopes of seeing him."

"Well, perhaps then you should have been more present in his younger years for him to feel a stronger connection with you."

The words were out before she could stop them, and

vaguely, she was aware of Sebastian's voice ceasing from somewhere behind her.

"Mother." His tone held no note of remonstration toward Louisa but was merely directed at the viscountess, who still focused her icy stare on Louisa.

Louisa casually took a sip of her wine, willing her traitorous lips to behave. It appeared she would simply be cursed with an impulsive nature and wayward tongue.

"Sebastian." The word was cold as snow and while she spoke to Sebastian, she kept her eyes riveted on Louisa. "Your wife seems to think I was a poor mother."

"Yes."

The single word drew the viscountess's gaze away from Louisa and up to her son. Her icy features cracked into a look of astonishment as her lips parted and her eyes narrowed at her son's response. Obviously the woman thought he would assuage her upset when, in fact, he'd done little more than acknowledge that the slight had occurred.

"I trust you are well," Sebastian said politely as he ignored his mother's expression.

Louisa took another sip of wine, willing her stomach to settle. They had only to get through this evening and then perhaps she would not be required to attend functions at this woman's home again. Hadn't Sebastian himself said he wished for them to lead separate lives? Perhaps this was a boon in disguise. Louisa would fulfill her duties as a newly married duchess and then she could slip blissfully into obscurity.

Alone and untouched, pining for a husband who couldn't love her.

"I am." The viscountess sniffed. "Sebastian, I think perhaps you should teach your wife her place. She seems to have forgotten it."

The woman spoke as if they were alone and not

surrounded by the woman's very dinner guests, members of the peerage and, likely, people she wished to impress. But perhaps that was just it. Louisa suspected that Viscountess Raynham enjoyed reminding people that they were below her.

Except...

"Do you mean my place as a duchess? Because the last I checked, a duchess outranks a viscountess." Louisa became aware suddenly of the quiet that descended in the drawing room, and she willed herself not to flush at the attention. While she had no issue defending that which required it, she did rather wish to do so without drawing attention to herself.

Viscountess Raynham's mouth opened on a silent word before she cleared her throat. "You should do something about her, Sebastian. If you're not careful, she'll become as wayward as your father."

Louisa wanted nothing more than to look at Sebastian's face, but she couldn't see him from where he stood slightly behind her without turning, and that would give an advantage to the viscountess she wasn't willing to concede. So she stood there and stared down this woman who had so succinctly constructed self-isolating behaviors in her only son.

Louisa could not at all be surprised. If she had been raised by this woman, she would have adopted some manners that would likely have been far worse than shutting people out.

"Are you not aware that it's unlucky to speak of the dead?" Louisa took the last swallow of wine and bestowed a sardonic smile on her mother-in-law. "You just might be haunted by their ghost."

The viscountess's gaze turned deadly, and the woman took the smallest step closer to Louisa. Even though the woman's shoulders stooped slightly with age, she was still a good two inches taller than Louisa, and she likely thought to use her height to her advantage. Except the woman didn't realize what it meant to grow up with Viv as an older sister.

Louisa didn't back down. Not at all. She stood her ground, standing perfectly erect between this horrible woman and Sebastian.

"Tell me, dear." The viscountess's voice dripped with polite derision. "Does your mother's ghost haunt you?"

Had the woman said anything else, Louisa would have been ready. But not that. Not her mother. The cold, menacing finger of guilt racked its way down her spine, and she feared at any moment her knees might give way and she would crumple to the ground in a heap of embarrassment and ridicule.

But she couldn't do that. She had to protect Sebastian.

"Yes." Louisa spoke the single word clearly and with enough power to be heard across the room. "She haunts me because I loved her."

She could not have been more accurate or deadly had she used a dagger to stab Viscountess Raynham.

The woman's eyes flashed with anger at the reminder of her damaged relationship with her son and the implication that she wouldn't haunt him with her memory when she was gone. But as Louisa knew only too well, sometimes the truth was far deadlier than any weapon.

The viscountess flexed her hands into fists, and Louisa readied herself for the next volley, but it never came. At just that moment, the Raynham butler announced dinner, and the viscountess was forced by propriety to lead her guests into the dining room.

Decorum dictated that Sebastian and Louisa enter after their hosts, and with sixteen pairs of eyes watching them closely, she had no time to do more than whisper to her husband.

"I'm sorry." She kept her voice low as the other guests assembled behind them.

Sebastian said nothing as he led her into dinner.

* * *

WHEN THEY STEPPED through the door of Waverly House what seemed an eternity later, the silence of the slumbering household was a welcome balm against his irritated nerves. Milton silently took their things, and by the time, Sebastian had shed his gloves Louisa was already heading up the stairs.

Once more she had been quiet in the carriage ride, and he was man enough to admit the silence was beginning to grate. After a year of intermittent exposure to the force that was Louisa, her quiet attitude toward their marriage was like an alarm bell being rung consistently in his ear. It was enough to drive a lesser man mad.

He watched her now, fistfuls of skirt in each hand as she methodically took the stairs, and he wondered if denying himself the very thing he wanted was just as bad as giving in to his temptations.

He had thought he wanted this kind of separation, a parting of their lives so he could live comfortably in the distance between them. He hadn't counted on the way it dampened her spirit, nor the way he would long to see her smile again, to hear her laugh, to kiss her. It was supposed to have been easy, but this wasn't easy at all.

Tonight he had witnessed that fire that now hid beneath her quiet exterior. The way she had stood up to his mother even when the viscountess chose to deliver such a cutting remark as to mention Louisa's poor, deceased mother. It was cruel by any measure, but unfortunately, quite usual when it came to Sebastian's mother. She had no standards by which she lived, and just as his father was known to say, his mother fell prey to whatever method devised the end she desired.

Why she would want to cut down Louisa he wasn't sure. Likely because Louisa wasn't able to go along with the polished exterior his mother had perfected over the years: doting mother and devoted wife. She was neither of those things if one knew her truly, but she was damned good at pretending otherwise. It had never bothered him before. He was too good at packaging up his mother and pushing her to the side so she could no longer interfere in his life.

But Louisa seemed to draw his mother out no matter how carefully he packaged her away, and he was forced to consider his real feelings toward her. He had always simply dismissed her as it was easier than confronting her and involved far fewer theatrics on her part. Tonight, however, had had a different effect on him.

He didn't like her attacking Louisa. It was as if a primal anger had surged through him at the first gambit his mother had laid down. He should have known Louisa would be more than prepared for such a battle of words, but it left him feeling unsettled. Louisa should not be expected to face such animosity and outright hostility should they need to interact with his mother in a social setting. Whether he liked it or not, he would need to address the matter soon.

Not tonight, though. Tonight he wanted nothing but a fire and a glass of scotch.

He found both in his rooms, and after dismissing his valet, he sank into his favored chair and let the warmth of the fire seduce him into a lulled state as the scotch warmed his insides. He sipped at it, feeling not at all the lure of its tantalizing effects the way he once did.

He wanted something much more powerful.

He recalled what Dax had said about Louisa fixing things, and while he had waited for some evidence of this nature, all he found was the fact that the house seemed to be the focus of her intentions. It bothered him little as he rarely spent time in the house outside his study and his rooms, and the rest he hardly noticed. She could do with it what she liked.

But was she expending her energy on the house to avoid him?

He didn't like how the thought rankled nor that his immediate response was that he'd welcome her attentions.

How, after eight years, was it possible for him to consider another avenue, another way to safeguard himself from the mistakes his father had made?

If he were objective, Sebastian must consider his mother's role in his father's death for surely she had played a part. Theirs had been an arranged marriage, and as a child, he was inordinately aware of the tension between his parents. It wasn't hatred, nothing so vile as that. It was a quiet distaste. His father avoided his mother just as she did him, and Sebastian did not miss that fact. Could his father have longed for someone else?

What had Louisa said earlier that night? Didn't her sister Jo find herself in the same position, longing for someone she couldn't have? What he knew of the girl seemed sound, and she didn't appear as though she would do anything irrational. But then, people tended to appear rational until the very moment they weren't.

He'd nearly thought himself into a downward spiral by the time the soft knock came on the door.

His first instinct was to pretend he was asleep. He knew he was tired, exhausted really, and his guard was feeling the effects of his dizzying thoughts. But he couldn't refuse Louisa any more than he could banish the memories of his father.

"Come in."

The door opened with a soft swish, and he did all he

could not to look at her. That damn virginal dressing gown haunted him, and he needn't look at it that night.

"I came to apologize."

Now he did look at her.

She was dressed much as he feared she would be, her body wrapped in snowy white satin, her golden hair plaited along one shoulder.

"Apologize?"

She pressed a hand to her forehead, so unusual a gesture for her it had him turning fully in his chair to face her. Propriety would have dictated he stand to receive her, but he found himself so entranced by her he forgot himself entirely.

"Yes, I shouldn't have acted the way I did. I'm terribly sorry. Jo upset me earlier, and I just wasn't myself this evening."

"I saw nothing wrong with your behavior. If anything, it is my mother who should apologize, but she will not because she's a narcissist. She likely enjoyed setting you down."

Her frown held a degree of self-deprecation. "Be that as it may, I promised I would act the part of the perfect duchess, and tonight I failed to uphold my end of the agreement. I only came to give you my apologies."

"I never asked you to play such a role." He wasn't sure why her words poked him more than they normally would, but there was something about this night that had his nerves raw and sensitive.

Her expression closed and a line appeared between her brows. "Be that as it may, I hold myself to a certain standard, and I failed to meet it this evening. I will strive to repair whatever damage I have caused on our next outing."

She turned, and he realized she was leaving. For some strange reason, he stood.

"Why do you feel you've caused damage and to what?"

He had never seen her appear so defeated. He couldn't

help but recall the way she had barged into his rooms on their wedding night. It seemed like an eternity ago and yet it could have been yesterday. So quickly and so swiftly was he able to extinguish her fire, and he had never realized what power he'd held over her.

But he couldn't help wondering—was it because he held such power over her or the fact that he'd robbed her of the possibility of love?

He should tell her to find a lover, find someone who could address her needs, but even as the thought entered his mind, he felt a cold rage seep into his bones, and he knew he'd never let another man touch her.

He could not have it both ways, he knew. It would be unfair to Louisa, and it would only serve to drive him mad. He had to do something, but he didn't know what. He was afraid of what might happen if he let himself go, but he was also afraid of what would happen if he didn't.

Her sigh was loud in the quiet room. "To the title and your reputation. What I do reflects poorly on you now. Surely, you understand that."

"You're assuming I care what other people think of me."

She met his gaze suddenly. "Do you not?"

"I wouldn't have cultivated a reputation as the Beastly Duke if I did, would I?"

She worried her lower lip, and he wanted to grab her then and kiss her, forcing away the phantoms that tormented her. He didn't give a damn what society thought of him or the title. It only rankled him that his mother had cut Louisa so.

"I disrespected your mother, Sebastian. She maligned your father, and I couldn't stand for it, but I shouldn't have taken my retribution there. It only served to harm you, and I'm sorry for that."

He recalled his mother's remark regarding Louisa's

behavior in comparison to his father's, but as his mother had spent so little time actually in his father's company, he'd come to dismiss her statements regarding his character. He'd nearly forgotten the remark entirely, so consumed was he by how she'd treated Louisa.

But apparently, that was what had triggered Louisa's response. She had come to his defense against his own mother because she thought his father maligned. The thought upset something inside of him, and he didn't like how it wore down the walls he'd erected, the rules he'd established to safeguard his objectivity.

She needed to leave, or he was going to do something entirely stupid.

"You mustn't apologize for defending my father's name. Not to me anyway. I should think, though, my father would tell you you're wasting your time trying to stop my mother's sharp tongue."

For the first time, Louisa's shoulders straightened, and her chin went up. "But somebody must try."

That was when he realized Dax was right. Louisa did fix things. Standing there in her billowy dressing gown, her hair loosely braided and carelessly tossed over one shoulder, she looked like he imagined a Viking queen would look, soft and snowy and dangerous as ice.

And that's when he realized what was happening. By telling her he couldn't love her, by showing her how adamant he was not to change, she was abiding by his wishes, and it was killing her. Her quietness, her one-word answers to his questions—she couldn't go on like this because he was stopping her from being who she was. He had robbed her of her spirit.

This was who she was, this warrior who defended those unable or unwilling to defend themselves; this was the woman who tore herself apart because her sister held a painful secret.

By keeping himself to himself he'd stolen away a chance for her to be herself. It wasn't about love. It was about Louisa and her beautiful soul.

Regret and anger washed over him, and he hated himself in the instant of realization. He couldn't let her go on as she had been. He could keep himself from falling in love with her. He had to because there was no other choice. He just wasn't strong enough to watch Louisa die inside because of him.

He didn't wait to convince himself otherwise. He strode over to her and pulled her into his arms, crushing his mouth to hers.

Sensation roared through him like a match striking dry hay, and he went up in an inferno of pent-up desire. This was what he wanted. This was what he craved. And Louisa needed him. He had to do this for her.

He just hoped he could keep his heart safe.

CHAPTER 10

*S*he was so surprised she didn't respond to his kiss at first.

But as soon as the warmth of his body spread through her, the feel of his hard muscles against her shoulders, her back, his hands clutching her to him—

Then she was lost.

What on earth was he doing?

He had said he wished for them to lead separate lives. She had spent the past several weeks steeling her heart for an empty and lonely future, and now he was—

Undoing the sash of her dressing gown.

She shoved him away so hard he stumbled.

Candlelight danced across his face, and she saw not only the shock of her pushing him away but also smoldering desire.

He wanted her.

The thought sent a thrill through her, and unconsciously, she took a step toward him and forced herself to stop.

"What are you doing?" She blurted the question out as if it

were her only chance of survival. "You said we were to live separate lives."

"I changed my mind."

Her gasp of surprise was audible. "You're Sebastian Fielding. You don't change your mind."

"I have done so in this instance. Now can we get on with it?" He held out his hands like a starving man would plead for bread.

Warmth immediately pooled low in her belly, and she struggled to push it away.

"No." She swallowed, licked her lips. "No, you said separate lives, and I am trying very hard to do as you wish. What about your father? I will not be responsible for causing you to do the very thing you have sworn never to do."

He didn't answer her. Instead his eyes shuttered, and a small grin came to his lips. Uneasiness shot through in sensual delight at the ideas that grin conjured. What was he playing at? She'd spent so much of her life making up for her impulsive decisions. Why would he tempt her like this now?

Because she had tempted him first.

The gasp stuck in her throat this time.

"Is this about what I said in the carriage? I apologize for that as well. I shouldn't have goaded you like that. I've learned my lesson." She spewed the apology even as he took careful steps toward her.

He hadn't removed his jacket, and it was rumpled now. In fact, he was deliciously rumpled like she'd never seen him before, and her body yearned toward him.

"Do you really think a few carefully planned words and a silly coquettish gesture—" He stopped here and turned his gaze to the side.

She followed it and watched as he took two fingers and pushed the lapel of her loosened dressing gown off her shoulder.

"—would tempt me." He was close now, close enough for her to see the shots of gold in his eyes. "I already told you, darling." He leaned in now, his lips so, so, so close to hers she almost whimpered. "I won't be tempted."

When his lips closed over hers this time, she was ready. She returned the kiss with all the pent-up passion she'd been resolutely ignoring these past few weeks. She practically assaulted him with her desire, her annoyance at trying to expend her lust on fabric swatches and paint colors fueling her.

She threw her arms around his shoulders, pulling him closer to her as his hands slid down her back, cupped her bottom and yanked her against him.

It was exhilarating.

Her head fell back as his lips left hers, trailing hot kisses along her jaw, down the line of her neck until he nibbled at the fine bones of her collar.

That's when her knees gave, and her hands clutched at his shoulders to hold her up.

"Sebastian." She poured her plea into his name, but she didn't know for what she was pleading.

This.

She wanted more of this, but she didn't know what to ask for. Memories of that night on the terrace rushed back to her, and tension coiled deep within her. He'd made her say it then. Say what she wanted.

She placed her lips close to his ear and whispered, "Sebastian, I want you."

The responding growl took her breath away, and his hands tightened, lifting her against him. No, not against him. He tossed her soundly on the bed.

Her hair came loose from its plait, and she shoved it from her face to watch him. He shed his jacket impatiently, and his fingers were on the buttons of his waistcoat before she thought to throw up a hand to stop him.

"Wait!"

His eyes flew to hers even as his fingers stilled.

She bit her lower lip, suddenly shy. "I've never seen you without your jacket. I just…I just want to look."

His smile was slow and devilish, but his fingers began to work at the buttons of his waistcoat again, except slowly this time, tantalizingly slow.

She swallowed.

"Are we demanding things now?"

She pried her eyes from his wicked fingers, heat flooding her cheeks. "Demanding things? I'm only making suggestions."

His waistcoat joined his jacket. "Your suggestions always feel like demands in disguise."

Oh God, his shirt was next.

She pressed a hand to her stomach, unable to bear the tightening there. He had to touch her soon or she would simply die.

"Sebastian." She hated how weak she sounded, but his fingers…his fingers…

His shirt fell away, and she saw all of him. Well, all of his chest anyway, but it was enough to send her into a frenzy. She came up on her knees, yanking her traitorous nightdress away from her legs as she scrambled to get closer to him.

"Sebastian, I—"

But he was already there, cupping her head so gently in his hands as he placed a soft kiss on her lips.

"I know, darling. I know exactly what you need."

She sighed against his lips, relief flooding through her at his touch.

Her dressing gown soon joined the pile of clothes on the

floor. The cool night air filtered through her thin night-rail, and she yearned toward the warmth of her husband's body.

His hands smoothed along the length of her back, and she pressed into him, her arms going around his neck to pull herself closer. But he didn't stop to cup her bottom this time. Instead his fingers traveled lower, finding the hem of her night-rail and carefully, achingly, pulled it up a painful inch at a time. When his fingers finally brushed the soft skin of her thigh, she whimpered.

He laughed softly, and the sound vibrated against her neck where he'd been plying sweet, hot kisses.

"Eager, are you? I should remember not to make you wait so long next time."

His words had the fire in her spiraling to a painful focus, and she pushed against him, seeking the thing he had only briefly shown her before.

"Easy, darling. You forget I've waited a long time, too."

He moved then, sweeping her night-rail over her head, and cool air rushed against her body, her nipples tightening instantly.

He stood there, her night-rail hanging from one hand, and studied her. She wanted to cover herself, suddenly feeling vulnerable, but he'd already seen most of her. But it was the way he looked at her that had her hands falling useless at her sides.

She had anticipated desire and passion and even lust in his gaze, but none of those things was there. Instead she felt cherished, she felt precious—

She might have even felt loved if she could have believed that.

"Beautiful." He spoke the word much as he had that night on the terrace, as if he couldn't quite believe it.

"Sebastian." It was the only thing she could say as her

heart squeezed in her chest from all the love he didn't want her to feel but she could see plainly on his face.

Her night-rail slipped from his fingers as he stepped forward and pulled her back into his arms. The rough hair on his chest chafed her nipples, the sensation so unexpected she looked down at where their bodies met.

She could hear the smile in his voice as he said, "Does that feel good, darling?"

"Yes." She felt ridiculous answering him, but she couldn't pry her eyes away from the place where their bodies met.

He was all hard planes and muscle where she was soft and curved. She ran her hands along the angles of his shoulders and down the contours of his arms.

"I didn't know this was hiding under that jacket."

"There's still more to see."

She couldn't keep her eyes from dropping to his trousers, but before she could ask to see what he still hid there, he captured her mouth in a searing kiss, nudging her lips open to invade her mouth. Sweet, sensual fire poured through her, and she clung to him as he bent her back, feasting on her neck, her collarbone, dipping lower until—

"Sebastian." She moaned his name, her fingers spiking through his hair as she pulled him closer.

After what seemed an eternity, he found her breasts with his hot, wet mouth. He traced kisses along their curves in circles, coming achingly close to the place where she wanted him most and always pulling away at the last moment.

"Sebastian," she pleaded. "Please."

"You're so polite, darling. Even in your desire."

He sucked one nipple into his mouth, and the heat made her buck against him. He held her still with his strong hands wrapped around her, but it was too much.

"Sebastian, I need—"

He reared back and for the first time, she saw the tension

in the muscles of his neck, the concentration in his gaze.

"Me too it would seem."

Gently, he lowered her back in the downy bed of pillows before going to work on his trousers. She lifted her head, curiosity making her want to see him. He shed his trousers much as he had the rest of his clothing, and she had hardly any time to study him properly, but what she did see frightened her.

"Sebastian, you're terribly—"

She couldn't finish the sentence as he slipped between her legs, his warm body coming fully along the length of hers.

"Do finish that sentence, my dear," he said, nuzzling at the sensitive spot behind her ear. "It's rather rude to leave a man in question about the state of his physical attributes."

"Well, it's just that you're rather large. I have an idea of how this is supposed to work, and I'm not convinced we're a proper match."

He pushed up on his elbows, hovering above her with a wicked grin. "We will fit. I promise you that."

He went back to nuzzling her neck, but her concern didn't fade until his fingers traveled their way down her hip, her thigh, slipping into that part where heat pooled. He was so very wicked in his intentions, swirling around that place where tension coiled but never touching her where she wanted it.

"Sebastian." She moved her hips against him, hoping to direct his hand to that spot, but he only laughed softly in her ear.

"So impatient."

He slipped one finger between her moist folds, prodding gently, and she started against his hand, the sensation too great. But then his fingers became focused, circling her sensual nub until she could do nothing but writhe beneath him.

"Oh God, Sebastian."

Her fingers dug into his back, but she didn't notice. She could only focus on the way he made her feel, the sensations rippling through her body, building and building until—

She came apart in his arms, but even as it happened, he pushed against her opening, and suddenly he was inside of her.

Her body, already aroused by what he had just done to it, slipped around him with ease, only constricting when he was fully inside of her.

She lay absolutely still, allowing her body to adjust to him.

"Are you all right, my darling?"

"I think so." She turned her head to see him better as he perched above her. "You are still so terribly big."

He leaned down and pressed a soft kiss against her lips. "Does it hurt?"

She'd felt a pinch of pain when he'd first entered her, but now the aftereffects of her orgasm echoed through her muscles, leaving her in a puddle of contentment.

"I don't think so."

He moved his hips ever so slightly, and the fullness inside of her changed, sharpening until she felt a spark of the fire that had so recently pooled there.

"Sebastian, I...I...well, it's just that that felt good."

"It's supposed to feel good," he said against her neck, the underside of her jaw, her mouth.

"You're very distracting with your kisses, Your Grace."

He laughed against her mouth this time, and she reveled in the sound of it, so free and unsurprising. That more than anything shot a thrill through her, and she wrapped her arms tightly around him as he began to move.

She thought it impossible, but the tension between her

legs once more pooled until she didn't think she could bear it.

"Sebastian, I need—"

"I know, darling. So do I."

He slipped a hand between them, and when his finger touched her sensitive nub, she exploded.

"Louisa." It was the last thing he said before his body tensed above her, and he collapsed in her arms.

As sleep wrapped its drugging arms around her, she had only one thought.

Maybe Sebastian could be fixed.

* * *

HE WOKE to the feeling of a warm body flung across his chest, and reality seeped back into his brain one piece at a time.

He'd made love to his wife.

Louisa.

His eyes flew open only to be met with muted candlelight. He must not have fallen asleep for long. The fire still burned, and the few candles that had been lit still glowed on the mantelpiece and nightstand.

He slowly became aware of other things. Like how tightly Louisa held him, her arm tucked around his side while her head pressed into his chest, her exquisite body fitting perfectly along his.

He *ached* just holding her.

Years of a loneliness he hadn't known was there flooded through him as his arm tightened about her shoulders, tucking her more squarely against him.

Loneliness was a physical thing, and that he could handle. He could allow her to take away the hollowness that had plagued him while still protecting his heart.

He remained that way for some time, listening to her deep breathing interspersed with the crack of the fire. Absently, his fingers twined in her hair, catching a fistful of the silky strands. God, he could stay like that forever. Just holding her. Just listening to the silence and feeling the beat of her heart against him.

He had expected fear, waited for it to rear its ugly, cynical head, but it never did. There was only the stillness of the night wrapping them in a sheltered cocoon of their own making.

He couldn't stop his mind from traipsing back over what she had said before he had thoroughly ravished her. He felt a lick of worry at her repeated use of the phrase *perfect duchess* and its implications. Why did she continue to say such a thing and what did it really mean? What could cause her to be so fascinated with perfection?

Not for the first time he wondered about her mother's death. Her reaction to the elderly aunts at the wedding breakfast was more than just the sudden grief that comes with the reminder of a beloved parent's death. It wasn't grief he had seen in her eyes that day. It was fear and even more strangely, guilt.

In the quietness now, he allowed himself to think of it, and worse, he wondered what could be done. He had tried to ask her of it, but she clearly wished to keep whatever it was that frightened her to herself. Even now, he didn't feel as though he could ask her again.

But there was someone else he could ask of it.

She stirred then, snapping his mind back to the present. Without opening her eyes, she reached downward as if searching for a blanket. They had failed to get beneath the covers in their earlier madness, and her search was futile.

He stilled her wandering hand with his own. "Shhh, darling. I will warm you."

He turned against her, wrapping her in the warmth of his body as her head fell to the pillow and he captured her mouth in a soft, exploring kiss. He felt her come awake by degrees, her eyelashes fluttering against his cheek as he kissed her temple, buried his nose in her luxurious hair. He pulled back to catch her gaze and found her studying him with a wondrous expression.

"You are here," she whispered.

He couldn't help but smile at her dreamy tone. "Where else would I be?"

Her arms slipped around his neck, holding him close. "I had feared it was all a dream."

He kissed her again, unable to stay away. "It is not a dream, my darling. I promise you that."

He traced the line of her jaw and found that spot he so liked just behind her ear. When he pressed his lips to it, she squirmed against him, and he hardened just anticipating what was to come.

He pulled back, smoothed the hair from her face. "Are you sore?"

She shook her head, stretching her arms in a glorious show of contentment, yes, but it did wonderful things to her beautiful breasts. He watched them rise as if she offered them for his tasting, and who was he to deny her offer?

He pressed his lips to one, tracing the delicate curve of the full mound until he reached the sensitive underside where he licked his way back up, teasing her nipple as she writhed against him.

"Sebastian."

He loved the way she said his name when she was caught up in her own passion—both plea and exclamation.

Not wishing to keep her waiting, he sucked her nipple into his mouth until she arched against him, her hands keeping his head locked against her. He cupped her other breast in his hand, kneading it before taking her nipple between his two fingers.

"Sebastian."

Now his name was simple pleasure, and he had to look up and study her face, her head thrown back in utter ecstasy. She opened her eyes when he stopped pleasuring her breasts, and she met his gaze, no longer shy.

"Sebastian, I want you to touch me."

He wrapped his arms around her and pulled her against him for a deep kiss, his erection pushing into the softness of her stomach until he thought he might lose control right then. He eased her back on the bed and broke the kiss to trail even more kisses down the column of her neck, along the fine bones of her chest. He swept through her breasts despite her mewling pleas for more, making his way along the roundness of her belly.

He didn't stop until he reached the pale, creamy skin of her thighs. He sucked on the skin in the delicate juncture between hip and leg, teasing the sensitive spot with his teeth. She grabbed his head, pinning him against her.

"Sebastian, you can't."

He peered up at her, a wicked grin on his lips. "Oh, but I can, darling."

He ventured farther, sucking and licking, biting and kissing, until he found her sweet mound.

"Sebastian?" Her voice held a question now, and he didn't hesitate, parting her folds to lick her nub with a single, hot stroke.

Her hips came up off the bed, only serving to drive her against his rough tongue. Her cries of pleasure were not at all muted with desire now. She said his name over and over again like an incantation as he swirled his tongue around her core. When he thought he'd tortured her enough, he focused on the nub until he drove her to climax.

She collapsed against the pillows, and he rose up over her, braced on one elbow so he could push the hair from her face.

"Jesus," she muttered with her eyes closed, and he couldn't help a laugh.

"I must say I had no doubt of my talents, but I've never before caused someone to invoke the name of God."

She opened her eyes, a slow grin coming to her lips.

"Then clearly you hadn't met the right woman."

Her words pierced straight through his heart, and for one precarious moment, he stood on the precipice he had feared, knowing only how quickly he could fall in love with her if he let himself. But then she reached up and dragged her fingernails down his chest, jerking him back into the cloying sensual fog that kept the rest of the world at bay.

He snatched her hand away and pinned it above her head as he came above her, sliding between her legs as if he belonged there.

"You minx," he growled as he teased her lower lip in a kiss. "You seem to have found your footing quite well."

"I had a marvelous teacher."

He kissed her furiously now, his hands sweeping down her luscious curves, finding all of those secret places that made her moan.

This time when he came inside of her he did it slowly, teasingly, until her legs came up to lock around his hips, holding him to her.

"Sebastian, please."

He laughed into the softness of her neck. "Oh, my darling, in such a hurry."

He pressed into her soft folds but held back, rocking gently against her as she tried to angle her hips to catch more of him. She was slick and tight, and he had to grit his teeth against his building climax.

God, this woman was trouble.

Finally, he gave them what they both wanted. He slammed into her, and she cried out, her fingers digging into his back. He was fully inside her now, and her muscles squeezed him.

"God, Louisa," he moaned against her neck.

He rocked against her, pulling out to almost the tip before pressing himself fully inside her. He repeated the movement, over and over, until she gasped against his ear.

"I want you with me."

Her words were his undoing. He lost what measured control he still had, and when she tightened for the last time around him, his name spilling from her lips like an oath, his whole world shattered.

The orgasm ripped him apart, left him gasping as he tried not to crush her. Slowly, realization dawned that it had never been like this for him. Before Louisa, sex had just been that, sex. A physical act of lips and tongues, legs and arms and such. It had never involved his emotions or his mind.

But making love to Louisa involved all of that. She made him laugh. She made him want. She made him believe that maybe he could be happy someday.

He rolled off her, willing his thoughts to scatter. He didn't want to think about that now. He only wanted to soak in the glow with his wife in his arms.

He felt the greedy fingers of sleep begin their crawl, and he nudged Louisa from his shoulder where she'd resumed her spot as if it were meant for her. He was coming to believe it, in fact, was.

"I must blow out the candles, darling," he whispered to her as he slid her head to the pillow behind him.

Reluctantly, he extracted himself from her damp limbs, padding across the room to extinguish the candles along the mantel. He added a single log to the fire to see them into the darkest hours of the night before returning to the bed.

She had both hands tucked under her cheek, her golden hair splayed over his pillow. She looked like an angel sleeping there, and he had no wish to rouse her. But again, they had failed to make it beneath the bedclothes, and he knew soon she would be woken by the chill.

Carefully, he bent over her, kissing her cheek, her ears, and finally her mouth. She fluttered, half awake, a smile coming to her lips so perfectly he felt a responding squeeze in his chest.

"You need to get beneath the quilt."

She seemed to understand him as she rolled, tucking herself up so he could slip the quilt out from under her. He had just tucked her in and turned to extinguish the bedside candle when her slight hand touched his back.

"Please don't leave me." She whispered the words with an urgency that pierced.

He blew out the candle and turned, sliding to join her beneath the quilt and pulling her into his arms. Her head found his shoulder as it was meant to, and he gathered her hair away from her face.

"I'm not leaving you, darling. I promise."

He expected sleep to take him, but he lay there for some time listening to the sounds of the house settling around him, Louisa's rhythmic breathing, and the sound of his own heart beating in time with hers.

She fit so perfectly there in his arms, in his house, in his life, and once more his thoughts began to wander and wonder.

He had made love to Louisa because he had convinced himself she needed it, but now he wasn't so sure. For the first time, he began to wonder if maybe he had made a mistake in believing he should never love someone.

He fell asleep, though, before he could convince himself of that.

CHAPTER 11

*W*hen she finally awoke the next morning, she became aware of several things at once.

Brilliant sunshine poured through the now open drapes, and she was forced to cover her eyes with a hand until she could properly wake up. She rolled, attempting to sit up and shield her poor eyes when she discovered the other important facts.

She was completely naked and very sore in places she'd never been sore.

She used the hand not shielding her eyes to draw the covers up to her chin. Had it been practical, she would have pulled them directly over her head. It would have solved the issue of the blinding sunshine, but it would have prevented her from discovering the final and the most favored of facts that morning.

Her husband, scampering about the room in what looked to be an attempt to collect their discarded clothing from the previous night. As the task involved a good deal of bending, she was treated to ample display of his incredible bottom.

She could easily have said she'd never noticed his bottom

before. Not before last night anyway. The man himself was what fixated her attention, but after spending a night in his arms, she was becoming increasingly aware of his other…attributes.

She had expected to find her husband to be fit of stature, but she hadn't expected the delineated muscles, the fascinating curves of his shoulders, and the corded strength of his forearms. Her favorite, though, was his sculpted chest. As she had only seen him last night without a coat, how was she to know it was there?

She knew now, and she planned to take advantage.

She only regretted that at some point this morning he'd donned his trousers from the previous day. They were wrinkled, a state so unsuited to the man she couldn't help but watch him.

So it was that he caught her staring moments later.

"I do beg your pardon."

Her eyes had been on the bits of him she enjoyed the most, which meant she had to force her eyes up to his and suffer the embarrassment, both from having been caught ogling him and for the heat that flooded her cheeks when he'd found her out.

She adjusted the covers against her chest primly. "I give you my pardon. A lady shan't expect to awake alone in her husband's bed after all, should she?"

She looked up to toss him a smirk and stopped, her eyes widening as she took him in.

"Sebastian, is that—" She didn't even know how to formulate the question that rampaged through her mind.

For it was not her husband who stood before her surely. This man was all muscle and sinew, true, but more than that, his hair was brown and fluttered about his face in glorious thick waves. Brown. Sebastian's hair was really brown.

For more than a year now, she'd only ever seen it

pomaded and swept severely back from his face, and in that time, *this* was what he'd been hiding. Glorious *brown* hair?

"Is that what you look like?" That was not at all what she meant, but it was the only thing her lips could form.

Sebastian Fielding looked like some celestial creature from a Renaissance painting, and nobody knew it.

Except *she* knew it.

It was as though he had a secret identity he shared only with her, and it sent a thrill through her. Only she knew the secret parts of the Beastly Duke, and they were far more tantalizing than his bite.

"Is something amiss with your eyes? I look the same as I always have."

She shook her head. "You most certainly do not." She pulled a hand out from under the covers to point at his hair. "You hide that beautiful hair."

His frown was swift but at least he took a step back, and she realized he was searching for his reflection in the mirror above a chest of drawers opposite the bed. When he turned back to her, his frown had only grown more permanent. "It's just hair. I don't see anything over which to be excited."

She put her exposed hand against her chest in mock surprise. "Then that's only because I can see beauty where you cannot."

His smile was slow, and heat instantly curled low in her stomach.

"I must point out the flaw in your argument as I see plenty of beauty right now."

Her hand fell limp to her lap as she stared at him. How could this be the same man who was so quick to cut himself off from society entirely?

"However," he continued, "in this case, you've already made me tardy."

She looked about them for a clock and realized this was the first she'd seen of Sebastian's rooms in the daylight. This room was much like the rest of the house, only here she would say the wear on the furniture and draperies appeared lived in rather than worn. It was a startling insight to realize Sebastian likely had only occupied this room and his study in the whole of the house for some time. It showed in the valley imprinted on the seat cushion of the chair by the fireplace and the disappearing pattern on the carpet in front of the door. Even the draperies showed worn patches where he must have stood at night, drawing the fabric aside to look out on a sleeping London.

All of the clues pointed to a solitary existence that he professed to be what he wished, but after last night, she knew it to be a lie.

Sebastian Fielding was lonely.

He might deny it, or more likely, he might not realize it, but he was, and she couldn't stand for it.

"It's half nine if you're wondering," Sebastian's voice interrupted her thoughts. "I'm due at Ashbourne House at ten. I promised Dax we would work on the agricultural bill votes this morning."

She sat up. "You're leaving?"

He paused, his hand on a discarded boot. "Yes. Was that not expected?"

She looked about her again for an entirely different reason. She was naked in his bed, and he was leaving?

"I suppose not." She didn't like how her voice shook slightly as she said the words.

After all, what had she been expecting?

She certainly hadn't anticipated what had occurred the previous night. She had only come in to apologize to her husband and assure him of her intent to do better. She had not thought he might pull her into his arms and make sweet love to her. That was the stuff of novels, and she had outlived those long ago.

Or at least she thought she had.

But that was something to be explored later. For now, she needed to address her wayward husband.

He seemed to understand her disappointment for he drew closer to the bed. "I did not plan the events of last night, and so I could not inform you of my obligations this morning."

She could not blame him for that. As she herself had just thought, nothing of the previous night had been planned.

"It's quite all right. I guess neither of us really planned this, did we?" She gave a self-deprecating laugh and a little shrug.

He continued to stand next to the bed, lone boot in one hand and discarded shirt in the other. It afforded her a glorious view of that magnificent chest he'd been hiding, but if they were to have this conversation, it would have been far lovelier to have it where she could touch him.

She patted the edge of the bed next to her.

"No."

He spoke the word before she could say anything in regard to her gesture, and her eyes shot up to his face. "I'm sorry?"

"I can't sit next to you. I have obligations to see to, and I must dress."

She couldn't help the flash of power that coursed through her as she realized what he said. "You don't trust yourself to sit next to me."

The statement hung between them like a matador's red cape.

His fingers tapped against the leather of his boot. "I find there's a great deal I don't trust about myself when I'm next to you."

She wasn't sure why, but this sent a spiral of hope through her now, and she felt a lightness she hadn't felt in some time. While she had always tried to make her sisters happy, she'd never thought she might one day affect a man so.

Was it happiness, though, that she inspired in him? He currently did not appear happy. Tormented was more likely.

But any affect at all was something surely.

She slipped her arm back beneath the covers.

"I will give you a reprieve this one time, Your Grace, but I shan't be neglected in the future." She spoke the words through a saucy grin with the faintest hope of eliciting one of his rare laughs.

He did not laugh.

Instead he dropped the boot and the shirt and sat down on the bed so quickly she dipped against the pillows. He had both arms wrapped around her, his mouth crushed over hers before she could draw a proper breath.

Heat and euphoria flooded her at the touch of his lips on hers, and she wanted nothing more than to wrap her arms around him, but as he'd grabbed her and the bed covers with her, he'd effectively trapped her arms in the blankets. She struggled against her prison, but he only deepened the kiss, and she was lost to it.

He shifted, cupping her cheek as he eased his way out of the kiss, breaking contact at the very last possible moment, so she inevitably swayed into him, chasing the echo of his kiss.

Her eyes fluttered open to find him studying her, something heavy wrinkling his brow.

"What is it?" She didn't know why she whispered. Only that the serious look on his face seemed to call for such a tone.

"I don't know what I'm going to do about you." It was

something someone deeply in love would say to their beloved in a fantastical way for surely their love meant more than any challenge that could come their way.

But Louisa understood that was not how Sebastian meant it. Sitting there on the bed, she understood he was actively attempting to decide what to do about her. He may have trespassed on his own steadfast rules, but she knew it was only temporary.

What had occurred last night was merely physical. It was beautiful and pure and right, and she would never degrade it like that, but she knew better than to believe in fairy tales. Sebastian may be able to make love to her, but it didn't mean he did love her or could.

Except now she knew something she hadn't known before.

He could be fixed.

She could feel it in the precious way he held her, in the moments when he seemed to understand her better than she understood herself.

She pried one arm from beneath the blankets and used it to reach up, grab hold of his wrist as he still cradled her face.

"Give me a chance." She poured all of her hope into those four words, willed him to understand what she meant.

His eyes moved back and forth across her face as if he were studying her features for the answer. She poured all she could into her own eyes, hoping he would see reason there. Only she knew now what she was up against. There was nothing that held faster than those events one experienced as a child. No matter what she told the logical adult Sebastian, small Sebastian was still inside him, waiting for his mother to come home and tell him she loved him. Small Sebastian still hoped to see his father again.

There was so much she would need to undo in order to

help him find himself, but if anyone could do it, it was Louisa.

She squeezed his wrist, and slowly a smile came to his face. It wasn't one of those coveted laughs, but she would take it.

Until he said, "Perhaps when I've more time."

He kissed her again and left her sitting there on the bed, still naked and still sore from his lovemaking.

* * *

GIVE ME A CHANCE.

The words haunted him as he stood in the foyer of Ashbourne House a half hour later.

Like most things about Louisa, she refused to stay carefully removed from his person as he preferred most people do. Instead, she rammed right into his heart like a runaway carriage.

He'd made love to her.

The notion still perplexed him, and if he hadn't been there himself, he would have denied it. But he had done it. He'd made love to her. Louisa, his wife. God, what had he been thinking?

But this morning, the old Louisa had awoken in his bed. The one with the playful banter and the quick wit, the one whose smile melted the ice around his heart.

Give me a chance.

God, he wanted to. That was the worst part of it. But still, something unanswered lingered in his mind, something that held him back. He wished he could say it was his own insecurities, but it wasn't.

It was about Louisa.

Louisa had a secret he still did not understand, and for some reason, it gave him pause. Did it matter? *Should* it matter? So when she'd asked him to give her a chance, he'd wanted to say yes immediately, but he couldn't. His own caution made him pause.

He stood in the vestibule of Ashbourne House, the chirp of birds from just outside the windows that flanked the massive doors disrupting his thoughts as he tried to focus on the matter at hand. There would be a vote on the agricultural bill soon, and he and Dax were no closer to formulating a plan to secure the needed votes.

The butler had only just moments before slipped off to announce his arrival and footsteps on the stairs had him turning.

"Sebastian." Eliza stepped carefully down to the floor, a smile splitting her face. "Dax didn't say you were coming today."

Seeing Eliza stirred something within him, and that needling finger of curiosity began poking him squarely in the chest.

He swallowed. "Eliza." He gave a polite bow. "Dax and I only decided we should have a meeting after yesterday's session."

Eliza's brow furrowed. "It's the agricultural bill, isn't it?"

Sebastian was not privileged to know how most societal marriages went, but he had witnessed his own parents' marriage, and that one was not so inclined to such intimacies as one knowing the other's professional concerns. And yet it didn't surprise him that Eliza knew. Was he then supposed to tell Louisa of his affairs? He was surprised to find he wouldn't mind divulging such facts.

"I'm afraid it is."

Eliza folded her hands in front of her. "He's not been sleeping, Sebastian, and I blame this bill."

Sebastian couldn't help a smile. "Your husband is determined to make this work. Improving the roads in this country will greatly reduce the cost of shipping goods to market without relying on the proximity of canals. The added benefit of—"

He stopped as Eliza's smile melted into one of doting warmth.

He coughed, suddenly embarrassed, as Eliza said, "You've been working very hard on this as well, haven't you?"

"It's what is best for commerce."

"It's what is best for the farmers." Eliza shook her head. "You're so determined to remain aloof, Sebastian. Wouldn't it be easier to just admit you care?"

"No." The word slipped free before he had meant it to, and Eliza gave a gentle laugh.

"Come. I'm sure Carver will find His Grace momentarily. Join me in the drawing room while we wait."

He allowed Eliza to usher him into the room immediately off the vestibule. He blinked upon entering as the drapes in the room were thrown wide, and as the house faced south, it was flooded with sunshine at this hour. Positioned just in front of the windows was a macramé of odd tables that had obviously been pulled from other parts of the house. Strewn across the tables were Eliza's watercolors.

Sebastian had come to know of Eliza's watercolors in the past year after frequenting Ashbourne Manor where Eliza had an entire room dedicated to their production. What had started as a way for her to create picture books to help children develop skills in reading and color recognition had turned into something more. He had heard whispers from society matrons wishing to have their own copies of Eliza's work and Dax urging her to require payment for them.

Again, he was struck by the difference between Eliza and Dax's marriage and that of his parents. Somewhere in the mix slipped the image of Louisa, and he swallowed, unable to swim in the turmoil that was his emotions at present.

"You seem to be quite busy." He peered down at a particularly intricate rendition of a turtle coming through the reeds of a lakeshore.

"Lady Danforth requested a complete set of books for the school in her village."

Sebastian turned a questioning eye to Eliza. "And have you agreed with Dax's idea to require a suitable fee for your work?"

She tried to purse her lips, but it was ruined by her smile. "I may have seen the wisdom of his suggestion."

"Lady Eliza Kane, embracing the wiles of capitalism."

She laughed as she scooped up a palette of watercolors from a single chair pushed to the side so she could sit.

She studied the watercolors as she responded. "It's hardly an adventure into capitalism. I'm only asking that those who wish for a set of the books pay for the cost of producing them."

"And you are not seeking compensation for your time?"

Eliza's look was sharp. "Hardly. I think it's more important that children receive the tools they need to learn to lead a happy and productive life."

At the mention of happiness, Sebastian's mood soured. The image of Louisa wrapped in blankets in his bed surged through his mind, and he wished he didn't want to know.

Except he did.

"Eliza, I wonder if I might impose a question upon you."

Her smile was swift as she looked up. "As your sister-in-law, a question is no matter."

He realized he didn't know what question to ask. How did he sum up the burning curiosity within him?

Give me a chance.

He kept his gaze focused on the watercolors as if to give the impression that he cared very little for the answer.

"I'm rather curious about your childhood. Were there

events that occurred which would have reason to cause painful memories?"

Eliza sampled a spot of color on a piece of paper next to her that seemed to be just for that purpose as its surface was a veritable rainbow.

"Painful memories?" Her voice was careful. "Why ever would you ask such a question?"

At the prodding, Sebastian found his sense of loyalty to Louisa roaring up as it had that day Dax had questioned him at the club.

Except was the need for loyalty the same when it came to Louisa's own beloved sister?

Sebastian gave up the pretense of disinterest and took a seat opposite Eliza, leaning forward on his elbows.

"As you know, I endeavor to be respectful no matter what the gossips of the *ton* have to say about me. A matter has come to light about which I do not know how I should tread. Your sister and I were accosted by a matronly pair of women at our wedding breakfast, and one of the women suggested they had not seen Louisa in some time. Louisa's reaction to this pronouncement was startling. She became suddenly withdrawn. I should wish to know if there is a topic I should skirt when in her presence."

Eliza's face had remained unchanged until he'd nearly finished, but as soon as he told her the whole of it, her expression closed.

She set aside her watercolors. "I should probably tell you I had some concern over this. Louisa's never spoken of it, but with my experience teaching her and Jo when they were very small, I had wondered how much of the matter Louisa had retained."

Sebastian's heart slowed, and his left hand began to tap a staccato against his knee. He willed himself to relax, but a seriousness had entered Eliza's voice he did not often hear.

"I assume you speak of Martha and Maude? They are sisters who resemble each other a great deal."

Sebastian gave a quick nod, gesturing for Eliza to continue.

"They are cousins of our mother, somewhat distant on our grandmother's side, but they tend to turn up at things like this. The last time they saw Louisa was at our mother's funeral."

Sebastian's chest tightened at the word *funeral*. He knew only too well how the loss of a parent could ripple its damaging way through the rest of one's life.

"How old was Louisa?"

"She was only four at the time, nearly five. We had hopes that she was too young to remember much of what happened. You say she acted strangely when the sisters mentioned our mother's funeral?"

Sebastian's nanny had often described being chilled as if having someone walk over her grave. It was a phrase that held just enough possibility and fright to be enticing to a young child, and it was a suggestion that had stuck with him. It was how he would have described Louisa's reaction that morning.

"She did. It was as if she were being confronted with painful memories."

Eliza nodded. "Perhaps she remembers more than she lets on. Viv and I had always wondered. Louisa is rather a cheery soul, wouldn't you say? Perhaps too cheery?"

He could picture her warm smile and wide eyes as if Louisa stood in front of him. It was such a startling contrast to how he felt about himself that he couldn't ever stop the image from forming. He marveled at such happiness at the same time he feared it.

"Louisa tends to see the best in all things."

Eliza gave a soft, knowing smile, and he wondered what he'd said to cause such an expression.

"Well, it's not for me to tell you family secrets, Sebastian, but I think it's best that you know something. You must swear not to use this against Louisa. I know you wouldn't, but as her sister, I'm fiercely protective and must ask anyway."

He felt a pulse of…something, knowing Louisa had someone to protect her, someone strong like Eliza, but even as he thought it he realized he was there to protect her now. The thought sent both fear and pleasure racing through him.

He swallowed. "I would never do anything to hurt Louisa."

"I know you wouldn't." Eliza shook her head and studied her folded hands for a moment. "Sebastian, our mother died of influenza. There was an outbreak in our village, and even though my mother ordered everyone to stay at the house, the disease still came. It took several of the servants. I'm not even sure how many as Father was always protective and shielded us from such things. My sister Viv got sick, but she was a strong child." She laughed softly, a faraway look entering her eye. "She still is strong." She shook her head as if to return to the present matter. "Louisa, well…" Eliza peered past him as if searching for the words. "Father had us all sequestered in the nursery, hoping to keep us from the sickness in the house. He didn't want us to see our mother die, you see. It was a hard choice for him to make, and while I wish I could have said goodbye to her, I don't think I would have been brave enough. She was very sick, and Father was so shaken. He just wanted us to remember how our mother had been, not how she died. Do you understand?"

Sebastian had spent a great deal of time with his father, unlike some sons in society. His father had enjoyed stalking in the hills that surrounded their country seat, and Sebastian had begun shadowing him as soon as he was old enough. That was the father he chose to remember. Not the one who had killed himself over his lover.

"Yes, I can," he said now, and Eliza nodded as if letting him know she believed him.

"Not Louisa. Louisa snuck into our mother's room. Sebastian, she stayed with our mother while she died. She was the only one who did."

A coldness swept over him, rattling him in a way he thought nothing could ever do again. He'd felt this emptiness before, but now it was greater, heart-stopping and fatal.

He stared at Eliza. "She was there when your mother died."

Eliza's features had tightened with memory, and she studied him in earnest now. "She was. She'd crawled into bed with her. They found her in our mother's arms. Because of Louisa, our mother didn't die alone."

He was suddenly bombarded with a million questions he wished to ask but because they all came at once, he couldn't get a single one out.

He was prevented from saying anything more when Dax stumbled in behind him.

"This bill is going to be the death of me. Have you seen the latest? That Bradburg chap has really been making the rounds."

Sebastian stood automatically at his friend's entrance and was grateful some sort of correspondence he carried with him had distracted him from seeing the tableau Sebastian and Eliza must have made. Sebastian didn't have any more room for questions just then. He was flooded with too many answers.

He was nearly to the door, following his rambling friend who had already disappeared into the corridor, when he turned back to Eliza.

"You think Louisa is too cheery?"

Eliza had picked up her watercolors again as if nothing had happened when Sebastian's entire world had just changed.

She seemed to consider her words before replying. "It's almost as if she's trying to make up for something."

CHAPTER 12

*S*he was sitting on the floor when he found her that evening.

She wasn't sure what the room had been used for by previous duchesses, but she had a mind to take it over for herself. It was a small room compared to the others, and it faced south, catching most of the light throughout the day. There was a small fireplace opposite her and a generous window seat in an alcove to her left. It looked over the street, but in the distance she could see the tops of the trees in the park, and it had a lovely, calming effect.

She wasn't sure if she'd ever sat in a window seat. There really hadn't been time, what with tending to Jo and then seeing to Viv's wishes when they were older. Now, sitting in the silence of the house in the early evening, it was the first time it occurred to her that perhaps she would have time to herself now, and she hadn't an inkling as to what to do with it.

She would need to attend to her duchess duties, of course, and it wasn't as if she'd divorced herself from her sisters by marrying. She would always be there should they need her. But there had been something about her wedding to Sebastian that had marked a space in time. She still had her sisters and Sebastian to tend to, and God willing, there would be children someday. But suddenly she found herself with time on her hands and not a single idea of what she might do for herself.

She'd never paid attention to herself really, and now the feeling was foreign and somewhat terrifying. How was she to fill the long hours between her social duties? Sebastian had his work and often left early to attend Parliament sessions or meet with his solicitors. What was she to do in this big empty house once she was finished reviving it?

She pressed her hands to her stomach, wondering if a babe already grew inside it. Surely one night of lovemaking was not enough to produce a babe so soon, but it had been passionate lovemaking. Did that make a difference?

She wasn't sure what she would do, but she knew she'd do it in this room with its tall windows and beautiful, intricate swirls of plasterwork on the ceiling, the small fireplace that begged for one to sit in front of, and the window seat, her very own window seat.

"Are you all right?"

Sebastian's voice startled her from her reverie, and she looked up from her place on the floor.

"Quite. And you, Your Grace?"

His face gave her cause for concern as he studied her with furrowed brow.

"You're sitting on the floor in an entirely empty room. Forgive me if I question it."

The room was entirely empty. She had sent what little furniture that had been in it out to be repaired and reupholstered. The drapes had come down that morning for mending and cleaning, and even the cushions on the loveseat had been removed for a thorough beating. The room was just a shell waiting for her to fill it.

"It's quite all right. I assure you." She patted the floor next to her. "Would you care to join me? I was just imagining what this room might have been."

He seemed to consider her words as if her soundness were still in question, but finally he moved into the room and settled on the floor beside her. Without removing his jacket. In fact, he tugged at the cuffs of his shirt once seated as if to ensure he were properly attired.

She, on the other hand, was mottled with dust and grime, having spent the day helping the workers clear the room and seeing to the mending of the drapes, which were thoroughly covered with dust.

She blew an errant strand of hair out of her face.

"So, Your Grace, by chance, do you know what this room was last used for?"

The sun had begun to set at some point, and she wondered just how late into the evening it was. She'd gotten quite lost in her work and was likely only still moving thanks to the attentions of Williams who had brought her tea and sandwiches along the day to keep her efforts up.

"I don't believe this room has ever been used."

His shoulder touched hers where they lounged back against the wall. Together they peered up at the empty space, their gazes traveling from one corner to the other. At this hour, the room was awash in an orange light that lulled one toward sleep with the pleasant feeling of a successful day. She wanted to be in this room to see all of its phases of light for surely they must be magnificent.

"Never been used? That can't be. This room is simply marvelous in the light."

He frowned in the direction of the tall windows. "You forget when my mother was duchess she was rarely in residence. I would think my father would not be the type of person to notice such a room."

He was right, of course. The room had an air of femininity about it, and it was that which likely drew her to it.

"Would you mind so much if I used it?"

He gave a shrug. "Of course not. I'm not sure I knew it was here until Milton told me where I might find you."

She could feel him tense beside her as if readying himself to ask a question he didn't wish to. The sensation gave her pause, and she became acutely aware of his breathing.

"Louisa," he finally spoke her name, his tone reluctant. "Should I be concerned about what you're doing to my house?"

Relief flooded through her, and she even gave a small laugh. "I should think so. I believe no one has touched this poor house in ages. It needed a thorough renovation if there is any hope of it continuing into the next century of Waverlys."

"You're sending the bills to my man of affairs, I presume."

"Yes, of course. Should I have done something differently?"

He tugged absently at the cuffs of his shirt. "No, I suppose not. Only—do you have any idea how much any of this costs?"

She finally turned to look at him. "Actually, I do."

His glance was pointed and questioning.

"I believe one should be responsible in renovating a house of this size. There is so much history to preserve and so much lost to time that must be recovered."

"What do you mean?"

She laughed again. "I wouldn't expect you to understand." She placed a hand on his thigh in understanding. "I know this is all commotions and costs to you, but I assure you it's important to keep the Waverly history intact."

He raised an eyebrow in disbelief. "Is it, though?"

She patted his thigh. "It is. For instance, the house has a great number of important pieces of furniture. It's only that they have been worn down with time and use. I'm having them refinished and repaired as I go room to room. There's no sense in replacing such fine pieces, and I'm sure at some point or another there was a duke who acquired it through some important means."

"I doubt it," he scoffed.

But she only brushed his comment aside. "Oh no, I'm quite certain about this. Families collect pieces for a reason, and rooms hold the history of that family. I think it's a great deal like how one might go about solving a mystery, uncovering the things a room has seen and heard."

He stilled beside her again, and she wondered what he could possibly be wondering now.

Like an owl sweeping through the night, her words from that morning came back to her. Had he considered what she'd said? Had he made a decision? Were they to go back to leading separate lives? She might very well be carrying the heir now, and if that were true, he needn't bother himself with marital relations until the outcome was determined. The thought sent an icy spike straight through her heart, and she swallowed, her eyes traveling to her husband sitting beside her.

"Louisa, I'm not…" His voice trailed off, and she realized he searched for a word, but still, she hung on the silence as though something truly awful were coming.

When he did not speak again, she feared the worst and steeled herself against it. But surprisingly, he took her hand, sending her stomach rolling.

"Louisa, I told you a secret I had not told anyone about my father's death. I must ask you something now that I have no right to ask, but I hope you know you can trust me with anything."

The unexpected course of conversation left her momentarily stunned. What was he getting at? She squeezed his hand to let him know he should continue, unable to form the words to tell him to do so.

"Do you remember anything of when your mother died?"

She had never heard such a somber note in his voice, and her chest tightened at the sound of it. It was several moments before she realized just exactly *what* he had asked.

"Why…" She licked her lips. "Why would you ask that?"

He turned to face her, the fabric of his coat rustling against the wall. "The morning of our wedding breakfast those women upset you. And not in the usual way family can be upsetting. You were honestly frightened by their mention of your mother's funeral. I didn't—"

His attention diverted to the ceiling as if suddenly exasperated by himself. The gesture was so unlike him it left her momentarily puzzled.

"Louisa, do you know before I met you I lived a perfectly calm and unexciting existence?" He pinched the bridge of his nose, which she'd never seen him do, before returning his gaze to her. "And now I upset myself over your reaction to a pair of exceedingly eccentric old women."

His honest declaration left her warm and somewhat hopeful for an instant before she realized he studied her expectantly.

"I don't like to speak of my mother's death," she whispered, afraid of speaking more or at greater volume.

He turned fully now, taking both of her hands into his.

"I know you don't. I *know* it, Louisa, because I went to great lengths to cover up the circumstances of my father's death so I must never speak of it. But I think there's something about your mother's death of which you've never told anyone. I think it…hurts you."

The setting sun poured through the windows, illuminating the planes of his face in oranges and golds. Sebastian. Her Sebastian. When had she fallen in love with him?

It was there all at once and all together, but she knew that wasn't how it started. That wasn't how love came upon a person surely. She loved him for the way he bantered with her sisters, for the way he protected his best friend, for the way he'd protected her, for his unfailing sense of loyalty and honor.

She loved him.

And it hurt so much more than she'd expected it to.

"I was so young." Still she whispered, and yet, she willed herself to find the strength, the strength she had used for so many years to keep moving, to keep going, to take care of her sisters, to pay the price for her crimes.

"I know you were. Are there things that happened then that you don't understand? That you don't truly remember?" He swallowed, and it looked like it hurt. He closed his eyes against it, and when he opened them, she saw a rawness to him she'd never seen before.

The Beastly Duke cared.

About her.

It rushed over her all at once until she almost drowned in it.

But somewhere out of the depths of emotions, she heard herself say, "I killed my mother."

* * *

HER WORDS MADE no sense to him, but the way her eyes fluttered shut as if she could not contain the pain her revelation had caused, the way her shoulders slumped, her body coiling against itself as if in protection, he understood.

He pulled her into his arms, wrapping them tightly about her until she was tucked safely against his chest.

"Louisa, my darling." He stroked her back. "Your mother died of influenza. I don't understand what you mean."

He thought she was crying as her shoulders shook against his arm, but he realized she wasn't. Her body shook with tremors she seemed unable to control as she let him hold her. One hand clutched the lapel of his jacket, dragging the garment down until it choked him. He unlocked her fingers, soothing her hand with the stroke of his thumb along her palm.

Whatever she had kept pent up inside of her had been there for a very long time, and he'd suddenly released it with his careless words. Eliza had been right to worry over what Louisa may have remembered and what she didn't. The loss of a parent was traumatic and life-altering. Louisa had been so preciously young and so incredibly scared. She must have been. How was a child so young supposed to understand what was happening? She'd probably been terrified.

And now, what was she saying about killing her mother?

Slowly, he eased her away from his shoulder, holding her in place before him.

"Louisa, my darling, you must tell me what is wrong. Tell me what this is about."

She heaved in his arms, her body bucking beneath the strain of whatever coursed through her mind. He searched her eyes, but they'd gone blank as if she'd slipped into a faraway time.

He set his forehead against hers, cradling her face in his palms.

"Louisa, you must tell me." He set his voice low, coaxing

her out of the abyss she'd fallen into. "Tell me the story just as you remember it."

Her eyes had fluttered shut, the brush of her lashes a phantom against his cheeks.

"I just wanted to see her dollies." Louisa's voice had gone soft and childish, a plaintive note as if she were once more a child being scolded. "Mary was my friend. I didn't think Mummy meant I couldn't see her. And the dollies were so pretty."

His mind raced, scrambling to put the pieces together.

"Where did Mary live, Louisa?" he asked, recalling what Eliza had said about their mother ordering them to stay out of the village.

Louisa's face constricted as he felt her brow bundle against his. He leaned back ever so slightly but never released her face from the cradle of his hands. He stroked her cheeks gently, willing color to return to her skin.

"Mary lived in the cottage at the end of the lane. Mommy said we weren't to go into the village, but Mary didn't live in the village. She lived on the lane where the steward's cottage was. I didn't disobey. I didn't." She shook her head violently at these last words and he loosened his grip so as not to hurt her.

"Mary was your friend." He spoke the words calmly, soothingly. "She was your friend, Louisa. You just wanted to see her dolls."

Louisa's eyes flew open, but she wasn't looking at him. She was looking at something else, something like the dolls of which she spoke.

"Her grandmother made them for her. They were knitted from the softest yarn and they had the most beautiful bows done in silks along their shoes and their dresses and in their hair. Peaches and pinks and blues, and they were so lovely. I just wanted to see the dolls."

"Did your mother forbid you from going into the village?" he asked, even though he already knew the answer.

Her eyes flashed at this, and he worried he'd said something wrong, but instead, it was the opposite. Color seeped back into her cheeks, and her eyes flicked back and forth over his face as if she saw him again for the first time.

"There was an outbreak in the village. Mother didn't want us to go there for fear we'd take ill."

"And you didn't go to the village."

Her eyelids slid shut. "I didn't go to the village, but I went to Mary's cottage."

Realization struck him all at once, robbing him of breath. Very carefully, he said, "Louisa, do you think you brought the influenza into the main house? Do you think your mother became ill because of you?"

Louisa jerked her head from the cradle of his hands as she swung her gaze away from him, a sound tearing from her mouth that was anything but human and entirely of anguish. He was faster, though, and caught her shoulders, drawing her back to him.

"Louisa, you know you can tell me anything. I've proven my loyalty to you, haven't I?"

For the first time in all of her weary tale, she looked at him, her eyes surprisingly dry and yet still haunted.

"I would never question your loyalty." Her words were low and fierce. "It's myself whom I do not trust."

"What do you mean?"

When she looked away this time, he let her. Her gaze roamed the empty walls of the room as if seeing something there he did not. The sun had set now, and only a small pink light hung far up in the room, and they were left shrouded in darkness along the floor.

"It's my nature, you see." She gave a soft, painful laugh. "I'm impulsive. I'm always harrying off on a whim, and someone is always inevitably hurt." She gave another laugh before facing him again. "I mean, look what I've done to you. I forced you into this marriage because I wanted to see puppies."

He couldn't stop the frown, his head jumbled with far too many things. He recalled she'd said the word that night he'd found her in the Lumberton drawing room, and still it made no sense that she should follow a man, alone, to these suggested puppies. But perhaps, that was the very thing of which she spoke, the danger of impulsiveness.

He touched her hand and gathered it into his when she didn't pull away.

"I hardly think wishing to see a friend's dolls or a litter of puppies is cause for a proclamation of such damnation."

A line appeared between her brows. "It is when you endanger your sister's happiness, her chance at a future." She grew somber, her voice softening. "It is when you condemn a man to marriage."

The agony in her voice was like a dagger in his chest, twisting until it struck bone.

"Marriage is not a condemnation. Especially not this one." He spoke the words to her hands, unable to meet her gaze as he wondered at the feelings coursing through him.

Once he may have agreed with her that marriage was a punishment he did not deserve, but now he was not so quick to judge. Marriage to Louisa was...well, fine.

He knew that was not the stuff of bards, and if he'd actually spoken such sentiment aloud, Louisa would be more than disappointed. She would blame herself for his unhappiness, but that was not at all what he felt when he thought of their marriage.

In fact, he might even be so bold as to apply the word *content* to his current state of affairs.

That word alone, so innocent and neutral, sparked a fear

in him he thought not possible. But he soon tamped it down, not wanting to allow it to vanquish the small bit of peace he'd managed between them.

She studied his face now as if to gauge the truthfulness of his statement, and he did not flinch under her scrutiny.

"Do you honestly feel that way?"

The wonder in her voice had his gut clenching.

"Of course, I do. I would not lie, Louisa." He spoke the words more harshly than he'd meant to, and unexpectedly, a smile broke across her face.

"No, you wouldn't lie." Her voice wobbled ever so slightly, and he forced himself to look away, feeling the tenuous grip on his emotions slipping.

This was what love did to a person. It made them question their every action, pour themselves out to another until they were at their most vulnerable. He couldn't stand for it. At least...perhaps not yet.

"Louisa, I think you judge yourself far too harshly." He spoke to the fireplace opposite in hopes he could steer the conversation to safer ground.

She followed his gaze as she reclined once more against the wall, her shoulder brushing his.

"No, I don't," she said softly. "It's difficult to carry the burden of your mother's death for so long." She turned, her hair rustling along the plasterwork at their backs. "Do you know I've never told another soul about what I did? You're the first to know."

He did look at her now, remembering the night he'd told her the truth about his father.

"Do you feel better for it?"

She gave a soft shrug. "Not really, but I guess it feels different now. Now that someone else knows. It still hurts me terribly."

Her gaze dropped to her lap, and he discovered she was

twisting her gown in her hands. Carefully, he slipped his hand between hers, capturing her warring fingers in his.

"It always will, I'm afraid." The words rung through the empty room with a quiet solemnity.

"I suppose it will."

Moments passed as they sat in silence, and he never let go of her hand. He let her revelation tumble through his mind, but it never quite sat well. Something wasn't right.

"Louisa, I know it must be an awful thing to speak of, but your mother—you think she became ill because you went to see your friend's dolls."

She gave a soft nod. "Even though I didn't go to the village, I still must have brought the disease back with me to the house. That's the only explanation. Mother forbid anyone, including the staff, to leave the house while there was an outbreak."

She turned her head to meet his gaze, and when he saw her eyes, his heart cracked. She looked so scared, like a frightened child.

"Mother was so very worried one of us children would become ill. Some would call what she did drastic, but she just wouldn't risk our health. And I—"

Her voice broke, and he pulled her back into his arms, pressing a kiss to her forehead as he tucked her head beneath his chin.

"It wasn't your fault. You were only a child."

"But that's just it. It's still my fault, and I was a child. I not only lost my mother, but I was the cause of it." Her voice was strained now, and he could hear the first hint of tears.

He kissed her temples, her cheeks, her closed eyes. "Louisa, my darling, you mustn't do this to yourself. You must let the past go or it will only serve to control your future."

Her head snapped up at this, and when she opened her eyes, the fading light shone from the moisture there.

"Says the man who cannot love me." The words were spoken with a ferociousness he hadn't expected, and he dropped his hands futilely into his lap.

"Well, that's...that's something else entirely."

"I see." She wiped at her eyes with quick hands before sliding her legs underneath her. "We should get ready for supper. I'm sure Milton will be calling it soon."

He helped her to her feet, their footsteps ringing in the quiet of the empty room. They stood facing each other for several seconds as he was unable to let go of her hands even after she proved to be safely standing.

The moon had begun to rise, and the beams of light struck her full in the face, illuminating the valleys and crests he found so fascinating. She glowed but not from the moonlight. She glowed from the weight of her secrets she'd carried for so long, from the fierceness with which she protected her family, from the love she kept held inside of her.

She was the Viking queen, robust and strong and beautiful.

Robust...

"Louisa, you say you brought the illness into your house." He licked his lips, realizing he was about to give himself away. "Only I know you didn't fall ill from it."

Her eyes became guarded, and she considered him carefully. "How do you know that?"

He'd never felt nerves the way he did now. "I asked Eliza why those women at the wedding breakfast might cause you to become so upset."

Her eyes widened at his revelation, and he felt a stab of guilt over his treachery. But then her features softened, and a small smile came to her lips.

"I have you so worried over me, do I? I hope Eliza was able to soothe your concerns."

"Not at all." He pulled his hands from hers and tugged at the cuffs of his shirt. "Louisa, you did not become ill. So how then can you blame yourself for your mother's death?"

Her smile faded as uncertainty took over her face.

"But I must have, Sebastian. I must have. It's the only way…" Her voice trailed off, but she continued to search his face.

"Louisa, do you think you may have been wrong? Do you think you've blamed yourself this whole time for something you didn't do?"

Her eyes narrowed, but then she shook her head.

"No, it's the only explanation, and I will not dredge up poor memories for my sisters by asking them for the truth. I just couldn't do it, Sebastian." Her voice was strong with her determination, and he knew he would not win.

"Then let's ready ourselves for supper," he said as it was the only thing he could have said.

CHAPTER 13

*S*he tried not to let her sudden suspicions cloud the happiness she'd fallen into, but it was difficult, especially when an invitation to tea from her mother-in-law arrived the next week.

She seemed to pass through the house like a ghost, not quite there and yet entirely haunting herself. The furniture she'd sent out to be reupholstered began to return in a steady stream that kept her occupied, and she willed her thoughts to be quiet. Except they wouldn't listen to her.

Her sister's confession of loving a man she couldn't have, exposing her lifelong secret to the husband she'd forced into marriage, and worst of all, she found herself in love with that husband.

How had it happened?

She'd accepted the fate of a loveless marriage as she'd never once imagined a life with love. When Sebastian had declared they'd live separate existences, she was only too quick to understand. After all, she'd never thought beyond her sisters to herself, and she had no formed idea of her life for him to destroy with his proclamation.

But then that night when she'd come to apologize, something had changed. Something was different.

She worried now it was something she'd done, something she'd said to cause him to break the oath he'd made to himself. But honestly, it was an oath meant to be broken.

How could he expect to live a life without love?

Couldn't she say the same thing to herself?

As she passed through wallpapering crews and dodged footmen carrying freshly beaten rugs, she wasn't sure how she'd missed it. This idea that one day she'd be gone from her sisters, and there would be someone else to care for but yet, she'd have so much time with the only person she'd failed to see this whole time.

Herself.

She existed in some kind of strange half state as she grappled with what to do about Johanna and her secret or her husband's unfailing attentions toward her now.

And the fact that she loved him.

She loved him for going to her sister when he saw her hurting. She loved him for choosing her over his malicious mother. She loved him for his loyalty, for his caring, for his understanding. She loved him, and he could never love her.

This should be a time of happiness and euphoria, and that was why she clung to that precious feeling of fleeting contentment because she knew just how unreal it was.

Because Sebastian did not love her in return.

He cared for her, she was certain, but he always held himself just a little bit away from her, held back just a small part of himself. She could feel it between them, the space he so carefully guarded, even when he made love to her, held her, cradled her in his arms.

She could feel the love pour through her at his touch, but she could also feel something else, and it was this other thing that dominated her thoughts.

So when the invitation to tea arrived, she nearly swallowed her tongue. As it was, she made a very unladylike pronouncement.

"Oh God, no."

They had taken to breaking their fast in the east drawing room as the breakfast room was currently having the floors redone. The light was magnificent here, and she wondered if they would ever remove themselves to the breakfast room again.

They took their meal at a small table nestled into the alcove of a large bay window, and the sun struck the correspondence Milton had brought with enough light to ensure she did not misread it.

"Has someone died?" Sebastian asked around the rim of his teacup as he'd been about to take a drink.

"Your mother has invited me to tea."

He swallowed and said, "Well, if someone hasn't died yet, they surely will soon."

She tossed him a frown. "That person is likely to be me."

"I hardly think so." He stood and set aside his napkin. "It will surely be my mother after you commit matricide over crumpets." He pressed a kiss to her cheek. "I am off. Dax is waiting."

She snatched his arm before he could slip off. "Good luck with the vote today." Something passed over his eyes that resembled confusion, and she smiled. "Eliza told me the vote is today. Dax feels as though you have enough support to get the bill passed. Do you really think so?"

"We should, yes." He answered the question as though he was surprised she'd asked it.

Not for the first time, she wondered just how much damage his parents' marriage had wrought on him. She smiled and patted his arm. "Good luck then. I'll see you this evening."

She kept her tone light, not wishing to frighten him anymore and hoping to keep her heart from breaking into a million tiny pieces.

She arrived at his mother's home promptly at the time specified as there was certainly no need to arrive early. She'd worn her best muslin gown in a shade of green Jo always said set off the warmth in her eyes. Louisa didn't know why she felt compelled to impress this woman. It wasn't as if the viscountess had earned Louisa's respect. Far from it. As she stepped through the front door, she very much worried Sebastian was right. She had never contemplated matricide, but suddenly, it seemed very appealing.

The butler showed her into a drawing room she hadn't seen before, but she was struck by the dull wallpaper and worn furnishings. It was as though she'd stepped into Waverly House on the day of her wedding. It became suddenly clear what had happened to the Waverly home, and Louisa's nerves grew even more taut than they already were.

"Louisa, child, so good of you to come on such short notice."

Viscountess Raynham's voice was melodic as she sailed into the room, her arms spread as though she planned to embrace Louisa.

Louisa stood next to the table that had been laid for tea and kept her arms tightly at her side, placing the chair between herself and the viscountess.

"Yes, of course," Louisa said with a small curtsy as was proper.

Suspicion flared its way up her arms as she took in the viscountess's unusually open expression. The woman wore a gown of faded lavender that had clearly been turned up at the hem and cuffs to hide wear, and strings of paste jewels hung at her neck, wrists, and ears. She very much matched the worn elegance of her home, and suddenly Louisa didn't feel quite so small.

She took the seat the viscountess offered and waited for the woman to pour.

"I thought perhaps we should get to know each other now that you've married my dear son."

"I told you that night at dinner that I will not pretend you were a doting mother to Sebastian." She kept her tone polite yet cool.

The viscountess didn't seem to notice. "Yes, well, people do change, and it would be suggested that we should make a good connection as we may be of use to one another in the future."

Louisa did not care for the connotations such a statement held. As she was now a duchess, Louisa was well aware of the power she held, socially speaking, and she was not so obtuse as to forget the viscountess had once been a duchess, too. Did the woman regret the loss of her social standing? Did she wish to use Louisa to regain some kind of control?

She sipped at her tea but did not take a single small sandwich onto her plate. "If you do not mind, I'd like to understand the true reason why you asked me here today."

The older woman's eyes flashed over the teapot. "Why, it's just as I've said. To get to know one another better. I must say I was quite surprised when I heard Sebastian was to take a wife."

"Surprised? Shouldn't you be elated that your son found a match?" Louisa watched her carefully, noting the way the teapot trembled ever so slightly at Louisa's reply.

"Well, you know how these things are. Time gets away from us, doesn't it? I hadn't realized just how grown up my son had become. He's been through a lot, you understand."

A prickle of suspicion made its way to the back of Louisa's neck, and she wanted to reach up and scratch at it.

"Yes, I am aware."

The viscountess glanced abruptly upward to sweep her eyes across Louisa's face, but she quickly returned her attention to the cucumber sandwiches as if nothing were amiss.

"I had worried that his father's death would adversely affect him. I mean, they were so close and all."

"I should think it would be assumed that one's father's death would influence the rest of one's life. I've lost both of my parents, you see, and I can say it does leave one changed."

The viscountess waved a hand as though to brush off Louisa's statement.

"Yes, but Sebastian's father died so tragically. I'm sure he's spoken of it." The viscountess glanced at Louisa from the side of her eye as she sipped at her tea.

Louisa set her teacup down with a clatter. "No, actually. Sebastian never mentioned it."

The woman wanted something from Louisa, and she would be damned if she'd give it away.

The viscountess set down her tea, her gaze suddenly riveted to Louisa.

"Is that so? Well, I hardly can believe it. I was so sure the experience must have left a scar."

Louisa shook her head and poked at a caramel biscuit. "No, I'm afraid he hasn't. Sebastian is rather close-lipped, as you can imagine."

This seemed to placate the woman as her eyes lost the roundness of surprise.

"Well, that is certainly true. I suppose I was merely concerned for his well-being."

That was an outright lie.

"I suppose you were," Louisa said.

The viscountess waved a hand. "It's just that men are such strange creatures. Wouldn't you agree?"

Louisa tilted her head coquettishly. "Oh, I don't find them all that strange. They are quite predictable beings."

This seemed to finally pierce whatever charade the viscountess was attempting for she abandoned her dainty perusal of the almond pralines to face Louisa squarely.

"Well, it's just that men do not have anyone in which they naturally confide. At least we have our lady's maids, don't you agree?"

Louisa's mind flitted to Williams, but while she understood what the viscountess meant, Louisa would not give anything away.

"I suppose one could. But that would be highly indiscreet. My mother always used to say one does not air one's dirty laundry on the front stoop. I would think she could agree with me on this."

The viscountess's mouth pinched ever so slightly. "Well, be that as it may, I had only a great concern for you settling into marriage with my son when I know he is ever so wounded from what's happened. You cannot fault me for caring."

Louisa could very well fault the woman for many things. Caring was not one of them.

"No, I suppose one cannot." Louisa finished her tea and carefully placed the cup back into the saucer. "I'm so very glad I was able to come today. I'm sorry I must make my visit so short. Duty calls, as I'm sure you understand."

The viscountess made no move to show her guest out as she sipped her tea. Her eyes became hooded as she regarded Louisa across the table.

"I think you should know I had nothing to do with it. With what happened to Victor. He made his own choices."

Louisa stilled, her back stiffening. Victor must be Sebastian's father. She'd never pressed Sebastian for his father's given name, but the way the viscountess spoke it with such fervor suggested Louisa was right. "I never accused you of having a role in the matter, did I? You're awfully quick to defend yourself from a slight that was not presented."

The older woman sucked in a breath at Louisa's statement, but it was low and harsh and could have been mistaken for a wheeze. Now the viscountess stood.

"Be that as it may, I should hope you understand you are free to talk to me about anything concerning my son. I imagine it's difficult being married to such a man. His father was the same way. So closed off and cold. Just know that you always have an ally with me." Her smile didn't reach the corners of her mouth, and her crooked teeth made Louisa nauseous.

Louisa didn't wait for her hostess to walk her to the door. She stepped outside the bounds of propriety and stood, discarding her napkin next to her place setting on the small table, preparing herself to leave.

Shaking her head, she said, "I'm sorry to not understand, but marriage to Sebastian is the single best thing that's ever happened to me." She gave a shrug as if to apologize again. "Good day, my lady." She gave a small bow and left before the viscountess could regain her wits.

* * *

HE WAS GETTING USED to coming home to her.

He wasn't surprised to find her in the little room she'd claimed as her own, standing by the tall windows still bare of drapery, the setting sun illuminating her like some kind of cherubic entity. He stood in the doorway for several moments, letting time slip by them simply for the pleasure of watching her unawares.

She held her arms crossed over her stomach, her fingers

still on either elbow. Her gaze studied something beyond the reach of his, and he wondered what so captured her attention. Was it the tops of the trees in the park or the heraldic spires of the palace beyond?

He had never thought to have such interest in another person, believing it safer to keep himself tucked away from human relationships. But he was finding it wasn't like that. Instead it was more like a steaming bath one expected to scald only to slip beneath its tantalizing surface to find it warm, coaxing, and comforting. That's what it was like to be with Louisa. That's what it was like to fall in love with her.

When she'd asked him that morning about the vote, he'd been startled she'd even known it was that day. He hadn't thought to tell her, but then, he'd thought she wouldn't be interested. He was beginning to understand he held a great deal of misconceptions about marriage, and Louisa held no qualms in showing him wrong. She was the perfect tutor for his icy heart, and he no longer feared what was to come.

Not that he was ready to declare his love from those very spires she viewed. It was more a shifting of something within him that allowed him to think of another possibility, another existence. One that included Louisa next to him for the rest of his days.

A small line appeared between her brows that had him straightening from his spot beside the door.

It wasn't the spires she studied then, but rather her own thoughts. They were likely troublesome as he'd not forgotten the unexpected invitation to tea his mother had sent that morning.

He gave no greeting but simply entered the room to take his place beside her, slipping his arms around her until he could set his chin atop her head. She fit so perfectly in his arms, and the scent of orchids flooded his senses.

She did not start when he touched her, and he wondered if she'd known he was there all along.

"A guinea for your thoughts."

He could hear the smile in her voice as she said, "If I accepted it, you would have overpaid."

"It's worth the price."

She sighed, relaxing into his arms. "I'm afraid it's nothing of interest. I simply find your mother vexing."

His gut tightened at the mention of his mother. "Tea was unpleasant, I take it?"

She hesitated for a moment as if mulling over her words. "It wasn't that it she was unpleasant. Although I would not call her affable. It was more that she asked the oddest questions."

"Questions?"

She slipped her hands along his arms as he held her. "She seemed awfully interested in knowing what you had told me about your father's death."

The tension in his gut grew to a roil. "And what did you say?"

She turned in his arms until she could look up at him. "I told her very little. It's not for her to know what lies between us."

The way she spoke made it sound as if there should be no question of what she would say to his mother. Being the receiver of such abject loyalty was new to Sebastian, and it unsettled him for a moment.

She played with the lapels of his jacket absently as she said, "Do you think it bothers her? The choice your father made?"

As always the shadow of his father's death loomed over him, but now it no longer held the bite it once did.

"I don't know. It never seemed as though my mother cared for my father in the least. I'm not sure why his death would cause her concern. Perhaps it was the potential for scandal it held."

Louisa's eyes were somber when she looked up. "That's rather selfish of her."

"She's rather a selfish woman."

Somewhere deep in the house a clock chimed, and Louisa groaned, laying her head against his chest.

"We must get ready. We have the Sloane ball this evening." She pulled back abruptly. "And you haven't even had time to tell me how the vote went." Her face was a riddle of banked excitement and consternation. He couldn't help but smile.

"The bill was passed."

Her face split into a smile so quickly his heart raced at her sudden joy. She threw her arms around his neck, and he was forced to catch her as the momentum picked her up off her feet. Her mouth found his in an exhilarating kiss before she pulled back, her smile bigger than ever.

"I knew you would do it! Does this mean the roads will be repaired?"

He held her against his chest, warmth and light radiating through him as if thawing him from a great chill.

"It means a committee will be formed to devise the funds for the project. You know how these government things work. There's always a committee."

She laughed and kissed him again. "But now you've made a start of it. You should be so proud of yourself and the work you've done for the farmers in—" Her brow furrowed, confusion painting her face. "Do you know I don't know where your country seat is? In fact, I know very little about you or your family, which I think should be concerning, don't you?"

Now he couldn't help but laugh.

"It's in Hampshire. Not more than a day's ride to Ashbourne Manor."

If he had thought her elated before, now she was a veritable surge of excitement at having heard her summer home would be so close to her sister's. That was, if she wished to summer there. Likely for the first time, he realized these decisions now involved another person. He had no issue with staying in London for the summer, but he thought Louisa would enjoy the respite and fresh air. They would need to discuss it soon as the season was already drawing to an end.

"Is it truly? I can't wait to see it."

"I haven't been there in some time. I'm not precisely sure as to its state."

Her eyes moved about him in a circular motion, a frown coming to her lips. "I can't imagine it's any worse than this."

He followed her gaze about the room. "Yes, there isn't even adequate furniture on which to make love to my wife. It certainly is a travesty."

Even though the sun had set, he didn't miss the blush that stained her cheeks at his words, and he loved having that effect on her.

"Do not make such suggestions, Your Grace. Not now at any rate. We're already late."

He was suddenly seized by the impossibility of the moment. Had it only been months before when he would not have conceived of this moment ever occurring? This beautiful woman, awash in moonlight, was his wife. By law she belonged to him, but it was so much more than that. He could feel it in the way he could breathe easier than he had in years, in the way he looked forward to waking up, finding her in his arms, in the way his heart skittered when she asked him about his work in Parliament.

It was the first time anyone had seen *him* and not the charade of the Beastly Duke.

She shifted as if to move from his arms, but he held fast,

suddenly gripped by a desire so strong he could never refute it.

"Wait." The single word shot through the empty room with a ringing echo. "What if we don't go? What if we stay in, just the two of us? One night without the *ton* playing witness to our every move?"

He cared not a whit what society thought of him or his doings, but he knew Louisa cared a great deal about her role as his duchess, and he didn't wish to upset her. The notion that he should care for another's feelings was utterly alien to him, so much so that his heart clenched against the idea. He willed it open, forced himself to take the next dangerous step in an already perilous dance.

Her face changed, right there before him, shifting in the moonlight. It was like watching a tulip open in the spring, its petals peeling away to reveal the vibrant center.

He had done that. With just his words, he'd transformed her face, and the feeling rocked him.

"What did you have in mind?" Her voice had grown soft and wondering, and instead of answering, he leaned down and captured her mouth in a searing kiss.

She rose up to meet him, returning his kiss with an ardor all her own. He caught her up, pressed her bodily against him and devoured her. He didn't know how much time had passed when he lifted her into his arms and made to leave the room.

"Wait."

He stopped, the movement sending her more tightly against his chest.

"What if we...well, there's..."

She pointed at a place behind him, and he turned to find a sofa set to one side that he had not seen when he'd entered. He looked back to find she'd gone entirely scarlet in his arms.

"Your Grace, are you suggesting we employ the services of that sofa for the purposes of our moonlit tryst?"

She opened her mouth, but no sound emerged. His darling innocent wife was dipping her toe into a sensuality she had only begun to explore, and he had to admit he was impressed by her boldness.

"Yes," she finally said as if she were doing nothing more than selecting a fish course.

He deposited her on the sofa before she could change her mind. Her hair had come undone at some point and hung in thick curls about her face. He slipped his hands beneath it, cradling her head so he could pull her into a kiss.

It wasn't long before his hands itched to explore, and they traveled down the length of her pale neck, loosening the ties of her bodice, his mouth following the trail. He nibbled kisses along the exposed line of her décolletage, savoring the smoothness of her pale skin. His hands had moved on, finding the hem of her skirts and pushing them up. He traced the curve of her knee through her stocking, tiptoed his fingers up the inner sanctum of her thigh. She moaned and arched against him.

"Sebastian, please."

He knew now of what she begged, but he still made her ask for it.

"Do you want me to touch you, darling?" he murmured against the soft column of her neck.

Her fingers were in his hair, her fingernails doing wicked things to him, and he shuddered against her until she pushed him back, her hands against his shoulders holding him steady.

"I want more than just your touch." Her tone was deep and beckoning, and he throbbed against the tight fabric of his trousers.

"Then you shall have it."

He made to resume his torturous work, but she stilled him, her eyes searching his face.

"I don't know why you do that to your hair with all this ghastly pomade." Her eyes moved back and forth, and he wondered just what she saw. "The real you is by far superior to the facade you've created." She placed a single hand against his cheek. "Why don't you let everyone see you?"

His heart squeezed so much he was sure it would stop beating entirely, and in that moment, with her spread out before him, bathed in moonlight, he knew.

He'd fallen in love with her.

He *loved* her.

The words came to his lips before he knew they'd formed, his body compelling him to tell her, only he couldn't. He stopped, the words lodging in his throat like a lump. Instead, he kissed her, poured all he was feeling into it, hoping somehow she'd understand.

Her hips came up off the sofa, grinding into him.

"Louisa." It was his turn to moan her name when his fingers found her hot core already wet for him.

He hardly had time to undo his trousers. He scrambled, his hands shaking like he was some unschooled dandy.

Sex had never meant anything to him beyond the physical release, and now it was the most important thing. He had to pleasure her. He *wanted* to pleasure her.

He had to make her see how much he loved her.

He entered her in a single, hard thrust. She bucked, clutching at his shoulders as she threw her head back. He knew he wouldn't last long and licking his thumb, he set it against her sensitive nub, rubbing in slow circles as he thrust inside of her.

"Oh God, Sebastian."

She was just as ready as he was, and when she convulsed around him, he let himself go.

He didn't know how much later, he heard her soft laugh through his sex-muddled brain.

"What is it?" he whispered, unable to pick his head up from where he'd collapsed atop her.

"You're still wearing your coat."

CHAPTER 14

*W*illiams brushed her hair the next morning as she sat in front of her looking glass, poking at the bruised skin beneath her eyes.

When Sebastian had suggested they stay in for the evening, she hadn't realized he did not have a restful night at home in mind. He'd kept her up most of it with his passionate lovemaking, and her body ached this morning for sleep.

But she didn't regret a single moment of it.

After they had thoroughly utilized the sofa in her small room, he'd carried her to his bedchamber where they'd locked themselves in until the sun rose, only ringing for a tea tray when their hunger grew insurmountable.

Her husband was a dedicated and generous lover. She wondered if other husbands were as attentive to their wives. Based on the whispers she'd heard at any number of society gatherings, she highly doubted it.

She let out a wistful sigh, her shoulders slumping.

Williams poked her ever so slightly between the shoulders, and she straightened again, repositioning her head so her lady's maid could finish pinning the curls in place.

"You're a right dreamy one this morning, madam."

"I suppose I am," she said, studying her reflection and hoping the bruised circles weren't so noticeable.

There was to be a luncheon of the Mayfair Garden Society that day, and the new Louisa was determined to try new things and perhaps discover something interesting along the way. She'd never had such leisure time to explore, and she would do her best with it.

Although if she were honest, she wasn't quite sure she cared about gardening overly much. It was all rather sad to watch the blooms die and the plants hibernate for the cold, dreary winter. Perhaps the joy was found in the plants returning in spring. She gave a mental shrug. She would just need to see is all.

"Marriage is sitting well with you, is it then, madam?"

The question might have been impertinent coming from anyone else, but Williams had been with her for years. They had practically grown up together, and the question slid into their conversation like any other.

"Oh, it is at that. His Grace is—" She struggled to find the right word to describe Sebastian, but everyone she selected seemed somehow unsuitable. "Well, he's…"

"Rather not like how he is to other people, wouldn't you say, madam?"

Williams picked up the hot curling tongs from the porcelain dish on the dressing table and tamed a particular errant strand.

"Yes, he is rather," Louisa muttered, watching Williams' reflection in the mirror.

That was precisely what it was. She felt as though every time she encountered him, she discovered him anew. Some hidden feature, some small facet, all of which he kept hidden from public view.

All of which she got to keep for herself.

While the thought warmed her, it also brought her a pang of sadness. It wasn't right that he should hide himself so. Sebastian was a kind, generous, intelligent man who, while rather direct in his manner, held honor and respect above all else.

Her warring thoughts matched her roiling emotions. She was still unsettled by what his mother had said at her preposterous, self-serving tea. Had the woman seriously thought to form some sort of alliance with Louisa? Against whom? Sebastian? The woman's son and Louisa's husband? How absurd. Perhaps it was flattering, though. They said if one could not defeat one's enemy, it was best to join ranks. But that was certainly ludicrous as well.

Louisa would never form any kind of relationship with the woman. She'd seen the evidence of the damage the woman had wrought. Louisa found herself the victim of the woman's machinations, doomed to love a man who could never love her in return.

She had been so certain something had changed between them last night. There had been a moment when she was sure something had shifted, something was different, and perhaps Sebastian had succumbed to the inevitable. But then the moment had passed, and no words were spoken. He'd made love to her just as ardently as he ever had, but there was still an unfathomable distance between them, and she feared there was nothing that could vanquish it.

She considered her own reflection. Williams had finished with her hair, and as usual, it was twisted up in the most divine creation Louisa had ever seen. Her skin was flawless, her looks fair if she were to judge although they had not really meant anything to her. She valued her health far more than her appearance, and that had always been robust.

The reminder of her good health had her thoughts skittering to what Sebastian had said so many nights ago now.

Could he have been right?

For the first time in more than twenty years, she pictured a different possibility. What if she hadn't brought illness into the house? What if she hadn't killed her mother?

She shook her head, a single curl bouncing free as she attempted to clear her thoughts. She couldn't ask such a question of her sisters. It was too painful, and they didn't deserve to suffer again. Louisa would just keep silent. She'd carried on for this long with the idea of what had transpired. There was no sense in changing it now.

Williams gave a soft *tsk*ing sound as she touched Louisa's shoulder to have her hold still while she fixed the curl.

"I'm terribly sorry," Louisa muttered to Williams' reflection, feeling every bit the recalcitrant child.

"'Tis no worry, madam." Williams' deft fingers plied the curl back into place, and with a small twist of a hairpin, Louisa was once more set to rights.

"Thank you, Williams."

Williams gave a nod of her head as she gathered up Louisa's night-rail for laundering.

"Madam, if I may."

Louisa turned, her fingers idly straightening the string pearls about her neck so that they lay just as she liked.

"Yes, of course, Williams, what is it?"

Williams gathered the laundry against herself as she prepared to leave. "It's only that you should think about getting better rest. The Kittridge ball is tomorrow night, and you know it's the event of the season. You shouldn't wish to be under the weather for it. It's your first one as a duchess, after all."

Louisa's face flamed at the intimation in Williams suggestion. It wasn't as though Louisa could very well hide the fact
that she'd been up all night making love to her husband, at
least not from her lady's maid. Lady's maids were privy to
far too much, and it was only a woman's skill at discretion
and a servant's aptitude for loyalty that kept a lady's secrets
safe.

Realization struck all at once and erupted in an exclamation from Louisa before she could stop it. Williams' eyes
grew round as she rushed to Louisa's side, laundry entirely
forgotten.

"Your Grace, what is it? Whatever is the matter?"

Louisa couldn't stop herself. She grabbed both of the
woman's arms as she gained her feet.

"Williams, you're brilliant. Of course! Why didn't I see it
earlier?"

Louisa searched the servant's face as though more were to
be found there, but she knew it wouldn't. She'd already been
given the biggest clue. She had only to know where to look.

"Her lady's maid knows the truth," Louisa hissed.

Williams' face grew concerned as she attempted to free
her arms.

"Whose lady's maid, madam? Are you all right? Shall I
fetch a doctor?"

Louisa shook her head so quickly she was sure she would
upset the pins Williams had just so carefully placed.

"No, it's utterly brilliant. Williams, you've done it." She
couldn't help it. She pulled the maid into her arms for a thorough hug. When she was sure she had scandalized the poor
servant, she released her. "Williams, I am going to need your
assistance."

Perhaps this was it. This could be her chance at uncovering the truth about the moment in time that had changed
Sebastian indubitably and forever. Maybe, just maybe, if she

could find out what had really happened that night, she could heal his wounds, and then maybe he could love her.

Her body flooded with hope, and she nearly danced with it.

"Williams, I must speak with the Viscountess of Raynham's lady's maid."

* * *

LOUISA HAD THOUGHT to simply arrange a meeting between the Viscountess Raynham's lady maid and herself through a discreet method of communication only to discover Viscountess Raynham's lady's maid had only been in her employ for the past six years. The maid they sought had moved on to a loftier position, that of housekeeper for an earl.

Louisa couldn't believe her luck when Williams brought her the news. It would be far easier for Louisa to arrange a conversation with the woman if she were not still under the nose of the viscountess.

Louisa was already shoving her arms into her pelisse when she asked, "And to which earl is she employed?"

"The Earl of Bannerbridge, madam."

Louisa went completely still in her mad frenzy to depart. "The Earl of Bannerbridge?"

Williams gave a quick nod. "So it would seem, yes."

Louisa left the house with far less enthusiasm as it was apparent she was to encounter the earl's insipid wife once more.

She was surprised to find herself received immediately upon brandishing her card at the earl's door. Louisa wasn't certain if it were her title or her name which gained her entrance, but she wasn't about to question it. She was shown into a spacious drawing room decorated in pale pinks and sage. She was too nervous to sit and so she was standing when the countess entered.

"Your Grace, I wasn't expecting you," the countess said by way of greeting, dipping into a curtsy as she entered.

Louisa hardly recognized the woman from the dinner party. Gone was the vapid mouse of a woman and in her place was a paragon of polite decorum with bright eyes and a wide smile full of confidence.

It took a moment for Louisa to return the curtsy. "Thank you for receiving me, my lady. I hope I am not inconveniencing you in any way."

The countess shook her head, her thick brown hair swaying gently where it was coiled about her face. "Not at all. It is I who must apologize for my appearance the other evening. It's this insufferable child, you see. I find I'm not quite myself."

Louisa felt a sharp pain of longing at the sight of the countess laying her hands against her rounded stomach.

How she longed for a babe of her own, one with Sebastian's eyes and smile. But her hope was somewhat soured as she recalled the distance between them. She had to discover the truth if she were ever to rid Sebastian of his curse.

"Shall I ring for tea?" the countess went on.

Louisa stopped her with a raised hand. "I'm afraid my visit is more of a personal one rather than social. I understand you might have a woman by the name of Tabitha Shaw in your employ."

The countess's smile dimmed somewhat, but she kept her poise. "Yes, she is. Is there something amiss?"

"Not at all," Louisa was quick to reassure her. She didn't wish to put Mrs. Shaw's employment at risk. "I had only wished to ask her a question about her former employment."

The other woman's face clouded with confusion. "Do you mean with Viscountess Raynham?"

"Yes. You see I had a question about an occurrence that neither the viscountess nor my husband seems to recall with detail, and I was hoping Mrs. Shaw might provide assistance."

"Of course. Allow me to fetch her for you and provide you with some privacy."

Louisa nodded her thanks as the woman left. She was alone only for a few moments before the housekeeper arrived. Louisa didn't know what she'd been expecting but it certainly wasn't the woman who stood before her. Housekeepers in her mind were older women who had been promoted to the position after serving for years faithfully on a staff. While this woman appeared older by the fine lines around her mouth and eyes, she was in no way decrepit or aged. She was beautiful with shiny, black hair held back in a simple chignon that accentuated the fine bones of her face and long neck. She carried herself with a regal grace, her chin high and steady as she curtsied.

"Your Grace. You wished to speak with me." Her voice had a melodious timber that curled around Louisa, and she couldn't help but hear the slight Irish inflection in the woman's words.

Louisa was suddenly gripped with nerves now that she faced the woman who could fix everything for her or destroy it entirely.

"Mrs. Shaw, thank you for speaking with me. I think you may know I am the Duchess of Waverly. I married Sebastian at the beginning of the season."

Mrs. Shaw gave a nod. "Yes, I had heard, madam. Congratulations." She spoke the words with graceful neutrality.

"Thank you," Louisa whispered, set off balance by the woman's steady tone. "You see I had hoped to ask you of a delicate subject. Please understand that my husband has already told me what he knows of the events that occurred that night, but I was hoping you might provide better insight as a servant in the household."

"You mean the night the duke killed himself."

The statement rang through the air between them even though Mrs. Shaw had spoken it in her soft and commanding way.

"Yes." The word came out as four or more syllables as Louisa tried to regain her composure.

She felt slightly ill. It only then occurred to her she was prying into family secrets that were not hers, and yet the price was too great if she did not proceed.

"What is it you'd like to know, Your Grace?"

"Well, I think I should like to know the truth."

The housekeeper smiled then. It was soft and somewhat beguiling as the woman seemed to consider something within herself.

"We all represent different versions of the truth, Your Grace. Which one do you seek?"

"The one that exonerates my husband from the prison he's built around himself." The words were out before she could stop them, and Mrs. Shaw's gaze grew pointed.

"His Grace has always chosen a more sequestered life, preferring to rely on his own merits rather than the attention of others. Has this changed?"

Louisa licked her lips, wondering if she could speak the words that burned through every day. "He says he cannot love."

She hated how her voice shook on the words, and she clasped her hands together in front of her, willing herself to calm.

Mrs. Shaw's eyes dimmed, a frown settling on her lips. "I see why you've come then. How can I help?"

"Viscountess Raynham suggested you might know something."

"I find it hard to believe the viscountess would give away her secrets."

"Oh, it was nothing like that," Louisa was quick to reassure the woman. "It was more that she gave it away unintentionally."

This seemed to strike a chord with the housekeeper as her mouth tightened.

"What happened that night is not what the current duke believes. Victor Fielding did not kill himself."

Again, she spoke as if she were doing nothing more than reading from a grocer's bill, and yet her words held the power to knock the strength from Louisa's knees. She sat on the sofa behind her before she could no longer hold herself up.

"He didn't kill himself." It wasn't a question. She'd merely needed to repeat the words.

"No, he did not. Of that I am certain."

So many questions poured through Louisa's mind, but only a single one stood out.

"How can you know that?"

"Viscountess Raynham told her son that his father killed himself when his lover wished to end their affair, correct?"

Louisa gave a quick nod.

"I can tell you that's not true. The duke's lover never ended their affair. Further, I can tell you there was another person in the house that night. The viscountess's own lover was present, a spiteful dandy who was enraged to find the duke in residence. You see, they had an arrangement of sorts. They kept their lives separate but discreet. Never should one life cross the other, if you are to understand my meaning."

Louisa's heart thudded harder at the mere mention of separate lives. With every word the woman spoke, Louisa understood with greater clarity every nuance of her husband, every moment in his younger years that had shaped the man he had become, and her heart ached for him.

"What happened?" Louisa couldn't stop now. She had to know.

"The young dandy became enraged, as I said. We were all below stairs then, you understand. We were under strict orders to remain in the servants' areas when the viscountess was carrying out her affairs. We heard yelling and doors slamming and then there was a single gunshot and the viscountess screamed."

Mrs. Shaw closed her eyes briefly, and Louisa knew she was reliving that night. She felt a stab of guilt at forcing the woman to endure it, but there was too much at stake.

When she opened her eyes, she said, "The viscountess sent the stable master to fetch her son at his club. No one was allowed in the room where the duke lay." Louisa wasn't sure, but she thought she heard the woman's voice hitch on the last part.

She'd heard enough, though. Louisa stood and went to the woman, taking both of the housekeeper's hands into her own.

"Thank you, Mrs. Shaw. You cannot know how much this means and what it will do for my husband." Louisa paused, searching the woman's face. "You're so very sure that the duke did not kill himself over his lover?"

The woman shook her head, her lips firm.

"How can you be so certain?" Louisa hardly whispered the question, the need to know burning through her.

Mrs. Shaw's voice was clear when she said, "Because I was Victor Fielding's lover."

CHAPTER 15

*H*e was surprised to find his duchess not at home when he returned after the morning session in Parliament. He recalled she had said something about a gardening society, but as he couldn't imagine Louisa gardening, he had dismissed the idea. In his limited experience with the female sex, he chalked it up to some kind of flight of fancy, a whimsical notion of attempting new things.

He sorted through the post Milton gave him as he made his way to his study. When he passed the small table in the hallway where he usually laid Louisa's letters, he found the table wasn't there. He stared at the spot where it should have been, his mind unable to figure out the void that he found.

He looked up, blinking, the post forgotten in his hand.

The vestibule had been transformed.

Gone was the water-stained wallpaper that had hung there since his boyhood. In its place was a simple silk paper of startling blue, so pale and yet so touching it expanded the space beyond one's imagination. The cramped and dark vestibule was now a grand foyer. The woodwork had been polished, the crumpling plaster repaired. He could even make out the individual panes of stained glass in the windows beside the front doors. Had he known they were stained glass?

Finally, his eyes set on the table.

He eyed it suspiciously as if he wasn't quite certain it was the same table. For one, it was gleaming like something entirely new when he was very well aware the table had sat in this same hallway for more years than he'd been alive. Inspecting it carefully, he found the place where he'd chipped his tooth on its surface when he'd carelessly chased their spaniel through these halls as a boy. She must have had it refinished just as she'd said. And it was in a much more advantageous place now. Tucked into the corner, it was closer to the door and anyone coming inside who needed it for packages and whatnot while also freeing the corridor itself for traffic.

The woman was a master at beauty and practicality.

He pressed a hand to his chest where a sudden pain throbbed, and he turned back into his study, Louisa's letters still in his hand.

This love nonsense was just as unpleasant as he had suspected. It interrupted his daily activities and clouded his mind. He didn't have time for it. And yet, he couldn't imagine his life without it.

He needed to tell her.

He needed to tell her he loved her just as soon as possible, but how?

Was he to simply blurt it out?

He was saved from such unwieldy thoughts by the sound of the front door being thrown wide, banging into the hallway beyond. He turned to the study door, which gave way to the foyer, and was pleasantly surprised to find his wife come sailing through the it.

She threw herself into his arms before he could stop her, her grip tight around his torso.

"Louisa, whatever is the matter?"

She didn't answer, merely shaking her head against his chest.

He held her tightly, attempting to peer down at her, only to be poked in the chin by the stone of the hatpin he'd given her. He reared back to look at the thing so innocently tucked into the brim of the small, purple hat perched on the front of her head. It warmed him to see it there, but he dismissed the thought as he attempted to unravel himself from his wife.

"Louisa, you must tell me what's happened? Is it the Garden Society? Was it really so awful?"

He pried her arms away so he could shift her back enough to see her face. Her eyes were squeezed tightly shut.

"Oh, Sebastian, it's terrible," she whispered.

A coldness began to creep through his concern.

"Louisa, is it one of your sisters? What's happened? Are they all right?"

She shook her head again. "It isn't them, Sebastian. It's you."

Trepidation replaced the concern that had built in him, and he dropped his hands from her arms, taking an automatic step back.

"What are you talking about?"

A line appeared between her brows, and like watching a spooked horse, he couldn't help but know what was about to happen with a growing sense of remorse. Dax's words whispered through his mind, and somehow Sebastian just knew.

Louisa had done something. She had tried to right a perceived wrong, had tried to cure him of something of which she thought he needed a cure. Years of protective instincts kicked in, and the euphoric feelings of only moments before evaporated as his need for survival over-powered it all.

"The other day at tea your mother said something strange. Only I didn't understand how strange until just this morning when Williams was doing my hair."

"I still don't understand, Louisa."

She pulled at her gloves, which he only now noticed she still wore. She'd been so hasty to get to him she was still entirely dressed for her outing. An outing he was coming to suspect had not been to the Garden Society meeting.

"I told you your mother had asked some unusually prying questions about your father's death, and at first, I just thought she was trying to squeeze her way back into your life, so I dismissed her and her foolishness. I would never do something to betray your loyalty, but I knew she thought otherwise."

She had said all this before, and while he still believed her, the sense of impending disaster overrode his feelings toward it.

"So what is it she said that has led you to this state?"

"She asked me if you entrusted me with your secrets because gentlemen have no one with whom to confide without their wives where as women always have their lady's maids."

Sebastian was uncomfortable keeping a valet, so he did not understand how a woman could presume to entrust anything to a servant. But then, he knew Louisa was vastly different when it came to such things and that included relations with her maid.

"Go on." This all seemed like utter nonsense. Perhaps Louisa was only misinterpreting his mother's words, reading into them something she wished were there.

"I found her lady's maid."

This statement meant very little to him. "I'm not seeing

how such a task would be difficult. I'm sure her lady's maid was in residence at Raynham House."

Louisa was already shaking her head as he spoke, prying the other glove from her hand. "No, the maid employed at the time of your father's death left her post as your mother's lady's maid some years ago. She's now the housekeeper for the Earl of Bannerbridge."

He blinked, his feelings too twisted up to speak. He willed Louisa to get on with it, so he could determine just how much damage had been done.

"Did you go speak with the housekeeper then?" It seemed the next logical step, and one Louisa would have no qualms in taking.

"Yes."

The single word pierced his heart like a dagger.

"What is it you discovered, Louisa?" For he was sure now she'd uncovered something. Something he would wish were kept buried.

"Mrs. Shaw—that's her name, you see—told me your father didn't kill himself over his lover, but rather she suspected he was, in fact—" She paused and licked her lips as if the next she had to say would take all her strength. "He was murdered, Sebastian. Murdered by your mother's lover."

The words seeped into his consciousness, but their unsettling effect left him uncertain if he was still even in his study or not, if he were standing or not. He reached out a hand as he turned away from Louisa, no longer able to look at her. He placed his palm on his desk behind him, the solid wood reassuring him that he was still alive and still in his study.

His father hadn't killed himself over his lover? He'd been killed by—

He whirled around, anger coursing through him. "How do you know this? How can you be so sure?"

He wasn't sure what showed on his face, but Louisa took

a step away from him, her hands going up to her breast as if to shield herself.

"Mrs. Shaw told me. She was there that night, Sebastian. She heard what was happening. She knew who was in the house."

One emotion tumbled over the next until he couldn't be certain what it was he felt. Anger, certainly, but there was also a numbness that clouded his thoughts. If what Louisa said were true, his father died at the hand of his mother's lover. His mother, who had been nothing but consistent in her abandonment of both of them, who had proven time and again that they were nothing to her—she would have been the cause of his father's death, the one parent who loved Sebastian unconditionally. The one parent he'd had to rely on, to teach him the things of the world, to teach him to be a gentleman.

Flashes of his childhood paraded through his mind, so many parts of it empty except for those with his father. Any moment worth remembering included his father, and his father died because of his mother's selfishness. A sense of powerlessness swept over everything, and through it, he saw Louisa, standing in front of him, biting her lower lip.

"Why?" The word came out strangled, and he cleared his throat, tried again. "Why would you do this, Louisa? Why would you go poking where you don't belong?"

Her mouth opened on a silent exclamation as her eyes grew wide. He'd surprised her, and somehow it sent a wave of calm through him.

"Sebastian, I thought you deserved to know the truth."

"I deserved to know the truth?" The part of him that felt violated and hurt that she would intrude into his life like this, that she would attempt to fix whatever she thought was wrong just as she'd torn apart his house, fueled his angry words. "I deserved to know that my father was murdered.

Did you ever stop to think what that means? That there might be a killer out there. That my father's death was never avenged."

She said nothing, only blinking as her mouth remained open without sound emerging.

"Did you not think about that because you were too concerned with fixing me?" The words flew from his mouth before he could stop them, and like an arrow finding its mark, Louisa's mouth snapped shut, her eyes narrowing in fury.

"No, Sebastian." She spoke the words calmly, carefully.

"You're so busy trying to fix me. Have you ever looked at yourself? Have you ever seen how you bow to your sisters' will? What about you, Louisa? Before you fix anyone else, perhaps you should fix yourself."

A distant part of his brain heard the words, and it squeezed his heart in pain, but at the same time he couldn't have stopped himself. Still Louisa didn't speak. She only stared, her eyes wide, her hand still pressed to her chest in defense.

"If you didn't think about the consequences of your action, then what did you think of?" Still no answer. "Then what, Louisa?" he nearly shouted.

His mind flew like a runaway carriage, careening from one thought to the next, unable to make sense of anything, and yet he hurt. He ached with the hurt of so many things. He ached with love for Louisa, love that he'd known would one day endanger him and now he knew he'd been right. She had no business prying into affairs he'd worked so hard to keep quiet, to keep at bay. He ached with the knowledge that his father may have been murdered. He ached and hurt, and no matter what, he must force that hurt onto someone else. It was the only way he could survive.

His words dripped with acid, and he flung them at her, hoping to cause her as much pain as she'd caused him.

"Then what, Louisa?" he repeated when she didn't answer yet again. When she continued to stand there, her chest moving with each shallow breath, her eyes locked on his even as he watched something inside of her build and grow until he knew it would consume her in a deafening crescendo. But even though he saw it coming, he prodded it until it did.

"Why would you—"

"Because I wanted you to love me." She threw the words at him so swiftly he didn't have time to avoid them.

They broke through him, splintering into a thousand shards that crumbled to his feet.

They each stood there in stunned silence, only the sounds of their harsh breathing permeating the room. Her proclamation echoed in his ears, and he wanted nothing more than to tell her he already loved her. But she'd proven him right.

Love was too dangerous.

So instead, he left, brushing past her without a single word. He didn't stop in the corridor. He continued until his feet hit the pavement outside and then kept going. He didn't know where he was headed, and he didn't care. He only had to get away from her and the pain and the hurt and the loss of a love he'd only begun to know.

* * *

SHE WOKE to a hand on her shoulder, shaking her far more violently than was really necessary.

She became aware of the cramp in her neck, the aches along her hips, and she knew she was awake but refused to open her eyes. She gave herself that one moment to collect her thoughts, reestablishing herself to where she was and what had happened.

Sebastian had left.

And he hadn't come home.

Her eyes flew open, and she sat up, pushing herself upright with her hands along the back of the sofa and the seat cushions.

Nearly toppling Eliza onto the floor.

"Sebastian!" Louisa cried as she awoke only to grab for her sister moments later as she nearly met the floor.

"Good heavens, Louisa," Eliza exclaimed, righting herself on the sofa. "Is that how you always wake up?"

"I thought you were Sebastian." She collapsed back on the sofa, her neck protesting the return to her uncomfortable sleeping position, but she didn't have the strength to move.

"I thought as much." Eliza studied her reclined pose for several beats. "Is this normally what you wear to bed?"

Louisa was still dressed in her gown from the previous day. When Sebastian had stormed out, she hadn't the energy with which to move, let alone dress for bed. She'd dismissed all of Williams' attempts to help her into a night-rail, and instead had come here, to her quiet little room on the south end of the house. She collapsed on the sofa where Sebastian had so recently made love to her and willed her heart to keep beating.

He was upset with her, that was all. Surely he would get over it in due time. Surely he would realize what gift she had given him, the freedom of knowing what had really happened to his father.

But no matter how she tried to reassure herself, she couldn't stop the feeling that she'd ruined this, too. She'd overstepped somehow, once more falling victim to her own impulsiveness. She could see that now. It wasn't her place to pry into Sebastian's past, especially into a subject so precious and personal.

Had she really been so desperate to get him to love her that she'd violated his privacy like that?

She groaned and threw a hand over her eyes, blocking out the sunlight that flooded the room.

"Louisa." Eliza nudged her when she didn't answer. "You must dress and break your fast."

Louisa peeked out from under her arm. "I will do no such thing." She put her arm back only to move it again a second later. "What are you doing here?"

Eliza reached over and carefully slipped off Louisa's hat, which apparently was still pinned to her sister's head. The morning sun caught the facets of the stone in the hatpin, and she jerked it loose from Eliza's grip, holding it close to her chest tightly.

Eliza raised a questioning brow but otherwise did not comment. "Do you know Sebastian asked me the same question when I woke him from where he slumbered on the sofa in our drawing room this morning?" She set aside the hat. "I must say you both look awful. How bad of a row was it?"

Louisa replaced her arm across her face. "Oh, Eliza, it's terrible."

Eliza picked up Louisa's arm to peer underneath it. "Nothing is ever that terrible, little sister."

She dropped her arm back into place as the sofa shifted. Eliza must have stood, which had Louisa removing her arm to watch her sister. A teacart stood in the middle of the room, loaded with a pot and all the trimmings, including Cook's decadent cinnamon scones. Louisa sat up, her stomach letting out a furious grumble.

She pressed her hand that still held the hatpin to her stomach as if willing it to stop. Eliza poured for both of them, handing Louisa her cup before taking a seat next to her.

The first sip of warm liquid poured through Louisa like a revitalizing elixir, and inch by inch, she came back to life. While it was restorative, she wasn't entirely certain she wished to be so aware of her surroundings.

"Oh, it was awful, Eliza. I'm afraid I've done something terrible."

Eliza reached out a hand and patted Louisa's knee. "Tell me what's happened, and I will tell you how the world will not end."

"I discovered Sebastian's father did not kill himself but rather might have been murdered by his wife's lover."

Eliza spat tea, hurrying to cover her nose and mouth as she coughed violently.

"Louisa!" she cried when she was able to. "What are you talking about?"

Eliza was the most conservative of her sisters, and witnessing her reaction helped Louisa to understand just what a grave mistake she'd made.

But what choice did she have? Was she to allow Sebastian to carry on with a life that was only a fraction of what it should have been? Was she supposed to allow him to live with a lie of his mother's construction?

"Sebastian's father was killed by his wife's lover. I only discovered the truth yesterday when I found the former duchess's lady's maid. She was in the house that night and overheard what happened. She only suspects it's the lover, though. She was ordered below stairs with the rest of the servants and can only surmise what happened." Louisa spoke to the tea she swirled in her cup, unable to meet her sister's gaze. "Do you know the lady's maid was Sebastian's father's lover?" She shook her head. "I had no idea these affairs could be quite so complicated."

Eliza still did not speak, and Louisa looked up to find her sister staring.

She patted her knee now. "It's quite all right, Eliza. I assure you I have not lost my wits. I'm sure Mrs. Shaw—that's the lady's maid although she's a housekeeper now—would be happy to discuss it with you as well."

Eliza shook her head. "Louisa, I had no idea..." Her voice drifted off as she considered her sister.

Louisa nodded and took a sip of her tea. "I didn't either." She gestured with her teacup. "Was...was Sebastian—" She had to lick her lips. "Well, was he all right this morning?"

Eliza set down her cup in the saucer on her lap. "I suspect he is the victim of a night of thorough drinking but other than that, I am sure he should be fine. He and Dax are teaching George how to tie a cravat as we speak. I'm sure that's helping his current state immensely." Eliza's smile was devilish.

Louisa's stomach tightened at the mention of her small nephew. Would she ever carry Sebastian's child, or had she ruined all chance of having a family of her own?

She forced a smile. "Isn't George a little young for such things?"

"He seems fascinated by the color and the fabric, I assume. He's mesmerized by the things." Eliza studied her again, and Louisa grew uncomfortable under such attention. "Louisa, you are saying Sebastian's father was murdered. You know that, don't you?"

Louisa gave a slow nod. "I'm very well aware of such things. It's just that—" She set aside her tea and turned on the sofa so she could fully face her sister. "His mother, a thoroughly unpleasant woman I assure you, said the strangest things to me about that night, the night his father died. I was just so certain there was something unusual about what she said. I had no choice, Eliza. I had to find the truth of it."

Eliza shook her head as she set aside her own tea. When she turned back, she took Louisa's hands into her own.

"Louisa, my dear, why is it that you always feel so compelled to rectify a situation? Why must you always try to help people? When are you ever going to learn to do something for yourself and leave others to their own means?"

A shadow passed over her mind then as her sister's words tumbled through it, Sebastian's accusation ringing in her ears. The question she must ask perched on the edge of her lips. She had only to ask it, and she would know. But she just couldn't. She couldn't revisit her own greatest mistake.

But was Sebastian right? Was she too fixated on correcting the wrongs of the past that she failed to see the implications they would have on the present?

She searched her sister's eyes. If anyone were strong enough to endure a visit to such painful memories, it was Eliza, and it was past time for Louisa to start recognizing her own flaws.

"Eliza, I brought the influenza into the house that killed our mother."

Eliza's brow wrinkled. "No, you didn't."

The words were spoken so matter-of-factly Louisa thought she misheard.

"No, Eliza, I'm speaking truth. It was me. I visited my friend Mary, you remember her, the girl with the brown pigtails, after Mother forbid us to leave the house. I brought the sickness back with me."

Eliza shook her head, her expression clear. "No, you didn't, Louisa."

Louisa pulled her hands free of Eliza's grip. "What are you talking about? I went to see Mary's dolls, and someone in her family must have been sick, and I caught it and brought it back to Mother. I killed her, Eliza." Her voice broke on the last words. She'd never spoken them before to one of her sisters, and fear and the possibility of recrimina-tions clawed at her throat.

Eliza pursed her lips in a frown. "Louisa, listen to me. You did not bring the influenza to the house. The scullery maid did. Lillian. You remember her. She was the gardener's daughter. She had a beau in the village and defied Mother's orders to stay away from there. Mother was already ill when you traipsed off to see those dolls."

Louisa could do nothing but blink for several seconds. "How do you know that?"

Eliza's expression turned pained. "You talked about those dolls endlessly after you visited Mary. I can remember precisely when you discovered them because Father had just given me a new set of charcoals, and all you did was chatter about those dolls and I wanted some peace to draw. Lud, you were an annoying child." Her smile was mischievous as her gaze seemed to recall a scene in her mind from their childhood.

Louisa still couldn't understand it. "The scullery maid brought the disease into the house?"

Eliza nodded. "Yes. Father was furious and would have dismissed her right then, but Mother said they couldn't turn her out while she was ill." Her sister shook her head. "Little did she know that was it. Mother caused her own death because of her simple human kindness." Eliza sat forward then, snatching Louisa's hands back into hers. "We had always wondered what you did and didn't remember from that time, Louisa. You've always been such a...well, you're always just so happy. We were worried it was forced." She squeezed Louisa's hands. "Please tell me what you remember."

Louisa shook her head. None of this could be true. It just couldn't. She was the one who disobeyed. She was the one who went down the lane. She was the one who—

"Louisa." Eliza's voice was stern, pulling her from her litany of sins. "Louisa, you stayed with Mother while she died, don't you remember? You were so very brave. Because of you, Mother didn't die alone."

The world which until that moment had somehow been canted on its axis righted itself, and Louisa saw things for what they really were.

"I didn't kill our mother." She spoke the words carefully as if by speaking them they might evaporate away the truth.

Eliza's smile was gentle. "Yes, Louisa. It wasn't you. You are the savior. You saved all of us."

Louisa's body flooded with heat, a weight lifting from her shoulders she hadn't realized she'd been carrying. But in its place swept the reality she now faced, and her shoulders slumped.

Eliza seemed to sense it and pulled Louisa into her arms.

"It will be okay, my little sister," Eliza whispered. "I promise you."

Louisa shook her head against Eliza's shoulder. "How can you say that? I went in search of his father's killer without telling him. How could I have been so stupid?"

"You weren't stupid," her sister said. "You were in love." She eased Louisa back and met her eye as she said, "And wouldn't you say Sebastian was guilty of the same when he asked me about the night Mother died?"

It was as if a bucket of water had been tossed on the fire that burned inside of her, and with utter clarity, she understood. She had done it out of love. It might not have been right. Perhaps she should have gone about it differently, but her reasons for doing it were the right ones.

Now she had to convince Sebastian of it.

Eliza eased her back to a sitting position.

"The Kittridge ball is tonight, and you know what that

means. It's time to get you ready." She hoisted Louisa to her feet, picking up their discarded tea things.

"I'm not sure I'm fit for a ball," Louisa muttered.

"Would you rather have all of the *ton* gossiping about your absence?"

Louisa cringed at just the thought, twisting the hatpin in her hands.

Eliza set the cups and their saucers down on the teacart and paused, casting her gaze about the room.

"Did you do this?" she asked, gesturing to the space around them.

Louisa looked about the room as if seeing it for the first time. The drapes had been rehung, and their soft hues of blues went well with the muted tones of the wallpaper, giving the space a feeling of being larger than it actually was. The rest of the furniture had returned as well, and the soft warm tones of wood gave much-needed highlights to the space. She still had the walls to fill, but she was in no rush. She wanted to select pieces that spoke to her instead of simply hanging those that looked nice.

"I did," she finally said, feeling a sense of completeness she didn't know she'd been searching for.

Eliza gave a sound of affirmation. "I should have you look at some of the drawing rooms at Ashbourne Manor. There are so many of them, and they are so sad and worn. I just don't know what to do with them." She looped her arm through Louisa's. "Come now. A bath is just the thing for you."

CHAPTER 16

*S*ebastian stood in front of the Bannerbridge home cursing the sun.

He wished the weather had the respect to match his inner turmoil. A good dose of rain and some thick gray clouds were just what he wanted right then, but it was not meant to be. The sun shone relentlessly down on him, warming his back and forcing him to rouse from the fog that still remained of his ill-advised night of drinking.

He had thought scotch would be just the thing to rid his mind of torturous thoughts, but it only served to make him ache with regret and want. Louisa's last volley rang over and over again in his mind.

Because I wanted you to love me.

Could he have stopped her from her inquiries if he had only told her how he felt? Could he right now be spending a lazy day in bed with his wife? Telling her how much he loved her, how much he looked forward to their long life together?

Instead he stood on the pavement in front of a near stranger's home, willing his head to stop throbbing while the sun lit a fire on his shoulders.

God, he had to get this over with.

He took the stairs carefully, all too aware of just how much scotch he'd drunk. Dax had been all too generous a host and had only stopped Sebastian when it was clear any more alcohol would have no more effect and sleep was the only thing left.

He tugged now at his clothes, aware of just how long he'd been in them. He ran a finger around his collar, the skin their chafed and raw. It only served to add to his annoyance.

The door was answered promptly, and at his card, the butler seemed not at all surprised.

"Should you like to see his lordship or is it Mrs. Shaw you seek?" the butler intoned ponderously.

The question startled Sebastian. "It is Mrs. Shaw I should like to speak with, but I will not disrespect the earl by going to his housekeeper directly."

The butler gave a nod. "His lordship and the countess left early this morning for the country, Your Grace. Her ladyship advised me to admit you should you seek Mrs. Shaw's audience."

Sebastian wondered what influence Louisa had wrought in such an arrangement.

"Very good," he said and followed the butler inside.

He was shown into a drawing room that, while tastefully appointed, felt cluttered and overdone. Louisa would never put such colors together, and she would never arrange the sitting arrangement so close to the door. He wasn't sure where these thoughts sprang from, and he swallowed them down, willing himself to focus on the present.

He didn't wait long. The precise tapping of heels on the wood floors greeted him first, and he turned to the door expectantly.

A flash of memory swept through him at the sight of the woman standing there. It was as if he knew her from somewhere but not entirely as a person. It was more that he'd seen her in different pieces of childhood memories. Like when he was playing with his toy soldiers on the back staircase because his mother didn't like to hear him in the house, and he had to hide where she wouldn't find him. This woman had passed him on those stairs, he was sure of it.

"Your Grace," she said as she curtsied. "I expected you would come. Should you like tea?"

He shook his head to tell her no and immediately regretted it. He must have given himself away because she folded her hands in front of her, a knowing smile on her lips.

"Your wife already told you what we discussed yesterday, did she not?" The woman's tone was deceptively neutral.

"Yes." He did not make the mistake of nodding again.

"And you imbibed hoping to erase the truths she told you?"

He did not wish to answer that.

She waved away his silence. "Your father was the same way. Never touched a drop unless circumstances overwhelmed him." She walked to the corner of the room where she tugged on a braided rope. "You look very much like him, did you know? Only he never wore his hair quite so severely." She sat on the chair closest to the door and gestured for him to sit on the sofa.

He didn't want to. He wanted to keep this conversation as brief as possible, but there was something about her voice which drew him in, and he found himself sitting.

"I've heard a similar comment recently," he said, trying not to remember how Louisa had looked in the moonlight.

"I was proud to work in the Waverly household, Your Grace. Your father was a well-respected man, and he treated his servants fairly."

"I should like to know then how it is you believe to know what really happened the night my father died."

Her mouth tightened, the lines around her lips growing more pronounced, but she did not back down from his bold statement.

"It's a rather obvious answer, Your Grace. I was there that night."

She was stopped from further explanation by the arrival of the teacart. She dismissed the maid and poured herself, handing him a cup. It was the exact shade at which he preferred his tea, and he looked up, meeting her gaze with a question.

"You might have forgotten, Your Grace, but I have served you tea many times. Do you not recall your mother's attempts to stay present in your life after you went to Eton?"

Honestly, he'd forgotten. When he was home on holiday from school, his mother would always arrange for them to take tea together as her way of catching up on his tales from school and how his grades were. Inevitably, his mother would become distracted, and he was left with her lady's maid. Another flash of recognition swept through him, and her face grew clearer in his memories.

"I do remember," he answered, taking the tea gratefully and sipping it. Warmth spread through him instantly, and he willed it to travel to his head and relieve him of the ache there.

"Did your wife tell you all that we discussed, Your Grace?"

He swallowed his tea. "I believe so." He felt a pang of guilt at the words. He hadn't given Louisa the chance to tell him if they had discussed it all or not. He'd run from the house instead, like the coward he was.

"Then you'll know there was a commotion that night. Your mother had taken to entertaining her lovers while your father was not in residence and he had returned early that evening. He was not expected. Your mother, she enjoyed the more passionate fellow for her bedmate, and when your father unexpectedly appeared, the man became enraged. He was a foolish young man who wanted your mother for himself." She gave a brittle laugh. "What a stupid man. He ruined so many lives that night with his brash selfishness." The woman studied her tea as if seeing another time, and something shifted inside him.

It was as if he'd finally broken free of a vise that he'd thought permanently squeezed around his chest.

When she looked up, the housekeeper's eyes were soft with memory. "Your father loved you very much, Sebastian." Her voice was thick with emotion, and he started at her use of his given name. It was as if she'd spoken it before, but there was more. It was if she'd spoken it before with...love.

He shifted on the sofa, unsure what to say. He had suspected his father loved him. There had been nothing to contradict that fact, but there was so much about Sebastian's childhood that had meant abandonment and rejection that it was hard to accept anything else, especially love. So he was not sure if he'd ever really admitted it to himself.

"Your father would be so happy to see you've wed, especially to a woman such as the duchess. She's a beautiful person, Sebastian, inside and out."

Again, the use of his given name uncurled something inside him, the tone of her voice, the softness of her gaze, it all came together at once.

"You loved my father." He spoke the words before he knew he was going to.

She wasn't startled by his outburst. In fact, she appeared puzzled, her brow furrowing.

"I thought your wife had told you."

Shame fell upon him, and he looked down at his tea.

"I'm afraid I am not very good when it comes to..." He couldn't say the word, choosing instead to let his sentence drift off.

"Love?" She spoke it with such clarity, he envied her.

He didn't answer. He merely studied his tea, thinking of the mess he had made with Louisa.

He looked up when Mrs. Shaw set down her tea and stood. When she took the seat next to him, he stiffened. She pulled the tea from between his hands and took his hands into hers. The gesture was so foreign, her concerned gaze completely alien. Nervousness crept through him, and he stilled.

"Sebastian, your father and I were lovers for many years. Louisa didn't tell you?"

He drew a deep breath. "I didn't let her."

Mrs. Shaw straightened and patted his hand. "I was concerned about as much. I knew when your father died you would be lost. I just hadn't realized how lost." She shook her head. "I should have told you. I just—" Her voice broke for the first time, and it suddenly occurred to him how much she had loved his father.

They had both lost someone that night. Lost someone they loved to another's selfishness.

He squeezed her hands, and she looked up.

"I think Louisa is trying to find me now." The words were almost too difficult to say.

Louisa wasn't trying to fix it. Louisa was trying to heal him.

Mrs. Shaw's smile was gentle. "I think she is."

He gathered himself to ask, "My mother lied about that. She didn't want me to bring justice against her lover, I imagine."

Mrs. Shaw's lips thinned. "Your mother is in possession an unspeakable selfishness, Sebastian. Your poor father tried to protect you from it."

He studied the older woman's face. "You and he...were happy?" He didn't know how else to ask the question, but somehow he needed to know. But he wasn't asking if his father was happy. He was asking if his father was happy *in love*.

Her smile was something unlike anything he had seen. It was pure nostalgia for a time when things in her life were better, when they were very near perfect.

"We were so very happy," she finally said.

He let the silence linger between them for a time before he brought himself to spoil her momentary bliss.

"Mrs. Shaw, you know who my mother's lover was." It wasn't the question he wished to ask, but he knew she would understand his meaning.

Who was the man who had killed his father?

Lines stood out along the corners of her eyes as she said, "He's dead, Sebastian. He died years ago when he was thrown from his horse and broke his neck. I am not decent enough to lie and say I mourned his death."

So much in his world had changed in a single night and yet nothing had changed at all. It had all already happened. It was only his understanding of it that was different.

Better.

It was better because of Louisa.

He nodded. "Then I don't need to know his name. It doesn't matter anyway." He stood abruptly, a sudden sense of urgency compelling him to right the things he could. God willing.

Mrs. Shaw stood with him. "What are you going to do?"

"It seems I must have a conversation with my mother." He was to the door before he turned back. "Mrs. Shaw, I wonder if on your day off if you should like to come to the house for tea. I'd very much like to share stories of my father with someone who knew him."

Mrs. Shaw's smile was slow and complete. "I should like that. If you can make me one promise." She stepped closer to him, laying a single hand on his arm, her eyes imploring. "Don't use the things that happened to you as an excuse for avoiding the things of which you are afraid."

He studied her imploring expression, and something unraveled inside him.

He covered her hand with his own. "I promise," he said and left, this time knowing exactly where he was headed.

* * *

SHE WONDERED how quickly one could get thoroughly soused from champagne.

She hoped it was very quickly indeed.

She had arrived with Viv, Johanna, and Andrew after Eliza had arranged it. There was no sense in Louisa enduring the scrutiny of arriving alone to the Kittridge ball, Eliza had reasoned, and as Sebastian had completely disappeared, Louisa was not one to argue.

Where was he?

The thought tumbled end over end through her mind. Dax said he'd gone off that morning after rousing himself from his stupor. Not a word was said on where he was going, and no one had seen him since.

Had he gone to see Mrs. Shaw? She couldn't remember much of their conversation the previous day, only the way it tore through her in regular intervals as she recalled his hateful accusations.

She was done fixing things. The truth of her mother's death sloshed through her like a rowboat on a stormy sea. One moment she couldn't believe it to be true and the next she couldn't imagine how she had believed otherwise. Her whole life she had directed herself based on the assumption of this terrible thing she did. But she hadn't done it. Instead she'd done something quite spectacular.

She'd stayed with her mother as she died.

It was this thought that played over and over again in her mind. She could recall it so clearly, and yet every time she had remembered that day, the noise around her had been scolding and cold. Now as an adult she pictured what everyone else likely had at the time.

A small child curled up next to her dead mother.

Wonder flooded through her. Wonder at how she had been so unknowingly brave at such a young age. Wonder at how she had sensed her mother was dying, how she had known she couldn't let her be alone. Wonder at how she'd carried on, making her sisters happy at all cost.

It was the same courage that had seen her seeking out the witness to the death of a man she'd never met.

The same courage that had her marrying the Beastly Duke and eviscerating the disagreeable façade he had spent years cultivating.

She didn't know anymore what to feel. Had she been right in finding out the truth of his father's death? Or had she overstepped? Sebastian was a private man. She knew that. But as his wife, shouldn't there be fewer secrets between them?

That was the crux of the matter. She wanted to be a part of his life, and he didn't want to let her in. She'd been wrong all along. Finding out the truth of his father's death wouldn't let him love her because he didn't want anyone to be that close to him.

She sighed and swallowed more champagne.

"If you're not careful, that will go directly to your head."

If she had taken a bigger gulp, she would have drowned. She spun in a circle toward that voice, a voice she hadn't heard in so very long.

"Margate."

Her heart dropped, not just to her toes, but clean through her slippers and down into the Thames.

Ryder Maxen, the Duke of Margate, stood before her.

Viv's husband was here.

She was absolutely going to vomit.

Of all the things to happen that night, she was the least prepared for this.

"Hello, little lady." His voice was exactly the same. The same enthralling drawl, the same one-sided smile that showcased that exquisite dimple. The jet-black hair that fell so artfully over his forehead, the way confidence dripped from his every pore.

Damn the man.

Viv did not deserve this.

"What are you doing here?" She ignored his attempt at civility and squared off.

His expression changed then. His eyes narrowed and his smile vanished.

"Ever the protector. I'm glad to see you haven't changed, little lady."

"It's Your Grace." She rolled back her shoulders, feeling her power as a duchess course through her.

"I had heard that somewhere. Congratulations. Waverly is a lucky man."

"You didn't answer my question. What are you doing here?"

His eyes easily traveled the room over her head as he was a good deal taller, and she hated how he ignored her. So she poked him.

He looked down at her, his hand going to where she'd jabbed him in the chest.

"What are you doing here?" She enunciated each word clearly, should he try to ignore her again.

"I must speak with my wife."

"Why?"

He raised an eyebrow. "I don't see how that's of your concern."

"You made it my concern when you hurt her."

If she hadn't been looking directly at him, she wouldn't have believed what she saw.

Remorse.

It flooded his face, soaking his eyes and dropping his mouth until she almost felt sorry for him.

Almost.

"Yes, well, I deserve that, I suppose." He gave her a nod and before she knew what he was about, he picked up her hand and placed something within it. "Good to see you, little lady."

He vanished into the crowd before she could uncurl her fingers to see the butterscotch candy he'd left there. Viv had married Ryder when Louisa was still in the schoolroom. He'd always called her *little lady* then and never failed to give her a butterscotch candy when he saw her.

Her heart ached for what might have been. Lud, why were men so difficult?

As soon as the thought crossed her mind, she saw a familiar face in the crowd, and her heart thudded to a stop.

Sebastian.

She'd only caught a glimpse of him and couldn't be quite sure, but she picked up her skirts, depositing her empty champagne glass on a passing footman's tray. He was headed out of the ballroom in the direction of the card rooms. She passed the wall of spinsters, lined up behind the refreshment table like spectators, and slipped into the relative quiet of the corridor between the ballroom and the card rooms.

That was when he grabbed her arm.

She turned around, an oath on her lips to tell him just

exactly how worried she'd been about him when she saw who it was.

"Devlin." She said his name in the same tone she would use to say *horse manure.*

His smile was cocky. "Heard you married that Waverly beast. Must be lonely. I'd be happy to give you a toss if—"

She was done.

She was done with everything and everyone, and in that moment, she would not stand for Jonathan Devlin to utter another word.

She reached up with her free hand, yanked her hatpin from her coiffure, and stabbed Jonathan Devlin soundly in the arm with it. He yelped, dropping his grip on her arm as he danced back in pain. She pulled the hatpin free and waved it at him.

"You will never learn to keep your hands to yourself, will you?"

She didn't wait for a response. She had a husband to find.

She walked away from Devlin, her focus on the adjoining card rooms. She peered into each with no luck and reached the end before she realized it. If she kept going, she'd find herself in the corridor with the retiring rooms, which was not at all helpful. She turned back and retraced her steps just as Sebastian emerged from the whist room.

She stopped dead.

"Your Grace." He gave her a neat bow and approached. "I trust you are well this evening."

She hadn't known what to expect when she saw him again. Perhaps an apology? Perhaps she should apologize. Whichever it was, it wasn't this jovial tone she had never heard him use in the entirety of their relationship.

And certainly not with that hair.

"Your hair," she whispered, receiving a swift frown.

"I'm receiving a good deal of comments on my hair," he

said dryly. "I'm beginning to think there is no pleasing anyone with it."

She placed a quick hand on his arm. "Oh no, it's not that. I quite like it. I was just surprised is all."

Surprised to find he wore no pomade in it whatsoever. His thick, deliciously brown hair hung about his face, making her fingers itch to run her hands through it. He looked so much younger, so much happier, almost as if he were a boy again.

No, he was probably sour and stern when he was a boy, too.

He looked better then, better than he had in all his life.

But...why?

"What are you doing here?" Once again, she found herself asking a completely absurd question of a man in her life.

Sebastian's smile was swift. "I've come to have a conversation with my mother."

Trepidation rushed through her from the top of her head to her toes in her slippers, but she didn't have time to revel in it because he took her arm and said, "Won't you join me?"

CHAPTER 17

*I*t was not at all surprising to find his mother in a card room, her husband nowhere in sight as her hand lay terribly familiar on the shoulder of a baron who held a hand of cards and a cigar.

"Viscountess," Sebastian said, stopping opposite his mother, the gaming table between them.

She looked up in surprise, her eyes flashing in the murky light of the cigar-smoke-filled room.

"Sebastian," she said, his name cool and clipped. "How lovely to see you."

"I wish I could say the same of seeing you, but I'm afraid not."

The conversation stilled at the table, and Louisa tensed against his side.

He hadn't missed how his gut had clenched at the sight of her tonight. Spending a night without her was pure torture, and he swore never to do it again. Never would he allow his past to separate him from her. She was his future, and he was going to damn well ensure she would always be there.

"I'm sorry?" his mother said, tilting her head innocently.

"I know what really happened to my father."

If the room had stilled before, it went absolutely silent then.

Louisa sucked in a breath beside him, and he felt more than saw her head turn, surveying the room. It needn't matter how many people heard him. With any luck, it would spread through the ball in its entirety before the night was through.

His mother's hand slipped from the baron's shoulder.

"Sebastian, I don't understand what you're doing. You can't mean to have a private conversation here." She gestured grandly to the room about her.

"I find private conversations with you tend to end in lies. I thought a public one would be a nice change of discourse."

There were several startled gasps around them, and Louisa's fingers dug into his arm.

"I spoke to your lady's maid today, Mother. If you should like to retain any amount of dignity, I shall allow you to speak the truth now. If you do not, I shall be forced to call you out for the liar you are."

His mother's eyes narrowed, and she came out from around the table to face him.

"How dare you." She hissed the words as if speaking softly would keep everyone from hearing her.

But even he could see that no one was about to miss a single word she spoke. Hands of cards hung suspended and forgotten in players' hands. Cigars smoldered in ashtrays. Drinks remained halfway to the guests' lips. All attention was on Viscountess Raynham and her son, the Beastly Duke.

He only hoped everyone had a good seat to the show.

"How dare I?" he asked. "I should ask the same of you. It's rather bold to suggest your husband has committed suicide in order to protect your lover who killed him."

The room erupted in a soft boil of whispers and exclamations.

"Sebastian!" She spat out his name as if the single word could stop him.

"There are witnesses to your machinations, Viscountess. It would do you well not to deny it."

She looked about her, her cold eyes scanning the room as if searching for an ally. But Sebastian knew the *ton* better than anyone. He knew they were only here for a good spectacle, and they were ready to believe anything, just like they believed him when he'd created the Beastly Duke.

Finally, she returned her gaze to him. "You don't know what I endured that night."

"You don't know what I've endured in a lifetime as your son." He could feel the tension in the crowd around him growing with every word he spoke. "Now would you like to tell these good people how you covered up the murder of your husband so your lover would not see justice?"

A gentleman to his left stood, and Sebastian recognized Baron Whitchurch, a magistrate from Hampshire.

"I suppose your lover had his own pistol that night. Did you use Father's dueling pistol as a decoy then?"

His mother's eyes flicked to the magistrate and back, her nostrils flaring but no defense coming to her lips.

"I'm still not clear on why you did it," he went on. "Was it to save your lover or the reputation of the title? I fear it's the second. Am I correct?"

Her nostrils flared again. "Sebastian, I demand you stop this at once. You've not been yourself since you married this harlot, and I—"

"You will do well, madam, to watch your words."

All eyes turned to the steely voice and the gentleman it belonged to in the doorway of the card room.

Andrew Darby, the Duke of Ravenwood, stood there,

flanked by his sister, the Duchess of Margate, and his brother-in-law, the Duke of Ashbourne. It was a formidable sight, and one Sebastian had never seen.

Allies.

Louisa's hand tightened on his arm, and he looked down at her.

"You have me, too," she whispered, and for a moment, he remembered that day so long ago when he'd asked her that fatal question, felt her hesitancy like a death blow. Hope surged through him, and he turned back to his mother.

"Your lover killed my father in a fit of rage, and you cried suicide to hide the scandal from the *ton*. Well, Viscountess, I am here to set the record straight. I'm not sure if I've made it clear or not, but I don't give a damn about the title's reputation and I don't give a damn about you. It's only luck that your lover is already dead, or I would seek a greater justice for my father."

His mother's cheeks flexed as he knew she was grinding her teeth.

"A greater justice? Just what exactly do you plan to do to me, Sebastian?"

His smile was genuine when he said, "I've already done it." Here he let his gaze cast about the room, taking in the astonished faces, the sneers of distaste, the looks of hatred, before turning to his mother's stricken face. "Your punishment is the worst I could think of." He leaned in, so she wouldn't miss his meaning when he said, "Public humiliation."

He didn't miss her sharp inhalation, didn't miss the way her lips trembled, but he turned his back on all of it and escorted his bride from the room. Ravenwood and Ashbourne stepped to the side to allow them egress, but he didn't miss the small smiles on either of their faces.

He heard the room erupt behind him. Chairs were pushed back, the sharp sound of glass breaking as drinks were abandoned. Soon he and Louisa were caught up in the exodus of ladies and gentlemen going to spread the gossip they'd just overheard.

His mother would be ruined utterly and completely before the night was over. He couldn't help but smile as the beginning notes of a waltz reached his ears, and he wondered at his luck. He headed straight for the dance floor, a mumbling Louisa at his side.

"Sebastian. Umph. Where are we going? You just—"

He swung her into the waltz before she could ask another question.

"Have I told you yet how beautiful you look tonight?"

His question stopped her completely, and she shut her mouth with an audible snap. She peered up at him, and he could see the questions in her eyes. He would answer every one of them, but not here. He had someplace else in mind.

He twirled her about, his feet sure as he carried her through the dance.

"Do you know I can't recall why I avoided balls and dancing?" He smiled down at his wife. "It's quite lovely when you find the right partner."

Her mouth fell open, and he loved every minute of it.

The song took an interminable time to end, but finally, the violins finished with an exaggerated flourish, and he could sweep them from the floor, pulling her in the direction of the terrace doors.

"Sebastian?" She said his name like a question, but his only response was to pull her through the open doors and into the cool air of the night.

He looked up, finding the full moon just as he'd expected it.

"Come on," he said, pulling her in the direction of the stairs. "We're almost there."

"Almost where?" She traipsed down the stairs beside him

and soon they were lost in the hedges of the Kittridge gardens.

Only then did he turn back to her.

Moonlight flooded her face, lit her up like the ethereal Viking queen she was.

Everything within him settled, and he knew of only one thing to say.

"I first fell in love with you in the moonlight, and in the moonlight was where I wanted to tell you how much I love you."

* * *

"Oh God, Sebastian, I'm so sorry."

His face fell at her words, and she was so overcome she laughed, finally reaching up to cup his face, run her fingers through his hair the way she'd longed to since first seeing him that night.

"I finally pour my heart out to a woman, and she expresses her regrets," he mumbled.

She laughed harder before finally pressing a kiss to his lips. She had meant it as a light thing, but soon his arms found their way around her, lifting her up to pull her more tightly against him.

She'd thought she might never feel this again, feel his body pressed against hers.

He broke the kiss, pressing his lips to her temple. "No, love, I am sorry. I should have told you sooner, as soon as I felt it. Only I was scared. I was so very scared that I...that I would—"

"End up like your father?"

He tilted her chin up, and she met his gaze.

"I went to Mrs. Shaw, Louisa. You didn't tell me she and my father were lovers."

Louisa frowned. "You cut me off if you recall."

He kissed her again, kissed her mouth, her cheeks, her temples.

"I'm so sorry for that. I'm sorry for my temper. I'm sorry for my insecurities. I swear to you I will never run away from you like that again."

She held onto him, holding his chin in place to meet his gaze.

"Do you promise me that, Your Grace? Do you swear to stay and speak to me about the things that scare you?"

He rested his forehead against hers. "I do. I swear I do."

Her smile grew slowly as she leaned in to kiss him. "Then I love you, too, you beast."

He growled as he kissed her. He picked her up and found the nearest bench on which to sit, cradling her in his lap. He savored the taste of her, plundered her mouth, trailed blazing nibbles down the line of her jaw. His hand found her breast, kneading it through the thin fabric of her bodice. She sighed, leaning into him.

"We can't possibly do this here," she whispered.

"I can recall another moonlit night when we did this very thing," he whispered back.

She sat up in his arms, her eyes wide. They studied each other before bursting into a snickered laugh at the memory.

She ran a hand down the side of his face, played with the fringes of his hair.

"That seems so very long ago," she said, transfixed by the way he looked with his hair loose and pomade-free. She stilled as she remembered something else. "Sebastian, you were right."

He raised an eyebrow. "Was that in question?"

She kissed him playfully before pulling away. "You were right about my mother. I didn't bring the illness into the house. It was the scullery maid." She shook her head. "I don't know if knowing the truth makes it better or worse. I feel so helpless knowing what really happened."

He cradled her face in his palm. "Louisa, you cannot blame yourself for events of the past just as I cannot use them as an excuse to hide from things. We both must move forward and forge the lives we want."

She studied his face, this face that was so dear to her now, so open when it had once been closed, so loving when it had once been so reserved. She kissed him softly, exploring every facet, every valley, and every crest.

Slowly she pulled away. "If we are to look to the future, I should like to start on another room in the house."

"Which room would that be?" he mumbled against her lips.

She pulled back to smile broadly. "The nursery."

His eyes widened, but before he could say anything, she captured his mouth in a kiss full of the love she couldn't wait to share with him for all the rest of their lives.

ABOUT THE AUTHOR

Jessie decided to be a writer because the job of Indiana Jones was already filled.

Taking her history degree dangerously, Jessie tells the stories of courageous heroines, the men who dared to love them, and the world that tried to defeat them.

Jessie makes her home in the great state of New Hampshire where she lives with her husband and two very opinionated Basset hounds. For more, visit her website at jessieclever.com.